By L.A. GILBERT

NOVELS
The Coil
Kieran & Drew
Witness

NOVELLAS
The Ghost on My Couch

Published by DREAMSPINNER PRESS
http://www.dreamspinnerpress.com

KIERAN&
DREW

L.A. GILBERT

Dreamspinner Press

Published by
Dreamspinner Press
5032 Capital Circle SW
Ste 2, PMB# 279
Tallahassee, FL 32305-7886
USA
http://www.dreamspinnerpress.com/

Kieran & Drew

Cover Art by Adrian Nicholas
adrian@cometfactory.com

ISBN: 978-1-62380-394-0
Digital ISBN: 978-1-62380-395-7

Printed in the United States of America
First Edition
March 2013

Dedicated to all the awkward teens who grew up to be awkward adults. You are awesome.

ChApteR OnE.

FRUSTRATION was becoming an all too familiar feeling to Kieran. School frustrated him—it was boring as hell and full of assholes who all had some sort of beef with him. Home frustrated him—there was only one asshole (infrequently) there, his dad, and that was getting just plain awkward. He didn't know when it happened precisely, but somewhere along the line, he and his dad had forgotten how to talk to each other. Now beyond the point of feeling hurt or actually caring, he was just eager to get out of Cedar Keys and Florida altogether.

The town itself was okay; it was just so... *small*. Boasting a population of around a thousand, Keys was a fishing town known for being a quaint and artsy kind of village with a thriving tourist trade for those looking for a laid-back vacation. The pace was so goddamn slow it was practically nonexistent. Everybody knew everybody. Everywhere was fish themed. Everywhere *smelled* of fish. Just... fucking *fish*! Morning, noon, and night. Even Keys's high school baseball team— yes, such a thing existed, though he didn't know why—was aquatically named: the Squids. The *Squids*.

And as much as all of this grated on Kieran, nothing nettled him more than being a senior and *still* a virgin. A friendless, gay, horny as hell virgin. If the small-town lifestyle wasn't enough to make him want to leave, then a desperate urge to have actual sex with another human being was.

It was an isolating feeling, seeing the people he'd grown up with suddenly pairing off, all boy-girl, boy-girl. He'd never been outright *bullied* for being gay—in fact, he'd never even announced or confirmed that he was gay to anyone (who would he tell?)—but people looked at him differently. As if they sensed he wasn't like them. It was the reason he felt like the school weirdo.

It wasn't always that way. Three or so years ago, round about ninth grade, he just stopped fitting in. One stupid incident set it all in place: the veritable *nightmare* that was the gym shower rooms. He hadn't meant to look at the other boys, and he certainly hadn't meant to get caught. He only realized he had a boner when the laughing and crude comments began.

He didn't get any hassle about it anymore, but it was the reason he recoiled from other students—other *guys* in particular. He'd become suddenly all too aware that he was never going to want to put his hand up a girl's shirt, and was instead exclusively interested in putting his hand down a guy's pants. He'd realized that he was different and that nobody was like him. Nobody. And no matter how many "it gets better" videos he watched on YouTube, he still felt alone and like an outsider.

So all of his hopes were pinned on college somewhere else, somewhere *not* in Keys or even Florida. The farther away, the better. He just had to stick out his senior year. He'd keep his head down, study enough to get passable grades, and fantasize about the day when he'd have himself some friends, maybe even a boyfriend, and about leaving Keys altogether for somewhere that didn't smell like the Little Mermaid's ass.

But for now, he'd go to lunch.

"Hey, spaz."

Kieran looked up just in time to see Adam Jefferson—a guy who innately hated him for no good reason—slam into him and send him sprawling into the lockers. His iPod he'd been scrolling through clattered to the floor. He looked up from where he splatted against the lockers and there was Adam, crowding close and getting in his face.

"Watch where you're going, freak."

The fist that slammed next to his head rattled the lockers and made him flinch. Adam smirked, pushing away, and before Kieran could stop himself, he did something very stupid: he spoke back.

"Fuck you," he whispered.

But Adam, who had a good few inches and thirty or so pounds on him, heard him clear as day. "The fuck did you just say to me?"

He recoiled against the lockers, immediately regretting his back talk as Adam leaned menacingly close, and Kieran's eyes widened slightly as he realized just what it was he said out loud. Giggling drew his attention to two girls standing close by, watching as the brawny Adam Jefferson tormented the weird kid nobody liked, and he suddenly hated people—all people and life in general. He wanted to call them bitches for laughing at what was happening. He wanted them to feel what he felt. But if he wanted to walk away from this without a limp, he needed to apologize; common sense and self-preservation dictated so. But his pride wouldn't let him.

"I said f-fuck you," he whispered back, waiting for his first-ever black eye.

"You in the mood to die or something?" Adam growled.

"I'm in the mood to get you busted for throwing the first punch," he said with more bravado than he felt. He swallowed hard and then gasped when Adam screwed his fist in the front of his shirt, pulling him close.

"I'm thinking it'll be worth it."

Kieran couldn't help but try to pull away from the grip. He squinted his eyes closed and braced for the fist that was surely hurtling his way, but another voice interrupted his impending pummeling.

"Hey, Jefferson!"

They both looked to see Drew Anderson—gorgeous, liked by all, pitcher for the Squids and all-around nice guy Drew Anderson— heading their way. Adam's fist slackened slightly.

"'Sup, asshole." Adam smirked.

"Been looking for you." Drew frowned, nodding toward Kieran but otherwise ignoring him. "Should you be doing that?" he asked Adam. "You know, with a game coming up this weekend and all. Last thing we need is you benched for roughhousing with your boyfriend."

Kieran very nearly fell on his ass when the grip on his shirt suddenly disappeared. He smoothed his shirt out and watched bitterly as Adam aimed a brotherly "fuck you" at Drew before diving for his middle to take him down. Drew easily shoved him aside, not even glancing at Kieran.

"You know I'm getting it good and regular from Tiff, asshole." Adam grinned, attempting to take Drew, who matched if not exceeded his height and build, in a headlock which Drew easily dodged.

Drew laughed. "Speaking of, I just saw your girl outside the science block looking *pissed*, man. You should probably follow up on that."

"Ah, shit. I was supposed to meet her for lunch."

"*So* fucking whipped," Drew teased.

"Yeah, and so fucking *laid*. Just you remember that. I'll see you later, yeah?"

"Yeah, later."

Kieran watched the exchange, trying his best not to feel pathetic and insignificant, before deciding to slink away just in case Jefferson changed his mind and gave him that black eye after all. He straightened the straps of his backpack and was already walking away when the sound of someone calling his name made him look over his shoulder. It was Drew.

"Hey, man. You alright?"

And goddammit, just like every other time Drew Anderson had so much as looked his way, he blushed. "Um. Yeah, I'm fine," he muttered to his shoes.

"Here." He held out Kieran's iPod. "This yours?"

"Oh, uh, yeah, it is. Thanks." He took the iPod, trying to not embarrass himself somehow when their hands touched accidentally.

"No problem. Listen, Jefferson's a bit of a caveman, you may have noticed." Drew shrugged one shoulder, looking almost apologetic. "You should probably just stay out of his way."

Kieran toyed with the tie that adjusted the shoulder straps of his bag. "I shouldn't have to."

Drew glanced around them, the hall thinning out as rumbling stomachs drew most students to the cafeteria. "I know," he said. "But just stay out of his way anyway, yeah?"

Kieran looked up to see piercing green eyes watching him, as if searching for something. He swallowed and nodded his head. "Thanks for intercepting."

Drew offered him a friendly, one-sided smile, a dimple showing in his cheek. "No worries. See you around."

I wish. "Yeah, see you."

Kieran watched discreetly as Drew turned, throwing a wave over his shoulder and heading off like most people toward the cafeteria. He let out a deep breath and slumped against the lockers. He hated school, and he hated almost everyone in it. He wondered if Drew would be as nice to him if he knew about the almighty crush Kieran harbored for him.

Drew. Freakin'. Anderson. Approximately five nine, a whole three inches taller than Kieran. Totally toned, with the kind of slim biceps that made Kieran hard from just a glimpse. Amazing green eyes, kind of dark blond hair that looked good even when messy. Fucking *dimples*, and a smile that was not only handsome but genuine.

He'd had a thing for Drew ever since Mr. Trinder, their art teacher, seated the class in alphabetical order at the beginning of senior year. This left him, Kieran Appleby, to share one of the high two-seater desks with the one and only Drew Anderson at the very back of the classroom. As soon as Drew smiled and introduced himself to Kieran, breaking all cliché jock rules, he was done for.

They'd never had a real conversation, partly because every time Drew nodded *hi* to him in art class, he'd turn into a blushing girl, managing a small nod back but otherwise leaning away from him on his stool, attempting to concentrate on not making a sound or moving in any way that would draw attention to himself.

Today's unexpected run-in with Adam, and ultimately Drew, left him feeling rattled. He'd actually played with the thought of skipping social studies that afternoon in favor of his one guilty pleasure: hiding under the bleachers with a sharpie, tagging the steps with doodles and his and Drew's initials in the hideaway he was sure no one would ever find, while watching Drew practice.

No one would ever see their names intertwined. It was the same pattern sprawled again and again on the underside of the bleachers, all grammar and punctuation disregarded in favor of erratic semicolons, quotation marks and capitalization that refused to conform, as was his way. He knew it was weird. Scratch *weird*, he knew it might be construed as downright creepy if anyone ever found out, but it was the one thing besides art class that he looked forward to while at school.

He'd see how he was feeling and decide later whether or not to skip class. Right now he was hungry.

There wasn't a chance in hell he was going to the cafeteria, though. He hadn't done that since he was a sophomore. He went where he always went for lunch. He left the corridor, travelled down to the basement, and walked straight up to the door marked "Janitor's Closet" and let himself in.

It wasn't a closet, as the sign indicated, but more of an abandoned office without windows. There was a bucket and mop, crap like that, but there were also damaged desks, spare chairs, and empty cabinets stacked up along the walls. In the middle, under a bare bulb, were two chairs and a table strewn with comic books. *His* comic books. He'd brought one with him one day and noticed how the janitor, Tony, kept trying to sneak a peek at the cover. He didn't come right out and ask if Tony liked comics. Not only because he wouldn't get an answer—Tony didn't like to speak—but also because he already knew. One comic book geek could easily spot another, even if the other was unaware that they were in fact a comic book geek.

Ah, Tony. Tony was probably the one friend Kieran did have, even if he didn't actually talk. He was a great hulking beast of a man, both tall and fat. So fat, in fact, that the zipper of his overalls stretched at the seams. Kieran often wondered if, were he to listen close enough, he would be able to hear that zipper screaming. Tony was big and fat, bearded and silent, and friendly. *Friendly.*

"Waddup, Tony?" Kieran greeted him, forcing a smile.

Tony glanced up, lifted his chin slightly in greeting, and then went straight back to his sandwich and comic. Kieran shrugged off his backpack and pulled out the spare chair and then his lunch.

"What you got today?" He knew better than to expect an answer but asked anyway out of habit. He unwrapped his own ham-and-cheese and craned his neck to try and guess what it was Tony was munching on.

"That bacon? Pastrami? Oh my God, are you rocking a meatball sub? Man! You always have better food than me." He couldn't be sure, but he thought he might have seen a twitch of the man's lips amidst the copious amounts of bristly black hair sprouting out of his face.

"What you reading today?" He fanned the remaining dog-eared comic books out across the table top. "You gone for the *Green Lantern* again, huh?" He plucked a comic out of the pile for himself. "That's cool, just means there's more *Hellboy* for me. Heh heh."

He ate his sandwich, read his comic and enjoyed Tony's easy company, and decided that, okay, there were a few things about school he didn't absolutely hate. He didn't hate Tony. He didn't hate art class, despite how on edge it made him to sit next to Drew, and he didn't hate sitting under the bleachers, watching Drew pitch. In fact, that was what he was going to do after lunch. Screw social studies.

DREW stood aside, letting the other students file out of class as he waited for Matt to finish up talking to Ms. Taylor, his math teacher. Sneaking a glance back through the doorway and judging by Ms. Taylor's expression, he could only assume Matt had done less than great on their last quiz. He watched Matt nod resignedly and then leaned back against the wall with a sigh. When Matt left the classroom but missed seeing him, Drew caught Matt's arm.

"Yo, I'm here." He grinned when Matt jumped slightly.

"Dick," Matt scolded. "You didn't have to wait; we'll both be late for practice now."

"Ah, fuck it. I'm sure coach'll let it slide this once, seeing as we're the best players on the team and all."

"Ah, very wise you are, yessss."

"Have you been hanging out with Travis recently, by any chance?" Drew asked, meaning Matt's little brother.

"Crap. Yeah, was I talking like Yoda again?"

"A little."

"Man. My little bro is a *geek*."

"Nah, he's okay."

Matt smiled despite his teasing words. "I guess."

"Must be kind of cool to have a nine-year-old worship you."

Matt shrugged, looking kind of smug. "It ain't bad. Though, come on…." He held his hands out to his sides, palms up. "It's pretty difficult to not admire perfection."

Drew laughed. "Perfection, huh? Is that what Ms. Taylor was calling you in there?"

Matt grimaced. "Not exactly."

"Do we need to make a study date?" he teased, batting his eyelashes.

Matt grinned and shoved Drew away a pace. "Yeah, seems like it. I hate math. I suck at it."

"Yeah, you do. Alright, get your ass on over to my place tonight. We'll crack the books."

"Can't tonight. I promised I'd take Travis to see the new *Iron Man* movie. Tomorrow?"

"Sounds good." They walked in silence for a moment as they approached the school's gym. "I think I'd like to have a brother," Drew mused.

"You wouldn't be saying that if he was bugging you to play with him every five minutes or making you watch *Star Wars* again for the fiftieth time."

"I don't know, I think having a big family must be better than having a small one, right?"

Matt glanced at him. "Maybe," he said a little more seriously. "Though, I mean, if you don't have siblings then that's what awesome, good-looking best friends are for." He gave Drew his most cheesy grin.

Drew snorted. "You have a very skewed, unhealthy perception of yourself going on in that little head, you know that?"

"Yep!"

Drew shook his head. "Come on, race you the rest of the way. On three. One, two—" He set off at a sprint on *two*, leaving Matt to cuss him out three paces behind.

Practice was good for a number of reasons, Drew decided two hours later while walking home. First, he loved the exercise. He loved the feeling of exhaustion after giving a game absolutely everything he had. He loved the stretch of muscle and the warmth it generated through his body. He also enjoyed the camaraderie with his teammates, either sharing a victory or leaning on each other through a loss. But mostly, he loved that it ate up the hours after school, leaving him too tired when he got in to do anything but eat whatever he could rustle up in the kitchen and then sag in front of his computer or TV in his bedroom. Overall, it meant less time spent with his mother, who would most likely be rattling around the house, mumbling to herself.

Goddammit, why'd things have to be the way they were? Why couldn't he have been born into Matt's family? Instead, he lived with his mom. Just the two of them. Or at least it was just the two of them while his uncle was away on tour, risking his life and being a hero in another part of the world, surrounded by sand.

He knew technically he *did* have a bigger family, but it was by blood only, and thin blood at that. His dad divorced his mess of a mother five years ago and went and had himself a brand new, undamaged family. New kids. New kids that were his half siblings and that he still hadn't met. He kicked a can across the sidewalk. His dad didn't really visit anymore. Didn't call all that much, either. Drew supposed that if he had a four-year-old daughter, twin two-year-old boys, and a pretty young wife, he'd probably forget all about him too.

It doesn't matter. I don't care, he repeated yet again in his head.

Things would be better when his uncle Rich came back. Just a few more months, that's what Rich had promised. Just a few more months and then back in time to see Drew graduate. He could make do. He could look after his mom until Rich was home, and then it'd be the three of them again and life would align itself into something manageable—something almost normal. He'd be able to breathe easier.

Uncle Rich made everything better. He moved in right after his dad took off, and having always been close to his sister—Drew's mother—there hadn't been a moment's hesitation on his behalf. Uncle Rich understood his mom's condition; he knew what to do to coax her out of her pajamas, and even on occasion managed to get her into the backyard for a little sun. Drew didn't know how to do that. He didn't want to let Uncle Rich down, but Drew didn't know how to keep her calm and happy like he did, and the pressure was starting to wear him down.

He only had the faintest of memories, but apparently things hadn't always been so bad when he was little. Her agoraphobia hadn't yet sapped the life and fun out of her completely. She was born in Cedar Keys and would certainly never leave the island, let alone the house she'd lived in her entire life, but he could remember as a child walking with her down the street to the local store on occasion. No farther, of course, but it was something. She wouldn't even open the front door now.

He could feel that tickle of muted rage in the back of his mind now. He had his theories. His father hadn't even waited for the ink to dry on the divorce papers before he married again. Just how long had he been unfaithful to Drew's mother, and how long had she been aware, and played along? Something had destroyed her fragile condition, which had at one time been manageable. Something as terrible as the person she loved most, the person who had vowed to stay with her through sickness and health, just up and leaving. *Abandoning* her. He imagined that would probably do it.

He hated his father sometimes. He hated him for marrying his mother to begin with, for telling her that her agoraphobia did not affect his feelings for her. He hated him for leading her on like that and then leaving. He hated his father for leaving *him*, for forgetting him, for not caring.

He took a deep breath, hesitating at the corner that would turn onto his street. He didn't want to be thinking all this bad shit when he got home. He wanted to be the guy his mother could rely on, just as his dad had been once upon a time.

He got his shit together. It wasn't that bad, he reminded himself as he turned the corner, his house coming into view. Other kids had mothers who were sick with a physical disease. Other kids had moms who were dying. Other kids had no mother at all. His mother wasn't dying; she just got a little lost inside of her head sometimes.

He took the steps two at a time up the porch and slung his gym bag just inside the doorway, where his mom would pick it up and add it to the laundry later. He took a cautious sniff and was relieved that he couldn't smell weed. Unfortunately, the house didn't smell of food, either, and he was starving.

"Mom?"

"Drew, honey? Where have you been?" She appeared at the top of the stairs, wringing her hands. "I was worried about you, I thought you'd left."

He held in a sigh and went up the stairs to hug her. "I had practice, remember? You should check the calendar on the fridge; it's all marked down when I'll be home late."

She covered her face with her hands for a moment, and his stomach turned slightly to see that they were shaking. "Oh! I'm so silly." She laughed, clearly relieved. "How are you, honey? How was your day?"

"It was fine, I'm… I'm kind of hungry, though. Is there anything to—?"

"Oh… *damn*!" she yelled at herself, screwing her eyes shut. "I was going to cook you my tuna casserole and I forgot, damn it!"

"Mom, it's fine," he said weakly, feeling guilty for even mentioning it. "I can just have a sandwich or something, it's no big deal."

"Yes, it is. You do so much for me and I can't even cook you a warm meal. I'm sorry, sweetheart."

"Really, Mom, it's fine."

"No, it's not. Come on, come sit at the kitchen table and I'll rustle something up." She took his hand and guided him down the stairs and to the kitchen.

He sat and waited patiently despite feeling tired and desperate for a shower, and chatted idly with her as she boiled him two eggs and cut up buttered bread for soldiers.

"There," she said happily. "Here are the soldiers, now we just have to wait for eggs. They're soldiers just like your uncle." She bit her lip. "I think he comes home soon."

"Yep," he tried brightly. "Just a few more months."

She nodded. "That's good."

He watched her, knowing she was trying to build up the courage to say something; he just didn't know what.

"Y-you'll be going off to college soon."

Drew sighed. "Local community college, Mom," he said softly. "I won't be far away, not far at all. I'll see you all the time, I promise."

At first, her shoulders drooped in obvious relief. Then she smiled brightly. "You'll be a wonderful fireman. I am so proud of you. *So* proud."

He smiled, feeling oddly bashful in the face of his mother's support of his hopes to be a fireman. "Thanks, Mom," he mumbled. It meant a lot to him that she wasn't just focusing on what she would lose when he left for college. He glanced at the clock. It was almost ten, and he was getting tired.

"Here you go!" she chirped, setting two runny boiled eggs down next to his soldiers.

"Thanks, Mom." He wolfed them down quickly and only happened to glance up between mouthfuls and notice that she was doing it again. She was sitting across from him, worrying her lip. "What is it?"

She startled slightly. "Oh, I was… I was hoping you could pick up a few things for me tomorrow."

He shrugged. "Sure, I'll go to the store after school. Then Matt'll be coming home with me. I said I'd help him study."

This only seemed to make her more uncomfortable. "Will… will Matt be going to the store with you?"

"I guess, why?"

She flushed and comprehension suddenly hit him. "Oh, do you need… you know, your… lady stuff?" *Lady stuff?* It didn't matter how often he did it, it would never *not* be mortifying to buy his mother's tampons.

She nodded quickly, eyes averted. "I'm sorry, Drew, honey. I know that's embarrassing. I don't want you to feel uncomfortable in front of Matt, either."

He coughed. "It's fine."

"I need some shampoo too, and we're out of baking soda and laundry detergent. Oh! And I need some new incense sticks."

"Why don't you write me a list and I'll pick it all up tomorrow." He hesitated a moment. "I'll tell Matt to wait outside."

She nodded. "You're so good to me, Drew. My own little hero."

He wouldn't go that far.

"Do you think… do you think you could nip over to Mr. Gullbeck's tomorrow and pick up a little—?"

"No." He cut her off firmly, feeling guilty for it but unwilling to bend on the issue.

"It's just for my nerves, Drew...."

"No, Mom. If you want something for your nerves, then we can call the doctor out again, but I'm not buying you weed. I'm not doing that."

She deflated, and he immediately felt guilty and ridiculous at the same time. He didn't enjoy playing the role of parent; it felt completely unnatural.

"Alright, I'm sorry I asked. I know how you feel about that."

He sighed. "Mom, you know Mr. Gullbeck is moving away soon, you can't rely on him to always be there to help calm your nerves. And I'm not willing to find a... a *dealer* for you either." He'd bet good money that none of his friends had ever had this conversation with their mothers.

"I just thought that maybe I could... stock up?" She shrugged, looking helpless.

"Or you could not smoke at all," he tried.

His neighbor, a middle-aged bachelor perhaps as strange as his own mother, was a good enough guy who, on the odd occasion, sold his mother weed for her nerves. He was, however, in the process of trying to sell his house. "We'll find a healthier way for you to get over your nerves, mom. I promise." He knew he shouldn't make such promises, but he was becoming desperate to just drop the subject.

"You're right. Of course, sweetie."

He took his plate over to the sink, ran it under the hot tap, and then left it on the draining board to dry. "I'm kind of tired, Mom. I think I'll turn in."

"Good night, honey. I'll see you in the morning."

"Night."

He made his way upstairs, leaving her to sit at the kitchen table alone. He took a quick shower and then pulled on a pair of boxers before plugging his headphones into his laptop and turning it on. He sat at his desk, checking his e-mail, and then, after a quick glance at his closed bedroom door, he typed the address of a porn site he favored into the browser.

He slumped in his chair, then flattened his hand against his stomach and slid it under his boxers to just gently roll his balls in his hand. He grimaced and turned down the volume when the woman on-screen screeched as the guy behind her took it up a notch. Drew felt a slight stirring but otherwise wasn't into it. He clicked the Home icon to return to his homepage, bit his lip, and then typed in something else.

Images appeared on screen that immediately made his mouth go dry. He clicked on a video, and ten seconds later his dick was as hard as stone. He quickly stood to find the moisturizer he kept in his sock drawer, and pulled his underwear down just beneath his ass when sitting back down.

His breath caught on the first stroke. He wanted to draw it out, but he was already sliding his hand up and down his cock in a firm stroke, picking up tempo and squeezing over his head. He focused on the man in the video who was bent over at the waist, and imagined what it'd be like to fuck him. He wanted to do that. He wanted it so bad.

He felt his groin tighten when the muscular man topping anchored the breathless, flushed guy beneath him by the shoulder and started to ram into him. He gasped as he reached climax and reached blindly for the box of tissues he kept by his desk.

His breath slowly returned to normal, and he cleaned up, deleted his browser history, and shut down his laptop. He climbed into bed and replayed the video in his mind. He wished there was someone he knew like that, someone who was like him who he could fuck. He placed his forearm over his mouth to stifle an unhappy groan. He was getting hard again.

He didn't want to feel this way. He just wanted an easy life, but his body was not confused and knew exactly what he wanted. He rolled over onto his stomach and closed his eyes. With no sounds in the house other than what he could hear of his mom tinkering about downstairs, he tried to unwind enough to sleep. He just wanted to sleep. He wanted an easier life than this, and he wanted to sleep.

ChAptEr TwO.

KIERAN wondered if it was normal for teachers to hate him as well as the students. To be fair, it was just the one teacher who always looked at him witheringly, and he knew he was probably being dramatic, but Mr. Trinder had never liked him, not ever. Perhaps it had something to do with Kieran thinking art was kind of dumb and never really making an effort to hide it.

If it weren't for the fact that he got to sit next to Drew Anderson for the next hour, he'd probably skip the class altogether. However, he noticed Drew was late. The idea was both a relief and a disappointment.

"Hey, Kieran."

Kieran looked up to see… what was his name? Oh, Toby Bennett. Toby was of the alternative persuasion and one of the few people who for some reason occasionally said hi to him.

"Hi, Toby, how's things?" he asked quietly.

"Not bad, not bad at all." Toby made his way over to his own desk, shooting Kieran a smile that seemed a touch smug, or perhaps knowing. Either way it was confusing, and Kieran shrugged it off.

While the last few students filed in, he opened his notepad and doodled. He rested his chin in his free hand. He was pretty sure they'd probably be deconstructing Picasso's cubism again today. Like he even gave a fuck. He'd rather be doing this if he had to be doing something artistic. He drew a heart around the initials K.A. + D.A., smiling faintly, and doodled "always" in stupid bubble writing underneath.

His crush was stupid, he knew, but he couldn't help finding Drew Anderson gorgeous any more than he could help breathing. It was the forearms that'd done it for him. While Drew was not stocky as, say, the almighty douche Adam Jefferson, Drew had a kind of sinewy muscled frame to him. His arms were thick, peppered with faint hair, and flexed in a way that made Kieran's mouth go dry. They brushed arms once, in fact, quite accidentally, and he'd had to excuse himself to the bathroom.

Drew was tall without being too tall, nice without being smug, and had an almost beach boy type of vibe without being too laid-back. He absolutely ticked all Kieran's secret boxes, but had to be (Kieran hoped) completely oblivious to his crush. He wondered what Drew, if he were likewise inclined, would see when looking at him?

One of the things he supposed made people think he was weird was probably the way he dressed. One day he might wear flip-flops, beach shorts, and a T-shirt. And on any other he might be rocking baggy, low riding jeans and a Hawaiian shirt and beanie hat. He supposed a nice way to put it was that he could be a little offbeat. A horrible way to put it was that he looked fucking weird at times. He didn't give it too much thought, really, and just wore whatever wasn't too creased and didn't smell bad.

Other than that, he was of average height and quite slim, had brown hair and blue eyes, and was super quiet. He shaded in the heart he was doodling and thought, *nah*; he wouldn't be into him either, in Drew's shoes.

He glanced up to check where the teacher was and noted that he was leaning over his own desk with a frown, reading something. He took the opportunity to lean down and snag up his backpack. Having missed breakfast that morning, he desperately needed to nibble on something. He took a bite of his Snickers.

"Hi."

And choked.

"Whoa, you okay?" Drew laughed, patting him on the back and setting his own backpack down under the table at the same time.

Oh my God, he's touching my back, was the thought running through his mind as he coughed. Eventually he managed to clear his throat, and with eyes watering and cheeks bright red, he looked at Drew and nodded. *Great, that's* gotta *look sexy. Well done, Kieran.*

"I'm fine, thanks."

"Appleby, are you quite done?"

With dawning horror Kieran looked to the front of the class where Mr. Trinder stood, one eyebrow raised in question. The rest of the students were turned in their seats, looking at him with various expressions that ranged from "what is wrong with that guy?" to "fucking freak." He wanted to curl up and disappear.

"S-sorry," he managed.

Mr. Trinder offered a final tired look before going back to handing out the large A3 pieces of paper draped over his arm. Looked like they were drawing again today. When the snickering eventually died down around him, he dared a look at Drew. Drew was frowning slightly, looking at something on Kieran's side of the desk. Kieran followed his eye's line and was mortified to realize Drew was looking at the notebook that lay open with its stupid but nonetheless damning doodles there for all to see.

With a quiet gasp, he slammed the notebook closed and folded his arms over it. At the same time, he sensed someone standing next to him and looked up to see Mr. Trinder staring back at him. He could tell by the tick in his cheek that the teacher was not having a good day and had quite obviously run out of patience.

"Passing notes, *really*?" Mr. Trinder asked, clearly resigned and beyond annoyed. He made a "give it to me" gesture with his hand. "Hand it over, now."

Kieran's eyes widened in horror, and he looked at Drew, who was staring back at him with a blank, unreadable expression. He looked back at his teacher. "I-I wasn't passing notes, honest," he choked out quietly. A glance forward confirmed that the class was once again watching him. *Oh God.*

"I said give it here," Mr. Trinder said firmly. "Now, Kieran."

"He wasn't passing notes, sir," Drew offered.

Mr. Trinder glanced between the two of them, and with a sigh, reached to take the notebook from Kieran. Kieran acted instinctually, and when the notebook was nearly out of his grasp, he scrambled and tore out the front page. Gasps and startled laughter erupted around him when, without thinking, he quickly crumpled the paper and shoved it into his mouth.

He could feel his face turning scarlet as Mr. Trinder stared at him, as shocked as the rest of the class. To his mortification, he could feel his eyes begin to actually sting as the laughter with intermittent whispered comments of "oh my God, he's so fucking weird" ricocheted around him. He cut a glance at Drew to see if he was laughing at him too, but was only further appalled to see a distinct look of pity instead. He looked back at his teacher when sensing Mr. Trinder leaning close.

The teacher spoke firmly and in a low voice. "I want you to collect your things, go to the bathroom, spit that out, and then go and wait for me in my office. Understand?"

Kieran nodded unhappily, gathered his bag, and left as swiftly as he could without running.

DREW had never in his entire life felt as bad for another person as he did for Kieran in art class that morning. He was still trying to make sense of what he'd seen in Kieran's notebook and which ultimately had ended up in his mouth. He knew he'd seen both their initials and a doodling of hearts. It was pretty hard to misunderstand what that meant. But he reasoned that he couldn't be the only person with those initials, surely? But then why would Kieran shove the paper in his *mouth*?

It'd been easy to see the clear-cut humiliation on the poor guy's face. Kieran had a hard enough time as it was, without drawing attention to himself like he had today. Though he'd never thought of the super-quiet guy he sat next to in art class as a weirdo like others seemed to, he had to acknowledge that Kieran was most definitely marching to a beat all of his own.

Thing was, he kind of liked that.

Yeah, sometimes he dressed a little… differently. And yes, Drew never saw Kieran hanging out with anyone else or even talking to anyone else, but that didn't necessarily mean he wasn't an okay guy. In fact, Drew sort of admired someone who was brave enough to break away from the herd. He thought about Jefferson, and how he put up with the guy's attitude and bullshit for the sake of keeping the peace. If he were braver, like Kieran, then maybe he too would have told Adam to go fuck himself a long time ago.

The idea of approaching Kieran now was an uncomfortable one. He couldn't do it without acknowledging what he'd seen in that notebook. But the idea of leaving him to stew and fret over the next time they bumped into each other seemed worse, somehow. He had to at least let him know it was okay. If the initials hadn't been his? Well then the decent thing seemed to be to tell him to pay no mind to what anyone else said or thought, and that he was okay in Drew's books. And if they had been his initials….

That required some thinking. It was a subject that he'd as yet been unable to acknowledge to himself. How did he feel about the prospect of another guy maybe being into him? He thought about it and had to admit, it was a little… stirring. Not exciting in a looking-forward-to-your-birthday kind of way. Exciting in an… off-balance, nervous kind of way.

All of his friends had had girlfriends; they'd had that exhilarated feeling of doing something sexual and new for the first time. His few (very few) fumbles with the opposite sex so far had been nothing but stressful and obligatory. So far, he'd felt nothing but resigned and almost cheated out of something he bet his friends didn't think twice about. The idea of there being someone else like him in school? It was nerve-wracking but kind of cool.

Kieran himself? He'd never given it thought. He never had a reason to. Put a gun to his head and… yeah, he'd have to admit the guy was kind of cute. Not hot as in porno-guy hot, but cute in a preppy and offbeat-with-big-blue-eyes kind of way. He felt himself grow warm; he'd never actually allowed himself to think that way… in a *gay* way.

He didn't want to get ahead of himself, though. For all he knew, he could be making shit up out of wishful thinking. But at the very least, he felt he should go check if Kieran was okay and all. A few more minutes and the bell would ring for school to let out. He discreetly pulled his cell out of his pocket and texted Matt that he'd be fifteen minutes late meeting him at the front gate.

He had a feeling he knew exactly where Kieran would be. Last year Drew and some other guys had been screwing around with a football outside the art department and the predictable happened: they broke a window, and as a result, he received detention by Mr. Trinder.

THIS was quite possibly the shittiest day of Kieran's life. He was used to feeling awkward and uncomfortable around other students, but today had to be one of the most embarrassing days on record so far for him. He couldn't decide what was worse; that he had shoved that piece of paper in his mouth, looking like a freak in front of everyone, or that Drew had seen what was doodled on the paper.

He was almost relieved when Mr. Trinder told him what his detention would be. Clearing out the art supply storage room for the next few weeks seemed to him to be getting off easy, considering his display of general mental illness earlier that morning. He'd been genuinely terrified that he'd have to do some sort of essay on art to read in front of the class. His relief was short-lived, however, when he actually *saw* the storage room.

It was a veritable *maze*. There were oil and watercolor paint supplies to separate. Shelves and shelves of unorganized works and sketch pads that needed filing by year and class. There were half-formed papier-mâché models that needed breaking down and canvas that needed to be stretched. This was a detention that would be ongoing, it seemed, for a while yet.

He was sorting through paint brushes that were stiff and practically fused together when he heard the storage room door creak open behind him. He glanced over his shoulder, expecting to see Mr. Trinder, but did a quick double take upon seeing Drew Anderson close the door behind him instead. Kieran turned around, gripping the paint brushes tightly with both hands.

"Hi," Drew offered quietly, digging his hands into his pockets.

"W-what are you doing here?"

Drew shrugged. "Just wanted to make sure you were okay. Art class was pretty brutal…."

"You're… you're not going to beat me up?"

"Why would I do that?"

Kieran flushed uncomfortably, letting his silence and averted eyes answer for him.

Drew had his answer. "So… that doodle thing, those were my initials, and yours?" he asked guardedly. "You like… have a *thing* for me, then?"

Kieran bit his lip, shrugged. "Sorry," he muttered.

"You don't have to look like you're gonna puke, you know. I'm not some homophobic dick."

Kieran looked at him, feeling exposed in a way he never had before. "My face is still in one piece, so I guess not."

Drew looked around the room, puffing out his cheeks and letting go of a deep breath in an uncharacteristically nervous gesture. "I had to clear this place out once."

"For far less humiliating reasons, I'm sure." Kieran spoke hesitantly, perplexed as to whether his crush had been addressed or not.

Drew grinned. "I accidentally broke a window in the art department." He strode over to one of the papier-mâché figures and, bending one of the arms, sent white flakes floating to the ground before abandoning it. "Had to break a load of these things up."

"Did Mr. Trinder make you do it?"

"Yep."

"So… that's how you knew I'd be in here?"

"Yeah, pretty much."

Kieran swallowed, bending the bristles on the brushes he held. "And you just came by to check I was alright?"

Drew looked at him a moment, shuffling his feet before shrugging slightly. "I… kinda wanted to let you know that if… if those were my initials, or whatever, then… you know, it's cool."

Kieran's palms were sweating. "Cool? As in… cool you don't care, or…?" He didn't know why he let his sentence trail off like that; what other reason could there be?

"Just-just… whatever, you know? I don't mind. It's okay if you like me, or whatever."

"Um. Okay, I guess?" He was more confused now than ever.

"I mean I'm not going to tell anyone, if you were worried about that."

"Oh." He nodded. "Thanks."

"And you don't have to avoid me, or anything."

"I don't make you feel uncomfortable, or weird?"

Drew shrugged. "No it's… it's flattering." He tried for a jokey smile, but it fell flat.

While Kieran was relieved that he wasn't having his ass handed to him, something wasn't sitting quite right with him. It upset him a little that Drew knew about his crush now. It wasn't his secret anymore, and any time Drew caught him looking, there would be no way to claim innocence. His one obsession didn't feel like it belonged to him anymore. It was an exposed feeling.

"I thought you'd feel better knowing I was okay with everything?" Drew frowned.

"Oh, no, no, I am. I just…." Kieran lifted one shoulder in a shrug and gave a sad, lopsided smile. "I just feel so dumb."

"You don't have to feel that way," Drew said, his tone more serious. "I don't…." He hesitated, unsure of how to word what he wanted to say without hurting Kieran's feelings. "I don't think like the others. I don't think you're weird."

Kieran swallowed, hating that Drew was shining a light on his obvious lack of friends, even if he was trying to be nice. "Thanks," he said stiffly, folding his arms across his chest and hunching his shoulders as if he was cold.

"I *don't*," Drew reiterated, at a loss as to how he was making things worse.

"I get it. Thank you." *Don't feel sorry for me, don't feel sorry for me.*

Drew sighed, feeling like he'd somehow made things worse, and dug his hands back deep into his pockets. "Okay. So, um… how long do you have to do this?"

"Until it's clear. May take a while, as you can see."

"Looks like." Drew rocked back and forth on his heels. "Well, anyway, I have to get going. I'm meeting Matt, so…."

"Okay, see you around, then."

"Yeah. Yeah, see you around." Drew turned and left the storage room, closing the door behind him.

Kieran groaned, feeling like an even bigger asshole and not even understanding why or what just happened. He suddenly couldn't deal with this shit. If Mr. Trinder came by and found the storage room empty, fuck it, he could call Kieran's dad or something, not that his dad would be home to pick up. He waited ten more minutes, figuring most people would have vacated the school grounds by then and he wouldn't have to run into anyone else, and then headed home.

Fucking come on, college. He couldn't wait to go. With no clear idea of what he wanted to do for a career, he figured a major in American Literature would suit him perfectly. He'd always liked English and reading; perhaps if he could learn to conform to "proper" punctuation he'd become a teacher, and then he could stand up for all the loner kids who had no one. His only stipulation was that it be a ways away from Florida. He was sure his dad wouldn't give two shits anyhow. He'd probably just be glad to have him out of the house so he could bring his not-so-secret girlfriend home once in a while.

The house he'd lived in his entire life came into view, and he was surprised to see his dad's car sitting out front. After such a horribly humiliating day, it really did make him miss the relationship he used to have with his father. In fact, a hug wouldn't go amiss right about now, but ever since he'd become old enough to not require supervision or a sitter, his dad was always at the restaurant.

"Dad?" He called out cautiously. As if he didn't quite believe he'd caught his elusive father at home. He walked into the living room just as his dad was finishing up a hushed telephone call. Probably with the girlfriend. He rolled his eyes.

"Hey, Kier. You're home a little late today, aren't you?"

"I was at the library." He didn't feel like being honest, and even if he was, it probably wouldn't matter.

"Good to hear. Listen I'm heading off to the restaurant—"

"What a shock," Kieran muttered, surprised when his dad actually stopped and looked at him.

"Everything okay?" His dad frowned.

Kieran swallowed. *No dad, it's not. I'm gay, I have no friends, you don't hang out with me anymore, and a whole class full of kids laughed at me today and called me a freak. I am* not *okay.* "I'm fine," he said quietly.

"You sure? You can come to the restaurant if you like. I have to go over the books in my office but I could ask the chef to whip up something special for you."

"No thanks."

"You sure?" His father looked uncharacteristically unsure of himself. "The chef's really settled in; he's a master in that kitchen."

Kieran bit his lip, then narrowed his eyes suspiciously before asking: "Who was on the phone?"

His dad stood up a little straighter, shrugged slightly. "Just restaurant business, why?"

Kieran swallowed the disappointment he felt and headed into the kitchen. "I'll just make myself a sandwich." He opened the fridge, using it as an excuse to hide the letdown he felt and that was surely written all over his face. He missed the worried expression on his father's face.

"Well, if you're sure...."

"It's fine. Go," he said without even turning around as he put a sandwich together.

"Okay, well... I'll probably be back late."

"Like every night," Kieran muttered.

"*Kier*...," his dad said softly.

Suddenly feeling just a little too overwhelmed by the world of hurt sitting on his shoulders, Kieran took his hastily made sandwich, snagged up his backpack, and headed toward his room. "Night, Dad."

He couldn't eat his sandwich. He could only sit on his bed and take deep breaths, trying not to cry like the little faggot he felt like as he listened to his dad's car come to life and reverse off the driveway.

Alone again.

He swiped angrily at his eyes with the heels of his hands. What was wrong with him? What was so terrible about him that nobody wanted to be around him? He toed off his sneakers and then lay down on his back, looking up at the ceiling. His dad didn't care. He didn't know where the fuck his mother was—in fact, he only knew what she looked like because he found a few old photographs once in his dad's office. She must have seen it in him from the beginning. She must have seen something was not right with him and decided he wasn't worth the time, so she just took off.

Well, it'd be his turn soon enough. He'd already applied for colleges as far away as Michigan, California, and Washington. He hadn't told his dad yet, but seeing as his father hadn't yet asked about his plans when it was already halfway through his senior year, he figured that, as usual, his dad didn't care.

And what was up with the secret girlfriend? *Still*? He couldn't figure out why his dad would think he'd be pissed at him for actually moving on finally and finding himself a girlfriend, so he could only conclude that he just didn't want Kieran involved with that part of his life. It fucking hurt. It'd been two years since he last felt properly connected to his dad, like he belonged with him. And a whole year had gone by where his dad had pretended he wasn't dating one of the waitresses at the restaurant. Like he hadn't heard him whispering on the phone, all smiles and flirty.

He reached under the bed and pulled out a *Hellboy*, volume one, "Seed of Destruction." There was a reason he loved comic books and other general geek paraphernalia so much. All the downtrodden, unnoticeable, unpopular protagonists had the most exciting alter egos. He decided that he really ought to get himself one.

TRUE to his word, Drew had made Matt wait outside the store while he picked up the odds and ends his mother needed. Though he still couldn't help but fidget uncomfortably at the checkout when the clerk rang up his mother's tampons and incense sticks.

Then at home, he helped Matt through some of the trickier math shit that even tripped him up from time to time. Now he was more or less letting Matt get on with it, just flicking through his English Lit textbook and offering input when asked for it, but for the most part, his mind kept wandering back to his conversation with Kieran in the storeroom.

He went there intending to reassure Kieran, but felt that he had only made things worse, somehow. He was torn between just letting it go and pretending it never happened, or approaching Kieran again. The former seemed the sensible idea, but left him feeling dissatisfied, and the latter ran the risk of embarrassing Kieran further.

He cut a quick glance to Matt, who was frowning in concentration. What he really wanted to do was talk to Matt about it. But then, he didn't even know what it was he wanted to say. *Matt? There's a guy at school who's into me, and I'm not totally against the idea of liking him back. What do you think?* Or even *Matt, old buddy old pal? I'm pretty sure I'm into guys. Can we discuss?*

"What?"

Drew was abruptly brought back to reality to find Matt staring at him. "Huh?" For a horrifying moment he wondered if he'd said any of it out loud.

Matt snorted. "You just laughed. What's so funny?"

He tried to downplay the relief that washed through him and realized right there that no, he wouldn't be chatting to Matt about his love life any time soon. "Nothing." He waved it off casually.

Matt raised an eyebrow in question, but then let it go with a "whatever" shake of his head. "Weirdo," he muttered.

"I'm cooler than you."

"You wish, butt-face."

"Butt-face? You're supposed to rub off on Travis, not the other way around, idiot."

Matt shrugged. "What can I say? Little dude makes me laugh." He grinned. "Speaking of, he's harangued me into taking him into that new comic book store in town tomorrow. You want to come with?"

"Do I want to come with?" Drew smirked.

"Ugh, fine. Will you please come with us and save me from total boredom-slash-geekdom? Plus my brother asked me to ask you. He thinks you're cool, though fuck knows why. Loser."

"You're such a sweet talker!"

"Just say yes so I can tell him you're coming."

"Fine, whatever. You'll owe me, though."

"I'll owe you shit. You're coming and you'll be happy about it."

"Why am I friends with you, again?"

Matt closed his math textbook and shoved it across the floor. "Because I am *fucking* awesome!" he declared with a flourish.

"Not to mention modest."

"That too."

"Your folks must be *so* proud."

"Hmm," Matt replied and gave him an odd glance. "You, uh… heard from your uncle recently?"

"Yeah, got a letter from him a few days ago, actually."

"You must be looking forward to him getting home."

"You've got no idea," Drew said, tension creeping into his voice.

"Is everything going okay?"

"Yeah, we're doing fine. I just worry about leaving her alone during the day."

Matt nudged him slightly. "She seems to be doing okay."

"Yeah, well. There are good days and bad days."

"There'll be more of those good ones when your uncle gets back, don't worry."

"Yeah, yeah, I know it. Thanks."

"No problem."

They went back to their textbooks. Within minutes, Drew's mind had wandered, thoughts of blue eyes and storage rooms distracting him.

ChaPtEr ThrEE.

DREW hadn't exactly expected an ecstatic greeting from Kieran in class, but he thought the guy would at least look at him and answer him with more than the odd one-word reply. He supposed Kieran's embarrassment was a little more acute than he originally thought. Though, casting a quick look around the classroom, he supposed he might want to keep a low profile too, if people were whispering about him.

He cut a glance to Kieran, who was more or less huddled at the other end of the desk, hunched over his sketch pad, and sighed. This was where small talk came in handy, surely? He heard Kieran curse quietly and watched as he examined the pencil with a now-broken nib. Seeing an in, he hurriedly pulled a spare out of his bag.

"Here," he offered, perhaps a touch too brightly.

"Careful, he looks hungry." Giggling erupted from the desk in front of them, and he glared at the two girls who sat there, smirking at Kieran.

He recognized one of them, Liz Sanderson. He leaned forward with a smile and nodded at her. "Hey, Liz...," he whispered with a small "come here" nod. A gleam of interest shone in her eyes. "Take a break from being a bitch, yeah?"

Her flirty smile turned sour, and both girls turned around with affronted grunts. He risked a cautious look at Kieran and was further annoyed to see that instead of looking amused or grateful, he seemed only uncomfortable to be the source of attention.

"Don't pay any attention to them," he tried, still offering the pencil.

Kieran took it and nodded his thanks, but otherwise went back to ignoring him. He sighed and supposed it would probably be best for Kieran if he played along and left him alone. Though the thought disappointed him, he turned his body away from Kieran, leaned his chin in his hand, and went back to his own work. He glanced up once more when someone else approached their desk—approached *Kieran*.

"Hey, Kieran, what's up?"

Kieran mumbled something back that Drew didn't quite hear, and he lowered his hand and faced forward in a discreet move to try and eavesdrop.

"I wanted to let you know I watched that film you recommended. It was awesome."

For whatever reason, Drew felt a dislike for this guy so instant it was dizzying. Here he was, unable to get a single sentence out of Kieran, despite knowing Kieran was hot for him, and this guy? This guy was carrying on like they were old friends. To his delight, however, Kieran seemed genuinely flummoxed.

"What film did I recommend?"

"That vampire film?"

Uh oh. Whether he could ever speak to Kieran again and still respect him all depended on whether the word *Twilight* was about to be uttered in his presence.

"You know...," the guy continued; Drew thought his name might be Toby something. "With the two kids, one's a vampire, the other's at school, he gets bullied and—"

"*Let the Right One In?*" Kieran provided, sounding a little impatient and glancing around them, clearly not wanting to draw any more attention to himself than he had over the past few days.

Two things happened. Drew quit eavesdropping at the mention of one of his *favorite* films and stared at them outright, and Toby snapped his fingers like a douche bag.

"That's the one. It was great. Though I hear there's actually an American version out on DVD too—"

"Don't bother," Kieran cut him off with a surprising level of authority in his voice. "I mean, it's okay and all, but it doesn't hold a candle to the original."

"Yeah, but…." Toby shrugged, actually glancing between Kieran and Drew. "The American one doesn't have *subtitles*." He grinned, as if he'd just made some sort of clever observation and they were all supposed to bow down to the intellectual and comedic giant that was Toby.

Drew, determined to not butt into a conversation that didn't actually involve him, held back a sneer, but could not stop himself from rolling his eyes. That film was boss. So what if it was in Swedish? He hated those stupid big blockbuster companies, taking an already stunning film and remaking it only two years later just so—

"They didn't need to remake that film, it was already perfect," Kieran answered Toby and, unbeknownst to him, only gained himself that much more respect from the guy sitting next to him. "And it held more true to the book, too."

"Oh, there's a book?"

Drew took a deep breath and held it in. *Don't punch the guy. It's not his fault he's a moron. Actually it is, but still, don't hit him.*

"Uh, yeah." Kieran kind of laughed. "The author's *John Ajvide Lindqvist*, and I sort of love him," Kieran deadpanned, obviously joking. It gained a small smile out of Drew, but fell flat with Toby.

"I'm reading one of his other novels right now, actually," Kieran continued, notably uncomfortable in how he shifted on his stool and cleared his throat.

"That a vampire book too?"

"No, it's called *Handling the Undead*. It's a zombie novel. Sort of."

"Huh, cool. Can I see?"

"Wha— Uh, you mean the cover? Yeah, I guess."

Kieran cast a quick look around at the rest of the class, who were busy and chatting quietly amongst themselves, as he pulled his backpack into his lap. Kieran handed the paperback over so Toby could check out the cover and read the back blurb, but Drew's attention was drawn to what he could see in the open backpack. He didn't realize he was almost leaning over Kieran to get a closer look until he heard Kieran clear his throat. Both Kieran and Toby were staring at him.

"Help you?" Kieran asked, clearly amused by Drew's faux pas.

"Oh." *Shit.* "Sorry, I was just looking at...." He gestured to where he could see a comic poking out.

"Oh." Kieran flushed slightly. "Yeah, I'm into graphic novels."

"What's that?" Toby smirked. "Porn?" Then laughed. Alone.

Kieran scratched the side of his neck. "No, it's a comic book," he mumbled.

There was an awkward five-second pause when no one said anything until Toby once again opened what Drew was starting to think of as the huge, stupid fucking hole in his face.

"Hey, have you seen those *Twilight* films? They're supposed to be cool."

Drew relaxed, knowing that despite the fact—for reasons not yet obvious—Toby was trying to impress Kieran, it didn't matter and he would not be successful. Kieran actually seemed to be one of the enlightened few when it came to truly great books, and quite astute in the world of ohmygodfuckingawesome films and ohmygodpiecesofshit films. Toby the *ass-hat* had just made a blunder.

Vampires. Do. Not. Fucking. Sparkle.

"Have you read *Harbour* yet?" Drew chimed in. Fuck being polite.

Kieran's eyes actually widened a little in surprise. "No, not yet. So... you like *John Ajvide Lindqvist?*"

"Absolutely. *Let the Right One In* is actually one of my all-time favorite films. And you're right about the remake, it's not as good." *Take* that, *Toby.*

"I want everyone in their seats, please," Mr. Trinder called from the front of the class. "Remember, you've only so much time to get your projects complete, so I suggest you spend your time wisely. Less chatting and more working, and I want to see all of you putting in a few hours after school."

Toby gave Kieran a nod and Drew a completely unreadable look. Drew tried not to smirk. He felt like he'd won something, he just had absolutely no idea what. He felt something kind of flip flop in his stomach when Kieran offered him a small smile. An *I didn't know you could be like me* smile.

Okay. Time to do something brave. Was Kieran actually kind of hot? Yes. Was Kieran already into him? Yes. Did he want to see what might happen if they were to hang out? Yes. But that last one was a bit nerve-wracking. He cleared his throat.

"So, hey… um. Me and Matt—you know, my friend Matt?" Kieran nodded. "We're taking his little brother and going to that new comic book store that just opened up, you know the one? It's by the—"

"I know it."

"Yeah, so, we're going tomorrow. You-you want to come with?" *Arrrgghhhgg.* There. He'd done it. No big deal.

Kieran was looking hesitant, however. In fact, he seemed almost suspicious. "You want me to hang out with you, your friend Matt, and your friend Matt's little brother?"

"Yeah, sure." He tried to shrug in a way that looked completely casual despite the fact that he was trying to figure out whether he'd just asked Kieran out on some sort of fucked-up double date.

"F-for real?"

Drew smiled. "Yeah, what's the problem?"

Kieran withdrew a little, looking away and lifting one shoulder like he didn't really care. "Just… I don't usually hang out all that much, with… you know, with people from school."

"Well, now you do," Drew said quietly. "Unless you have plans, or whatever."

Kieran was quick to shake his head. "No, no plans. But, um… I mean, I don't want to intrude, or anything."

"Kieran, it's a comic book store, not dinner and a movie." He laughed and was pleased when Kieran smiled.

"And this isn't like… some sort of trick where you two stand me up or whatever?"

Drew frowned. "Are you serious?"

Kieran pressed his lips together in a straight line, glancing away and shrugging again. "People do that to other people." He scratched the side of his face. "I hear."

Whoa. He knew Kieran was a bit of a loner, but that sucked. "We're not like that. We don't do that."

"Yeah?" Kieran asked so hopefully that Drew wanted hug the guy. "This doesn't have anything to do with…." He suddenly blushed and looked around him quickly, lowering his voice. "Anything to do with what-what we talked about in the storage room?"

Drew caught the drift. He knew Kieran was actually trying to figure out whether this was a trick—whether he and Matt wanted to prove some sort of point outside of school without getting in trouble. The idea of it made him feel kind of shitty and only reinforced his resolve to make this guy his friend, if nothing else.

"Okay, I'm no longer asking, I'm telling you to meet us outside the store. There will be comics, a nine-year-old who will most likely hang on your every word, and a greasy burger somewhere along the way."

Kieran's smile started off small and unsure, but then quietly grew into something that had Drew wishing he were braver, and that they *were* discussing some sort of date.

"Okay." Kieran nodded.

"Okay." Drew nodded back, pleased as shit.

KIERAN was nervous. They were late. They were late, or Drew was full of shit and they were somewhere else right now, laughing that he was here, standing all by himself and waiting for them. He was considering just turning around and going back home when he saw them. Judging by the somewhat nervous glance Drew shot Matt and Matt's subsequent frown, he could only assume that Drew hadn't mentioned his inviting him or he'd forgotten altogether. Great. What was Drew's deal? Why invite him to hang out with him and his friend but then look all uncomfortable when he actually turned up? He dug his hands deep into his pockets. It was the kid who darted ahead of the other two and spoke to him first.

"Hi, I'm Travis."

"What's up, Travis? I'm Kieran."

"Hey, you're here." Drew smiled, looking nervous.

He suddenly felt doubtful. Had he imagined the entire exchange in art class? Had Drew just been playing polite but ultimately didn't want him there? He should have stayed home. "Uh, yeah. You... you asked me, right?"

"Yeah. Of course I did."

Kieran worried his lip. What did that mean? Did that mean "no, I was just being polite," or did it mean he'd forgotten altogether? The awkward silence was broken none too gently by Matt slapping Drew's arm with the back of his hand.

"*Ow*. What?" Drew frowned, rubbing his arm.

"Oh for—never mind." Matt rolled his eyes at Drew and held his hand out to Kieran. "Hey, man. It's Kieran, right?" They shook hands and Kieran nodded. "I've seen you at school, but I don't think we've ever actually met." He looked at Drew, who was rubbing his arm still. "And that was for not introducing us, moron. Didn't your momma teach you any manners?"

"Not really." Drew grinned.

"Can we go in now? *Please*?"

"All right, butt-head, just stay in sight."

Kieran looked at Drew, who inclined his head in an "after you" gesture. Kieran followed Matt and Travis through the doors and consoled himself with the fact that even if they ditched him at some point, he could still look for the new *Walking Dead.*

"SO, KIERAN seems like an alright guy," Matt said.

Drew glanced over to where Kieran and Travis were leaning over opposite sides of a desk, both skimming through a large, open file of labeled comics. Kieran was grinning and Travis was laughing at him. "Yeah, he's not bad."

"Are you gonna tell me why you invited him?" Matt asked, picking a large plastic sword up out of a barrel, frowning at it and turning it around in his hand.

"I need a reason?" He shrugged. "I saw one of those comics Travis likes in his backpack and thought he might want to come with." He chanced a look at Matt, only to see him looking back at him suspiciously.

"You don't *need* a reason, I was just wondering. I didn't know you two hung out."

"We don't, we just got talking in class, that's all," Drew kind of mumbled. At the time, he'd felt a victory of sorts for having invited Kieran, despite not knowing what he wanted out of doing such a thing. But when it came to mentioning it to Matt, he backed out. He'd grown nervous, and a part of him wanted to know what Matt's reaction and attitude to Kieran would be without forewarning.

If he were to be honest with himself, he was kind of disappointed at his own actions. He'd always been the type to try and keep the peace, and he hated confrontation, but not mentioning Kieran to Matt until the last second smacked a little of cowardice. And as much as he initially liked Kieran, he was a little bit embarrassed when explaining to Matt that Kieran would be there waiting for them. What kind of guy did that make him? He turned it over in his mind and rationalized that though he was a bit of a chicken, he didn't know Kieran all that well and was still feeling him out himself.

"What class do you have with him, again?" Matt asked.

"Art."

"Ugh. Mr. Trinder?"

"Yeah."

"I hate that guy; he made me stay behind class once and wouldn't let me go until I could draw a perfect circle. Fucking Nazi."

"Yeah, I don't like him much. Kieran neither, actually."

"So, you guys know each other from just art class?"

Drew felt himself grow warm and turned away. He plucked a flyer from a stand and pretended to study it. It advertised the date and time for some sort of comic-book signing in a couple of months' time. He shoved it into his pocket. "Pretty much. He mentioned a movie and an author I liked." He shrugged. "We both like the creepy shit." He looked at Matt and made a scary oogie-boogie face, laughing when Matt glared.

"I don't know how you can like that stuff, man." Matt shivered. "I had to sleep with my fucking lamp on for a week when you made me see that *Paranormal Activity* movie."

"That's because you're a pussy."

"No way. You have to be twisted in the head to like that shit."

"What shit?" Travis asked.

They turned around to see Travis standing behind them, his arms full of comics, and Kieran beside him, suppressing a smile.

"*Stuff*. I said stuff," Matt amended quickly.

"No," Travis said in a sing-song voice, clearly enjoying his brother's discomfort. "You said *shit*."

"Am I gonna have to beat you up?" He crouched and grabbed the front of Travis's shirt, making his brother giggle. "Huh?"

"Not if you buy me this one." Travis nodded to one of the comics he held.

"That's called bribery."

Drew grunted. "That's called keeping your little brother quiet."

"Fuck." Matt sighed.

"I'll have this one too, please." Travis preened. Both Drew and Kieran laughed.

"I like this kid," Kieran said to Drew.

"Oh for—" Matt began.

Drew put a hand on Matt's shoulder. "Dude, stop while you're ahead."

Matt took the two comics, messed up his brother's hair, and then told him to put the rest back while he headed over to the counter to pay.

"Find anything you like?" Drew asked Kieran, feeling oddly nervous when it was just the two of them.

Kieran shrugged, but he looked to be enjoying himself. "Not today. You?"

"Uh. No…." He laughed.

Kieran gave him a knowing look. "Not your kind of thing?"

"Not really."

"Well, at least you have good taste in movies."

"We're going to see a movie?" Travis asked, now back and smiling at Kieran.

"Uh…." Kieran hesitated.

"We hadn't planned on it, Trav." Drew nudged the kid.

"Planned on what? *Here*…." He handed a plastic bag to his brother. "Take this, you little gangster."

"We're going to see a movie!" Travis literally hopped from one foot to the other.

"What?" Matt looked between Kieran and Drew. "You just fleeced me for two comic books; I'm not taking you to the movies as well." He looked up at Kieran and Drew again. "Which one of you assholes put that in his head?"

"You said *asshole*!" Travis chimed happily. "We get to go see a movie!"

"Oh, for fuck's sake."

Travis threw his hands in the air in triumph. "And now I get popcorn!"

"This kid has a life of crime ahead of him," Drew stage-whispered to Kieran.

"Look, let's just go get something to eat for now, yeah?" Matt dragged his brother by the back of his T-shirt out of the store.

They made it to the burger house, but fries and a Coke weren't enough to satisfy a nine-year-old who had his mind set on what he wanted. Travis's insistent pleas had them standing outside the movie house, looking up at the dot-matrix text of what was showing.

"Oh man!" Kieran grabbed Drew's arm unconsciously and shook it. "They're showing old Hitchcock movies!"

"You like the old scary films too, huh?" Drew asked, feeling unexpectedly pleased as Kieran gripped his arm, and disappointed when he dropped it.

"Yeah, I love them." He looked at Drew. "I never thought I'd meet another weirdo my own age who likes old cinema like me."

"I love scary shit and old shit. Hitchcock, Frank Capra films…."

"Look!" Kieran pointed at the billing. "They're showing *Rope*."

"No, no. Let's see *The Birds*."

"Um, when you say old *scary* movies… how scary are we talking?" Matt asked, playing it casual. His brother leaned against his leg, munching on popcorn. He nodded down at Travis. "You know, because of the T-man."

Drew snorted. "Yeah, because of *Travis*." He looked at Kieran, grinning. "Matt's actually a throwback from the eighties. He loves all those corny films where the kids wear oversized sweaters and legwarmers."

"Oh, oh!" Kieran laughed. "Films where the guys hold boom boxes outside the girl's bedroom window, and walk across the football field with their fist in the air?"

"That's it!" Drew laughed.

"You both suck, you know that?" Matt griped.

"D'awww," Drew pouted, slinging an arm over Matt's shoulders. "Are widdle us being mean?"

Matt shoved Drew's arm off of him and nudged Travis in the butt with his knee for laughing. "Say what you like, but I'd rather be a throwback than a freak who watches the kind of shit you two do."

"You know…," Kieran began. "Statistically, as teenagers we're supposed to be into action junk, like *Transformers* or something." He laughed when both Drew and Matt shivered dramatically.

"Fucking Michael Bay. He gets a pass on the first *Transformers* film, but not the second or third," Drew stated with utter authority.

Matt laughed. "Yup. Getting rid of Megan Fox? Dumb. And dare I mention *Pearl Harbor*?"

"I think *Team America* summed up that movie quite well—" Drew began.

"What's *Team America*?" Travis asked.

Matt immediately pointed a finger at Drew, shutting him up when Drew grinned wide and opened his mouth to speak. "It's nothing, kid," he said to Travis, and then to Drew: "He is *not* seeing that film. I'd be grounded for a week, so don't go getting it into his head."

"What is it?" Travis chimed impatiently.

"It's nothing; it's just a film with puppets."

"Like with Kermit and Miss Piggy?"

"No, it's by the guys who make South Park," Matt provided with waning patience.

"Cool!" Travis tugged on his brother's arm. "I want to go see that."

Matt groaned. "We can't, it's not showing. But there's others...."
He looked at Drew and Kieran. "So this bird film, I don't suppose it's
animated, with an after-school-special vibe?"

"Well," Kieran answered, "*The Birds* is about this woman that
turns up at this place called Bodega Bay, just as these bird attacks start
happening...."

"Bird attacks?" Matt asked hesitantly.

"You okay there, Matt?" Drew asked in a teasing voice. "You're
looking a little green."

"Soon enough the birds are killing everyone," Kieran continued
with relish. "You know, swooping down at them in the thousands and
poking their eyes out and stuff. It's awesome."

"Sorry, Matt." Drew grinned. "It's not quite *Pretty in Pink*."

"One of these days I'm going to beat you so hard, Anderson."

"I want to see the bird movie," Travis whined.

"No, you don't." Matt said firmly, glaring at both Kieran and
Drew when the pair cracked up. "Look, they're showing the new
Chipmunk movie, you want to see that?"

"Yeah!"

The relief on Matt's face was unmistakable. "Thank fuck," he
muttered, and shoved Drew when he started to crack up. "Okay, looks
like your movie's a little longer than ours, and I'll have to get him
home after this so...."

"Yeah, cool. We'll say 'bye here, then. I have to get back after
this too. You busy tomorrow?" Drew asked while messing up Travis's
hair with both hands.

"I'm free in the afternoon. Meet you at the usual place?"

"Sure thing. Bring your mitt."

"Cool." Matt purposefully knocked Kieran's shoulder with his
own as he shepherded Travis past them over to the separate ticket
booth. "Good to meet you, Kieran. See you at school, yeah?"

Kieran smiled, looking a little surprised, but nodded his head yes. "Yeah, see you around."

That left the two of them. They stood there awkwardly for a moment before Drew gestured for Kieran to go first toward the ticket booth.

They bought their tickets and then Drew asked, "So, how far have you gotten with the storage room?"

"I haven't even made a dent."

"Yeah, you might be at that for a while." Drew grinned. "Does Mr. Trinder have you clearing it out every day?"

"More or less. Though he hasn't come to check on me once. I'll be clearing that room out after graduation at this rate."

"What are you doing after graduation?" Drew nodded at the concession stand. "You getting anything?"

"No, I'm good." He showed his ticket to the usher and waited a second for Drew to do the same before continuing. "And I'm getting out of here after graduation," he said with conviction.

"Where are you headed? Have you had any offers come through yet?"

"No, I'm still waiting but I've applied all over. Washington, Michigan, everywhere."

"Whoa, you really do want to blow this joint."

"Yep. Where do you like to sit?" He nodded out at the sea of empty seats. "Looks like we have a choice."

"I like the back. What do you want to major in?"

"I was thinking English Literature. My plans haven't really extended past just getting out of Keys, really. What about you?"

Drew smiled. "I want to be a fireman."

"Seriously?" Kieran asked as they took their seats. "That's so cool."

Drew nodded. "Yep."

"I thought for sure you'd want to do something with baseball, you're so good at it."

"Thanks, but nah. I enjoy it and all, but I've wanted to be a fireman ever since I was a kid."

"Where are you thinking of going?"

Drew was quiet for a second. "The local community college. Here. In Keys."

"You don't want to get out of here?"

Drew shrugged. "Family commitments kind of have me glued to Keys for the time being, plus, I kind of like Keys, so…."

Unsure of what to really say to that and not wanting to pry, Kieran nodded. "I see. Well, I'm sure the fire department here could use more men."

Drew nodded. "I hope so."

The room darkened, and they eased into a comfortable silence as the trailers began. It was kind of cool, Drew decided, being here with Kieran in an empty theater and watching an old film they both happened to admire. He couldn't help but think that this would have been a great first date. But even as he thought it, some squeamish, straight-laced and eager-to-please part of him rebelled against the idea.

Part of him wanted to do what seemed to be a rite of passage for all other guys his age. He wanted to lay his arm across the back of Kieran's chair and have Kieran rest his head close against his shoulder. Or even just reaching across the armrest and taking Kieran's hand would have felt both natural and arousing for him. Instead he sat in this empty theater, barely paying attention to the film with every sense hyper-aware and preoccupied with Kieran sitting so close.

The whole afternoon had been a tug-of-war with what he wanted. He'd wanted to hang out with Kieran today to test the waters with Matt. He wanted to know what his best friend thought of Kieran, but at the last minute he almost lost his nerve. Kieran was actually funny and sort of cool in his own way, but he was also kind of hot and completely frustrating to Drew at the same time. He wanted to put his hand on Kieran's leg in the dark theater, but then horse around with the guy like he was Matt in the daylight so no one would look at them weird. There was no manual, no set-out rules of conduct, and it wasn't something he could ask Matt about.

He'd told Kieran it wasn't dinner and a movie, and where were they now? He was about to finish school having never truly kissed someone he'd wanted to kiss or touched someone who honestly made him hot under the collar. It didn't feel fair. So... fuck it.

With his heart in his throat and staring straight at the screen, he slowly inched his hand off of the armrest until the back of his hand touched Kieran's. He felt Kieran start, sensed Kieran turn his head ever so slightly to look down at their hands and then look back at the screen.

Glad that Kieran didn't look right at him or say anything, because he knew he'd lose his nerve if that happened, he knew that all it would take was one movement, one movement and he'd have Kieran's hand in his. He stared ahead at the screen, turned his hand, and then touched his palm to Kieran's. He threaded their fingers together.

He felt another involuntary jerk in Kieran's hand, but then he was relaxing, and there it was. They were holding hands. It sounded so juvenile and simple but felt so dangerous and out of bounds. He let his thumb gently rub against the side of Kieran's hand, took a breath, and chanced an embarrassingly inhibited look at Kieran.

Even in the dark, he could see the blush in Kieran's cheeks and the pleased smile that he was trying to tamp down by biting his lip. The second Kieran looked at him, he felt a strange mix of panic and amusement rise up, something that must have been identical in Kieran's mind, because they both looked back at the screen at the same time, smothering nervous grins.

He didn't know if this had been his plan from the start, or even what his intentions would be outside the movie theater, but for right now he didn't care and allowed this one small thing; just for now he didn't let go of Kieran's hand.

CHapTEr FOur.

KIERAN felt as if everything he did was in slow motion and seemed to be merely a reverse countdown from when it had happened. Two hours since Drew knocked him on his ass by holding his hand. Twelve hours since Drew—*bam*, out of nowhere—held his hand. Sixteen hours, forty-eight minutes, and thirty-two seconds… and so on. He went about clearing the storage room in a daze, or, to be more accurate, he didn't so much clear as sluggishly move the mess from one place to another.

Hell no, he hadn't seen it coming. But he supposed the fact that Drew had been so understanding, so *okay* with his crush should have tipped him off that perhaps he and Drew weren't so dissimilar after all. Honestly, he'd just assumed Drew was a decent, uninhibited, okay guy, rather than the standard jock cliché. Now he wasn't so sure.

Of course, everything had felt so different when they stepped out of the theater. Inside the dark theater Drew made that first move, Drew reached for his hand and held onto it for more than an hour while watching thousands of birds lose their shit on-screen. As soon as the lights came up, Drew seemed embarrassed, but that was okay because Kieran was too. But as soon as they were outside the theater where the weather was warm and they had to squint a little while readjusting to the daylight, things changed. It was as if it hadn't happened at all.

He hadn't exactly expected Drew to whip out a rainbow flag or anything. In fact, he still didn't know for sure what the deal was with Drew's sexuality, but what confused him was Drew's utter discomfort as the two of them stood there on the sidewalk, him nervous but still feeling a little giddy, and Drew looking like he wanted to run away as quickly as possible.

Their good-bye wasn't frosty, exactly, but it felt perfunctory and rushed at best. Had their hand holding in the theater been Drew's little experiment? If so, he felt the beginnings of resignation and letdown set in. They'd only held hands, and he felt juvenile and silly that such a small thing could hold such importance for him; it wasn't like they'd gone down on each other in the theater, but all the same he was at a loss.

What was really bugging him, he supposed, was the uncertainty. What would happen the next time he saw Drew? Would Drew flat-out ignore him, or just pretend it never happened? He didn't for a second want to let on that they were more than friends (if they in fact were); the idea of drawing more attention to himself than he inadvertently sometimes did made him feel itchy and warm. But he didn't want to be used like that. He wasn't some... some sort of hybrid pregnancy test— minus the babies and peeing, of course. Drew couldn't just hang out with him and try a little hand holding to see if the results were positive.

He was considering calling it a day and heading home when he saw the door to the storeroom creak open a fraction and then close again. He frowned, craning his neck to try and see who it was.

"Mr. Trinder?"

The door creaked open again to reveal Drew, loitering and looking like he hadn't made his mind up whether to walk through or bolt. Eventually he walked through the door and closed it behind him.

"Hi," he said quietly.

Kieran stared at him before jolting out of his stupor, and put down the crumbling plaster he held to wipe his hands on his jeans. "Hey."

Drew ventured a little further into the room, taking in the mess. "I figured I'd find you in here."

Kieran shrugged. "I'll probably be here until I'm old and gray; I think Mr. Trinder's actually forgotten I'm even here."

"It doesn't look like you've made much of a dent yet."

Kieran glanced away, rubbing his hands together to get rid of the dust in the small creases of his skin, and sat on one of the stools. "Are you okay?"

Initially Drew was startled, obviously not expecting Kieran to go straight for the meat of the discussion they were inevitably going to have. For a second it looked like he might play at being oblivious, but then his shoulders sank, his hands dug deep into his pockets, and he crossed the rest of the room to sit on one of the stools a little way away from Kieran. He mostly kept his eyes averted, only offering Kieran an occasional glance. "I thought I'd be the one asking that."

Kieran lifted one shoulder, sensing nothing but regret in Drew and feeling a crushing disappointment. "Nothing happened. I'm fine."

"It didn't?"

Kieran looked at him. "Isn't that what you want to hear?"

"I don't know."

Kieran sighed, and spoke softly. "It was just my hand, Drew. Not my dick. Relax."

Drew stared at him. "Maybe I don't want to relax."

"Then why did you practically sprint home after the movie?" Kieran managed a small smile despite himself.

Drew groaned quietly. "Because I'm a coward, maybe?" He lifted a shoulder apologetically.

"You're not a coward," Kieran tried to reassure him. "I think you were just… and I kinda hate this word because of how overused it is, but I think maybe you were confused."

"Uh, not so much confused, I think. Just a little freaked out."

"Because…?" Kieran encouraged.

"Because…." Drew swallowed. "Because it felt so easy." He looked at Kieran and clarified. "With you."

"You mean…?"

"I don't think anything through. I mean I never think *anything* through. So I didn't have any expectations. If I had, then maybe I wouldn't have taken off so quick, you know?"

Kieran frowned, turning on his stool slightly to face him better. "We had a good time, right?"

Drew nodded. "Sure."

"Okay good, because me too. And I'm not talking about…." He gave a short, breathless little laugh, looking away briefly. "I mean, y-you know I've got this dumb crush on you. But, it was really cool to just hang out with someone, *anyone* that just likes the same dumb stuff I do, like movies or whatever." He wet his lips, feeling kind of sick for admitting the following: "I-I don't have many—*any* friends," he said with a shrug, and let out a deep breath. "It fucking sucks and it's pathetic, but you say you freaked out because it felt easy with me? Well, me too." He shook his head. "God, I'm acting like a freak but I'm just trying to say that whatever you want is cool. Friends or… the other. But if you want neither then say so, so I don't make an idiot of myself. I've done that before."

Drew frowned at him. "What do you mean?"

"Just… just mistaking politeness for friendship, that sort of thing."

"Why the fuck do you have such low self-esteem? It's frightening."

Kieran looked at him uncomfortably for a second, then said, "Because I'm the weird kid. I'm the kid that gets bullied and called a freak! I'm the kid that wears weird shit and says stupid things and is obviously gay and *eats his lunch with the fucking janitor.*" With each sentence, his voice rose until he was uncomfortably loud in the small room. "*That's* what happened! Alright?" He stood, snatched up a cardboard box, and stomped a few paces away.

"*Whoa.*" Drew stood and followed after him. "You don't have to get all defensive and shit. I came to… to…."

"What?" Kieran turned, letting his hand go limp and the box drop to the floor.

"I've… what? I've embarrassed you now? I don't even know why. I thought we'd just talk about what happened or some shit, but you just blew up out of nowhere."

Kieran flushed red. He'd wanted to act casual and cool the next time he saw Drew. He wanted to be the one all put together, reassuring Drew that everything was fine. But here he was, an insecure freak. "You-you started talking to me out of nowhere, then you asked me to hang out and then you fucking…." He gestured helplessly with his hand. "With my hand. So maybe someone else would have taken that as nothing, but that sort of thing never happens to me. And now I'm just acting like a massive freak and you're never going to talk to me again and—"

Drew abruptly shut him up with an impulse he'd been fighting since the conversation with Toby, when Kieran smiled at him. He kissed him.

DREW took him by each arm, his fingers digging into Kieran's slim biceps, and pulled him into a rushed, unromantic, and hard kiss. He frowned into it, exhilarated and terrified by what he was doing as their lips pressed too hard. Kieran, after an initial quick intake of breath, held still and exhaled heavily when Drew broke the kiss, still holding him.

"Ow," Kieran whispered.

"Shit," he laughed quietly, nervously. "That was terrible, wasn't it?" Drew's smile lifted at one corner of his mouth.

"What was that?"

"A really bad first kiss, I think."

"No, I mean—"

"A combination of trying to shut you up and wanting to make out with you. Sorry it sucked."

"You want to make out with me?" Kieran repeated, baffled.

Drew nodded. "Ever since I knew I could."

Kieran blinked rapidly for a second and then wet his lip. "You can have a do-over, if you want," he said quietly. He wriggled his shoulders. "This is uncomfortable, though."

"Sorry." Drew quickly let go of Kieran and looked him in the eye briefly before dropping his own gaze to follow what his hands were doing. He put them on Kieran's hips, delighting in the nervous intake of breath this caused Kieran, and then pulled him a little closer. "Better?" he asked, and Kieran nodded.

The slight height difference meant he had to tilt his head down a touch. He didn't have much time to think about it, but he knew he liked that. He came in slowly and brushed Kieran's lips softly this time, once and then again, lingering a moment. He pulled back a fraction just as Kieran let out a shaky breath, and gently brushed his nose alongside Kieran's.

"That was unequivocally better," Kieran whispered, a sound like a breathless laugh leaving him before he bit his lip.

Drew swallowed hard, realizing that he was suddenly very turned on. His arousal stemmed partially from kissing another guy, *finally*, and realizing that was exactly what turned him on—not girls. Guys. One hundred percent guys—and then partly from seeing Kieran blush like that, breathing unsteadily and biting his lip all nervous and giddy-like. He knew he wasn't alone in this.

He couldn't say a word; all he could do was slowly walk Kieran backward—delighting in the way Kieran clutched his arm when he stumbled slightly—until he was up against the wall.

Arousal washed through him and he crowded Kieran against the flat surface, his lips a hairsbreadth away as he savored Kieran coming apart right there before him. He touched Kieran's cheek, his own hand not completely steady as his thumb brushed the underside of Kieran's lip.

He exhaled hard and dove down for a slightly more urgent kiss. Kieran opened up to him, and he slid his tongue in to search for Kieran's. In that instant, in that exact fucking *second* he finally understood what the big deal was. He breathed heavily through his nose and deepened their kiss, lifting his hand to hold the nape of Kieran's neck.

He was more turned on than he'd ever been in his life and he didn't know what to do with it. His own groan when Kieran tried to push back just as hard against him turned into something like a growl. Kieran's surprised whimper went straight to his groin and made him want to pin him down. Hard. It made him want to fuck. Instead he broke away, breathing heavily. He took Kieran's hands, which were clutching the front of his T-shirt, and slid them up his chest and onto his own shoulders.

"Put your hands here," he said in a rough voice.

Kieran did as directed, but then went one further and slid one hand along his shoulder and up the back of his neck to grip what he could in a fistful of short hair. Drew grunted, pushed Kieran back against the wall with a curse, and gripped Kieran's waist tightly. He hesitated a second and then slid his hands around, and down over his ass, and *squeezed*.

The noises Kieran made weren't loud, but they were breathless and needy and drove him crazy. His feet somehow situated themselves between Kieran's, and without even meaning to or without realizing what he was doing, he crushed his groin against Kieran's. They both had to break away from the kiss, gasping.

With his hands on Kieran's hips, practically holding him there, he could feel Kieran rigid against him and knew Kieran could very well feel him too. He moved his thigh against Kieran's, encouraging him to spread a little. Afraid that Kieran wouldn't let him do what he wanted to do next, he attempted to distract him with a kiss as he shifted his stance lower, just as he slid his hand under Kieran's thigh and hiked it up against his hip.

He kissed him deep as he took that first good rub. He didn't know if Kieran wanted it; he didn't know if Kieran would be embarrassed to be the one against the wall with his thighs pressed apart. He didn't know if it made Kieran feel like a girl to have him rubbing his groin between his open legs and against Kieran's erection, but it made him feel like he never had before.

He felt completely and utterly *male*. He felt alpha. And for those first few inexperienced rubs, Kieran was his, like he belonged to him, like Drew owned him and Kieran was his for fucking. He'd take the time to feel embarrassed by such caveman thoughts later, because right then, Kieran was gripping his shoulders, trying to move against him.

Feeling reassured that Kieran was okay with what he was doing, he slid his free hand down Kieran's other side. They broke the kiss for a millisecond, their eyes meeting.

Kieran's lips were open, plump and glistening. He just nodded quickly. Drew didn't hesitate; he shifted and then lifted Kieran by the backs of his thighs, making him gasp as he pushed him up to equal height against the wall. The feeling of being between Kieran's thighs, of those legs being spread for him and wrapped around his waist, was sublime.

"I fucking love this," he growled as he began to dry hump against Kieran. "Oh my God."

Kieran grunted and then pulled Drew close for a kiss that was as messy as it was desperate. Drew's arms began to shake despite using mostly his own weight to press Kieran against the wall. Unable to keep on kissing Kieran when his groin was tightening as it was, he broke the kiss, pressed his brow to Kieran's as he ground against him, and then moved his mouth against Kieran's neck.

Kieran gasped and clutched at his shoulders, and Drew's hands tightened their grip on Kieran's thighs as a result. Drew mouthed Kieran's neck, his breath coming hot and fast against warm skin as his hips began to lose rhythm.

He barely registered Kieran's hands trying to squeeze between them, pressing at his chest, and his breathless voice trying to get his attention.

"Wait, stop—*stop* or I'm gonna come!"

"Then come." He growled, trying to crane his neck forward to kiss him, but Kieran's hands were pressing him back again.

"What, just... just come in my fucking pants?" He gasped, managing a shaky smile. "I have to walk home in these pants."

Drew groaned as if in pain and crowded Kieran flat against the wall again. "I don't care." His breath caught on a particularly good rub, and he moaned, enjoying Kieran's hands against his chest. "*Fuck, please! Please?*" he begged, so desperate to finish, but needing Kieran to let him.

Kieran's cheeks were flushed, and there wasn't one thing that didn't scream that he was as desperate to come as Drew was, but he could tell Kieran was enjoying making him wait. There was a certain level of power there, and though it might drive him insane, he had to give those few seconds of control to him. Finally, Kieran nodded ever so slightly.

With a groan of relief, he shifted Kieran higher against the wall with shaking arms. He touched his brow to Kieran's, enjoying the tight grip in his hair from Kieran's fist when their eyes locked, and he began the slow grind once more.

There was something utterly heady about watching Kieran's expression as Drew rubbed his throbbing groin between his spread legs. It made him feel in control and in charge; it made what they were doing feel wicked. It made Kieran look kind of… *slutty*.

He groaned. Just that word in his head, with Kieran in the position he was in, was enough to begin the irrevocable slide that was gearing up to be the best orgasm of his life. When the coil in his groin became too tight, he had to press close; he hid his face against Kieran's neck and screwed his eyes shut.

Kieran's whimpers were becoming drawn-out groans. Suddenly desperate to get as close as possible and rub as fast as he could, Drew wound one arm around Kieran's back, absolutely loving that Kieran's arms instantly wrapped around his neck. He held one of Kieran's thighs up and against his own hip as he ground as hard as he could in a stuttering rhythm, but with the shift in balance, they slowly slid down against the wall. Drew went down to one knee just as Kieran clenched his hands tightly, losing rhythm in his hips and screwing his eyes shut as his mouth fell open in a silent cry.

That was all Drew needed to send him over. He came in hot pulses, his breath catching and his eyes watering.

They lay in a crumpled heap, gasping and pressed flush against one another as they found their bearings. Eventually reality began to set in, and Drew couldn't help the slow smile that spread across his lips, realizing that they had just made each other come in the art storage room.

"That," he said in a garbled, breathless voice. "That was… that was *porno* hot. Oh my God, Kieran." He felt Kieran laugh against him.

"That wasn't making out," Kieran giggled, his voice sounding far away and very light and happy. "That was much, much more than making out."

"You were egging me on." Drew smirked, shifting to lean up on one hand so that Kieran was beneath him. "Kieran?"

"Yeah?" Kieran looked a little nervous now that the heat of the moment was gone.

Drew went from leaning up on one arm down onto his elbow, and pressed a kiss to Kieran's lips. "You are fucking *hot*."

Kieran's cheeks, which were already flushed, suddenly burned red. A delighted smile and an embarrassed, shy laugh escaped before he bit his lip, shook his head and kept his gaze level with his hands, fiddling with the hem of Drew's T-shirt.

"*You're* hot. And you know it."

"I'm okay-looking...." Drew continued, enjoying how coy he'd made Kieran. "But you got this almost...." He chewed his own lip and grinned, wondering how far he could go, and what he could say before offending him. He leaned closer and stole a chaste, simple kiss before continuing in a lower tone. "You have this innocent, cute thing going, but when you're about to come?" He licked his lips quickly. "You kind of get a little slutty." He snorted when Kieran turned beetroot red, and kissed his cheek. "That's what made me come so hard."

Kieran was shaking his head. As red as a tomato but looking distinctly smug about it, he plucked at Drew's T-shirt. "There's, uh... there's something I've always wanted to see...." Kieran looked up at him, playful and daring at the same time.

"What?" he asked, and looked down when Kieran tugged at the hem of his T-shirt.

"Can I?" Kieran asked, and pulled the hem up an inch to demonstrate.

Drew snorted and then shrugged one shoulder as he shifted slightly. He watched as Kieran lifted his T-shirt to slowly, teasingly unveil his flat, toned stomach beneath. Seeing Kieran bite his lip with clear admiration and excitement was enough to get him turned on all over again.

"That something you've been fantasizing about, or something?" he murmured as he craned his neck to nuzzle against Kieran's collarbone, enjoying being ogled by the same (the *right*) sex for once.

"Yes." Kieran's hands splayed across his stomach and moved up to his chest .His touch was soft but still managed to have an effect on Drew. "Oh my God, look at you."

Drew's stomach caved slightly, his breath hitched, and he opened his eyes (unaware that he'd closed them) and looked down at Kieran to see him looking rather pleased with himself. He felt his own cheeks burn and caught Kieran's hands.

"We need to find something to change into."

Kieran groaned unhappily and shifted his hips. "I don't have anything."

"I have some spare shorts in my gym bag, *in* the gym. Let me go grab it." He gingerly stood, stretching his back, and looked down to see Kieran sitting up and plucking at his jeans where they clung to his groin. "A good thing school let out ages ago; otherwise this would be an embarrassing trek."

Kieran snorted. "Yeah, I think I'll wait here."

Drew bent and snagged a quick kiss. "I'll be right back."

KIERAN took advantage of the time alone to collect himself while Drew was off finding them clothes to wear. He sat on the floor, crossed arms resting on bent knees, and grinned like an idiot. He wondered if he looked different, because he sure as hell felt it.

That was… *insane.* He hadn't expected the kiss, let alone the frantic dry humping against the wall; his cheeks flushed just thinking about it. He hadn't known he could *feel* that sexual, but then he supposed it took the right person to bring it out of you. Drew was that person. He'd been assertive and growly and strong, holding him up like that… Kieran grinned, feeling himself getting worked up again.

He knew all of the doubting "what now" questions were there, waiting to be addressed. But for right now he didn't want to think about that. Right now, all he wanted to think about was the last twenty-four hours. The last twenty-four hours where he'd held a guy's hand, been kissed, and been made to come so hard he'd nearly seen God, all for the first time. Those were things to savor.

He looked up and then gingerly stood when Drew came back in, clothes in hand, and was surprised that the insides of his thighs ached a little. "Ow," he mumbled quietly as he rubbed his thighs.

"Are you okay? Did I hurt you or something?"

Kieran glanced at Drew and couldn't help a small smile. The guy looked cute, standing there, holding clean pants with both hands and looking worried. "I'm fine. I'm great, actually."

"Oh." That smile that lifted just at the corner of his mouth made an appearance. "Good. Um… I had these to spare. They're probably going to be a bit long on you, but I figure they're better than nothing." He held them out for Kieran.

Kieran took the sweats, and then there was an awkward pause between them where he was supposed to be stripping down. It was stupid to feel shy about getting naked after what they'd just done, but there it was anyway.

"What's up?" Drew asked, having changed back at the gym and now waiting on Kieran for them to leave.

Kieran worried his lip and then smothered an embarrassed smile. "Are… are you just gonna stand there, or…?"

Drew frowned, but then both his brows rose in amusement and comprehension, and he turned his back with a small laugh. "Sorry, I'm used to hanging around guys who strip off after games and stuff… guess I'm not that shy." He waited a heartbeat, then shrugged with his back to Kieran. "That, and I wanted a sneak peek at the goods."

Kieran slid his jeans and—after casting Drew a quick look—his underwear down, but snorted at his words. "Maybe some other time," he said, feeling daring as he pulled on the sweats. "Okay, I'm decent. Modesty maintained."

Drew turned around, smirking. "Some other time, huh?"

And there it was, the big question that would have to be addressed before they parted ways. "Well, I-I don't know. What do you think?"

"I think I definitely want to do that with you again. Soon."

Kieran couldn't help the bright smile that bloomed instantly on his lips, but quickly dialed it down to a casual nod. "Cool."

Drew laughed. "Cool," he repeated, and then snagged up Kieran's jeans for him and rolled them up. He frowned when something tangled, then offered a confused grin. "Suspenders? With jeans?"

Kieran shrugged, taking the jeans. "I don't wear them on my shoulders or anything."

"But, suspenders?"

"I like wearing different stuff."

"Now that you mention it, I'm pretty sure I saw you wearing a bow tie once."

"Probably."

"You really do march to a beat all of your own, don't you?"

"They're just clothes," Kieran said, his voice a touch uncertain.

"No, I think that's cool. Fuck it, do your own thing. Whatever makes you happy, you know?"

"Thanks," Kieran said quietly, appreciating the uncritical words. "Did you mean it when you said you might want to... you know, again?"

Drew stood close, wet his lip, and tilted his head for a soft, lingering kiss. "Yes. Though...."

"What?" Kieran asked, his eyes blinking open slowly.

"Though maybe we don't jizz in our pants next time. Just a thought."

Kieran laughed, just pleased there would be a next time. "Okay, okay. So... so we're what? Just hanging out sometimes and...." He trailed off, shaking his head. He didn't want to seem insecure, but he needed to know what to expect.

"Are you asking me if we're dating?"

Kieran lifted one shoulder, looking for pockets to hide his hands in and then crossing his arms when not finding any. "I just want to be clear. I don't want to overstep or something. I mean... are you—are you gay? Or just...."

Drew stepped back a little, taking a deep breath and letting it out slowly. It was a fair question. "You know what? If you'd asked me that yesterday, or even half an hour ago, I would have told you I didn't know. But now? Uh... yeah. Oh hell yes, I'm gay."

Kieran visibly sagged in relief. "That is so awesome. Can I please go on record for saying I *love* that you are gay."

Drew laughed. "Glad you approve, but we should probably be... discreet? I mean I-I really only realized this for sure here, with you. I don't want to *out* myself; I'm totally not ready for that."

Kieran held his hands up, palms forward. "Oh, hey, I'm right there with you. I think you know firsthand how much I hate to draw attention to myself."

"So... we're doing this just in private?"

Kieran nodded. "I can do that, though...." He bit his lip. "I mean if you just want to hang out like normal, that'd be cool too," he said, meaning how they had that weekend.

Drew pulled him close, looking pleased, and kissed him. "That's perfect." More of what they'd just done but somewhere not at school, with maybe Hitchcock, privacy, and a mattress? Fuck. *Yes.* He kissed Kieran, taking his time and sighing into it. He pressed his brow to Kieran's, and laughed softly. "How awesome is it that I can do that with you."

Kieran rose on his toes slightly and bravely wound his arms around Drew's shoulders. "It's pretty awesome."

ChaPteR FiVe.

THIS was the best freaking part of his day. What had started out as a punishment from his art teacher was now a blessing. However, for the most part everything was much the same. He didn't really run into Drew save for their one tense lesson together. Their lunch periods alternated and were never at the same time, so he maintained his usual routine of hanging with Tony. And their lockers weren't even remotely close, so they didn't have cause to run into each other.

During the last three weeks, he'd passed Drew a total of once in the hallway, and for whatever reason it felt uncomfortable. Maybe it was company, or the unfamiliar and unexpected meshing of two totally different people in front of others that made it so. They said "hi" to each other, but he soon lost his nerve and moved on, and though he might have imagined it, he thought he'd sensed relief in Drew.

He'd made one definite change though; he no longer went to his hiding place under the bleachers to watch Drew. It didn't feel quite right now. Whereas before it was weird, now that he had something going on with Drew in secret, it crossed the line into flat-out creepy, and he didn't relish the thought of explaining it to Drew in the near-impossible scenario that he found out.

So now was their time together. School had let out, and he came here to the art storage room under the guise of clearing it out. It looked virtually the same. He couldn't even bring himself to clear a little of the mess while waiting for Drew, his nerves were so jangled. His entire day dragged and whittled down to the hour, hour and a half they'd spend together three times a week.

He didn't want to think about how they hadn't really hung out outside of the storage room, because to do that would maybe risk what they had going on. He knew Drew had baseball practice two days a week, and it pleased him that the other three were spent with him. But it was only for so long and always here. He wasn't sure what Drew's situation at home was, but he got the impression that something required his time and attention there and that it was a sensitive subject matter, so he let it be. They didn't see each other on the weekends. But he was gathering his courage to broach that subject to try and remedy that.

The door opened, and his heart jumped into his throat just like every time Drew came through that door. He watched Drew close it securely behind him, that small action just turning him flat on. Drew turned to him, and a glance down below the athlete's waist told him Drew was ready to go.

They reached each other at the same moment, falling into what was becoming Kieran's nirvana. He loved, loved, *loved* that Drew got as hot as he did. He loved that Drew was unmistakably what would be called a "top," he supposed. It made him feel powerful when Drew got worked up and so turned on that it was just grunting and kissing and desperate hands scrambling at zippers.

He moaned into Drew's mouth when feeling his hands, larger than his own, sliding down his back, straight for his ass. He could feel Drew smiling against his lips, and knew he got off on his every reaction to what those hands did to him. He could do this all day, every day, just kissing Drew Anderson. If it were possible to have a career in kissing Drew Anderson, then he'd be set for life.

"Do you wanna go get comfortable?" Drew asked, his voice all husky in a way that made something somersault in Kieran's stomach.

He nodded and took Drew's hand to more or less drag him to the back end of the storage room, where there was a small nook surrounded by easels and a large, cracked wooden desk. They'd laid down some sheets that were spattered with dry paint, folding them so there was something between them and cold, tiled floor.

He lay on his back immediately, and then Drew was there, carving a space for himself between Kieran's legs, to lie comfortably.

But Kieran's hands on his chest stopped him from going in for a kiss. Kieran bit his lip to suppress a distinctly mischievous grin and pulled the front of Drew's T-shirt by way of asking him to remove it.

Drew knelt up on his knees, smirking. "Careful, I might think you only want me for my bod."

Kieran snickered. "Come on, take it off. Please."

Drew slowly pulled the T-shirt up and over his head, and Kieran groaned, making him laugh.

"Oh my God," Kieran breathed. "You could be in *Playgirl*." He couldn't help it; his hands went straight for where he could see a modest six-pack. He curled in a half sit-up to take hold of Drew's hips and press his mouth to Drew's stomach. He grinned when Drew sucked in a sharp breath, his stomach caving slightly against his lips.

Their brief time together so far had been spent realizing just how good it was to touch and be touched by another person so privately. Only recently had Drew been brave enough to unzip Kieran's jeans, startling him by slowly jacking him off. That's what Kieran's world was now. Kissing Drew, rubbing off on Drew, jacking off with Drew. He wanted something else, though, and knew for sure that Drew would want it too; it was just a matter of one of them being brave enough to ask.

He wanted to taste him.

He'd always wanted to try it. In every porno he'd ever seen, he always wanted to be the one on his knees. Just the sight of Drew's long, thick, and glistening dick sent his heartbeat racing. It made him want to forget all pride and just beg to go down on it.

He groped Drew through his jeans, earning him a grunt from above as he kissed that flat stomach. He glanced up, saw the look in Drew's eye, and took note of the position they were in. They both did. With Drew kneeling above him and his head level with Drew's stomach and hips, it was the perfect moment to be brave and make a move.

He swallowed hard and slowly pulled down Drew's zipper, the noise seeming to echo in the room. He eased Drew's jeans and underwear down his hips, and Drew's dick, hard and twitching, curved up directly toward his mouth.

"Kieran… y-you sure?" Drew asked, sounding adorably flustered and uncertain.

"Do you want me to?"

Drew let out a short, abrupt breath. "*Yes*," he hissed, his trembling hand ghosting across Kieran's jaw.

Kieran wet his lips. "Say it. Say it and I'll do it."

Drew groaned a helpless noise. "Do it, suck me off. *Please* suck me, Kieran."

Biting back a whimper, Kieran shifted to kneel up and encouraged Drew back a few steps so he could lean against the broken desk and Kieran could settle in front of him. He took Drew's dick in his hand and brought the tip to his lips, the unique scent of Drew, warm and musky, making his mouth go dry. He couldn't hold back a moan at finally having the head of a cock—*Drew's* cock—in his mouth.

The head was plump, bulbous almost, and glistening with precum. He licked it off with one swipe, glancing up at Drew as he did it and feeling ten feet tall when Drew gasped and gripped the edge of the desk tightly. The taste, salty, was even more exciting than the scent of him.

He licked under the helmet and along the underside of Drew's cock, tasting every inch of him, all while saving the best for last. He placed his mouth back over the head, took it into his mouth and, covering his teeth, slowly took Drew down as far as could. Not wanting to gag, he stopped when the head of Drew's dick touched the back of his throat, and with a moan, drew back, hollowing his cheeks and sucking. He heard Drew cry out above and felt him grip his shoulder as an anchor.

"O-oh my God." Drew gasped.

He drew back, suckling once more on the tip. "Is that good?"

Drew gave a breathless, almost hysterical bark of laughter. "Good? I'll cry if you stop, how's that for good?"

Kieran grinned and wasted no time in going back for more. He suckled on the head and gently cupped Drew's testicles, barely believing what it was he was doing and loving every damn second of it. He felt a thrill as soon as he began to move his head in an up-and-down slide, a rhythm he'd seen plenty of times on the Internet and had fantasized about actually doing more times than he could count. He was doing it. He was blowing someone. He was giving head. He was sucking cock and it felt unbelievable.

He barely registered the hands in his hair or the restrained jerks of Drew's hips. He breathed heavily through his nose and could feel his saliva dribbling down his chin, but he kept going. He used his hand to stroke the base he couldn't reach with his lips, and sucked hard. Nothing had ever felt as incredible or empowering as having Drew's dick in his mouth, having Drew himself panting and grunting above him. He loved the feel of it, how hot and *hard* it was. How uneven it was with veins, but then smooth and fat on top. He loved how it tasted and how precum would cling to his lip like a spiderweb as he pulled back a fraction. He fucking *loved* it.

"Kier-*Kieran*! You gotta sto—oh *shit*," Drew ground out and had to ease Kieran away from him and hold him by his shoulders. "You're gonna make me come." He panted, eyes closed as Kieran slowly jacked him.

Kieran looked up at him from down on his knees, his hand on the root of Drew's cock. "How do you want to finish?"

Drew stilled, and he looked down at Kieran, who was flushed, his mouth and chin glistening. "That's totally up to you."

Kieran hesitated a second, his own erection pounding in time with his heartbeat in his pants. "I-I want to swallow you. Can you tell me that it's safe?" he said quickly before losing his nerve.

"Totally, 100-fucking-percent safe."

Kieran took him back into his mouth and bobbed his head, feeling dizzy and a little scared that he'd just told Drew to come in his mouth. It didn't take long for Drew's breath to catch and for his hips to begin to stutter beneath Kieran's touch that held him more or less still. In fact, it took only for Kieran to roll his balls on a particularly hard pull up, and then Drew was coming. The feel of Drew tensing, of his balls pulling up tight in his palm and of Drew's hands in his hair, preceded the gush of come, salty and thick, hitting the back of his throat.

Drew's cry as he came was partially a grunt and an expletive of Kieran's name. Kieran actually managed to swallow most of it down, and only coughed when attempting to take a breath. He let Drew's dick slip from his lips, noting how his jaw ached a little, and swiped a hand over his mouth and chin.

Drew hauled him to his feet, encouraging Kieran to lean against him as they slowly caught their breaths.

"That was... *fuck*." Drew laughed. "I've never in my life... Kieran, that was incredible."

Feeling pretty damn fine, Kieran gently tucked Drew back into his pants and lifted his chin to press a kiss to his lips. He paused when Drew hesitated, not even considering that Drew may be uncomfortable tasting him after what they'd just done. He was about to apologize, but then Drew leaned close, his kiss tentative at first, but soon growing into something deep and lingering.

Kieran sighed when they parted. "That's the best thing I've ever done in my entire life."

Drew grinned lazily. "You were really, really into that."

"So were you."

Drew snorted. "Yeah, no kidding. But you were really... I mean you were so good at it." He bit his lip, unsure if he should go there. "Have you done that before?" he asked quietly, his hands resting on Kieran's hips, just under his shirt and with this thumbs dipping under the waistband.

Kieran shook his head. "No. First time."

"Goddamn. Talk about a natural-born talent."

Kieran flushed, ducking his head as he trailed his hand up Drew's bare chest, which was now damp with sweat.

Drew tilted his head to try and catch his gaze. "I didn't mean that unkindly or anything," he said softly.

"No, I know. I just… I *loved* it, Drew." He cupped Drew's face and kissed him firmly, trying to convey what it was he was feeling. "I've always wanted to do that, and I loved it. I want to do it all the time…." He kissed him again, a touch urgently. "God, I just want to be with you…." He kissed him again, shifting his hips against Drew. "Be with you and suck you whenever you want it, anytime, anywhere."

"God," Drew breathed, feeling a twitch in his groin. "I'll be sure to remember that." Another shift of Kieran's hips against his own and he suddenly realized that he'd left Kieran out in the cold. He slid his hand between them to cup his groin. "What can I do for you?"

Kieran looked him in the eye and unbuckled his pants. He saw Drew glance down nervously and with obvious trepidation. He knew what Drew was thinking; he knew he was nervous to return the favor and maybe not ready to, but probably would anyway. Kieran shook his head. "There's something else I've always wanted."

"Tell me, I'll do it."

"I don't want you to… I don't know." He hesitated. "I don't want you to be weirded out."

Drew raised an eyebrow. "Okay, now you have my attention."

Kieran laughed quietly but then grew serious again as he looked Drew in the eye, took the hand that was resting on his hip, and slid it into the back of his jeans, over his ass. Drew's hand naturally curled and stroked over the curve, squeezing a little, but it was clear he didn't know what it was Kieran wanted. Swallowing hard and fighting a blush, Kieran went up on his toes to whisper in Drew's ear and to hide his face.

"I want you to put your fingers in me."

Drew immediately pulled back a fraction to look at Kieran, and though Kieran braced himself for mortification, he was relieved to see nothing but hunger in Drew's expression.

When Drew spoke, his voice was a fraction deeper, his eyes seeming darker. He glanced between Kieran's eyes and his mouth, his hand still curved over his bare ass. "You want me to finger you?"

Kieran closed his eyes, feeling embarrassed despite Drew's obvious interest, but a heat rose in him regardless from the words alone. He nodded his head. "Please," he whispered.

"Have you done that to yourself before?" Drew husked.

Kieran instantly looked away, cheeks flaring bright as he bit his lip. Drew laughed quietly at him and nudged Kieran to make him look him in the eye. Kieran shrugged, but may as well have screamed yes.

"Maybe."

A low groan came from Drew's throat, and he spread his feet apart a fraction. "Rub off on me," he encouraged, pressing his thigh against Kieran's groin even as his fingers pressed between Kieran's cheeks, touching his hole and making him jolt with a gasp.

"Th-they need to be wet." He pulled Drew's hand free by the forearm and brought his hand and first two fingers to his lips. He looked at Drew from under his eyelashes as he sucked those fingers just as he had his dick moments before.

Drew dug his hand into the back of Kieran's jeans once more, going straight for his hole and applying light pressure against him. "I've never done this before," Drew warned.

"It's fine," Kieran lightly panted as he rubbed against Drew's thigh. "One, and then two."

Kieran gripped Drew's biceps as he rode his thigh, and gave a quiet whimper when feeling the tip of his forefinger enter him. "Keep going."

With Drew's gentle pressure and his own encouraging pleas, Kieran soon had two fingers inside of him, thrusting gently in and out. Drew's lips on his neck sent his eyes flying open, and he cried out.

"You love this, don't you?" Drew growled, and Kieran could only nod. "You are so hot." He accentuated the word with a more insistent push of his fingers, and Kieran clutched at Drew, his fingers winding through his short hair at the back of his head as the desire to push back against those fingers conflicted with the desire to rub against his thigh.

"Have I got that spot? You know—"

Kieran nodded his head vigorously. "You've got it, you've got it!"

Drew pressed his brow against Kieran's, watching him as he worked Kieran's ass with his fingers. "I bet you look amazing when you're having sex."

Kieran bucked. "I-I'm going to—!"

Drew quickly moved his free hand to cover Kieran's dick. With his other hand he moved his two fingers in and out rapidly, stroking him firmly like he really was being fucked, and massaged over the small lump inside. Kieran hid his face in the crook of Drew's shoulder, and with a garbled cry, came into Drew's cupped hand.

It took him a moment to come down, and he hissed quietly when the fingers slowly pulled out of him. He melted against Drew, his breath coming in pants. "Wow."

Drew laughed and kissed his forehead. "I need to go wipe my hands on something."

Kieran reluctantly moved and pulled his jeans up over his hips and zipped them up as he turned and leaned against the desk. Drew wiped his hands on one of the sheets with dry paint all over, and then snagged up his T-shirt and pulled it on over his head. He pulled Kieran close by the belt loops of his pants.

"Wow is right." Drew smirked and then kissed him softly.

Kieran flushed, hardly able to believe everything he'd just done.

"Hey," Drew said teasingly, ducking to meet his gaze. "No need to get all shy on me. You're incredible."

Kieran couldn't think of a thing to say, so just shook his head.

"Yes, you are," Drew continued, and then took Kieran's hand and placed it over his groin. "Got me all hot and bothered and ready for round two."

Kieran laughed, and decided to be playful and gently *squeezed*.

Drew hissed and then moved his hand away with a pitiful groan. "As much as I'd love to do every bit of that all over again, I have to get home." He pressed a kiss to Kieran's neck. "Are you going to stay here to actually *do* a bit of clearing up, or do you want to walk out with me?"

Kieran sighed unhappily. "I should probably stay and actually clear a bit up; I don't want to be in any more trouble than I already am."

"Poor baby," Drew teased.

"You could always stay and lend a hand."

"*Pft*, yeah, right." He turned back to Kieran. "So, um… tomorrow?"

Kieran bit his lip. "Come here."

Drew strode over, and when close enough, Kieran pulled him close by the front of his T-shirt and kissed him. Drew hummed happily.

"I have to leave and you keep making me want to stay."

"Then stay."

"I can't, I really have to get home, but tomorrow…."

"Just like I said," Kieran murmured against his lips. "Anytime, anywhere."

HE WAS embarrassed at exactly how eager he was to see Drew. They were supposed to have met up two nights ago, but Drew hadn't showed and Kieran didn't have his cell number to text or call him. Art class wasn't until tomorrow, and he didn't think he'd be able to sleep without knowing what was going on.

He had to admit he was feeling particularly vulnerable, considering everything they got up to the last time they secretly met up in the storage room. He didn't want to think it, but he couldn't help but wonder if, after the heat of the moment, Drew wasn't a little ashamed with what had happened between them and was now avoiding him. Just the thought of Drew avoiding him made him want to go home and curl up in bed. As it was, he stood in the hallway he believed Drew's locker resided in, hands dug deep into his pockets and hovering nervously around the water fountain as he discreetly scanned the hall for any sign of him.

With a start he spotted him standing next to an open locker with Matt and... Matt and Adam Jefferson. They were laughing at something, and for a horrifying moment he wondered if they were laughing at him—the weird kid Drew had gotten to blow him. He dismissed the thought almost immediately. Not only was Drew not like that, but Drew wouldn't want that sort of attention. He wouldn't want people knowing about him being gay or at least that he let a gay guy give him head. It was something they'd touched on, and they both agreed that they wanted it to be kept a secret, but just leaving him in the dark like this? He was beginning to have doubts.

Mustering up his courage, he strode over there, his steps faltering slightly as he approached them. He hesitated just on the perimeter of where they stood, all of them taller, broader, and louder than he was. He didn't have a clue how to get Drew's attention. They all seemed to be talking about some party at this kid Thompson's house next week. It sounded like they were going. He never got invited to things like that.

He tried a quiet "hello" but went unheard. Feeling the beginnings of mortification, he'd just decided to turn and take off before he was spotted, but was bumped into by Adam, who was backing up as he laughed at something Drew had said.

"What the—" Adam began, turned, and spotted Kieran. The look in his eyes instantly shifted from amused to something unkind. "The fuck are you doing standing so close to me, huh?"

Kieran froze up and glanced helplessly to Drew and Matt.

"Hey, I asked you a question, fag."

Kieran jolted backward, his backpack sliding off his shoulder to the ground when Adam's meaty hand pushed him in the center of his chest. Nearly tripping up on his own feet, he took several steps back, alarmed when Adam followed.

"Hey!" Matt gripped one of Adam's arms and hauled him back. "Take a breath, Jefferson. *Fuck*."

He felt an odd mixture of relief and betrayal when Drew snagged up the backpack.

"You okay?" Drew asked, sliding the backpack back on his shoulder for him. Kieran nodded, though he didn't feel it.

"The little freak was creeping up on me!"

"*Hey*, Jefferson," Drew said firmly. "Cut it out, alright?"

"And he *knows* me and Drew," Matt jumped in, gesturing between himself and Drew.

This seemed to not only stump Adam, but make him uncomfortable and pissed at the same time. "Fucking *whatever*, man." He pulled his arm out of Matt's grip and glared at Kieran. "Do yourself a favor and stay out of sight, reject." He slammed the locker door closed and strode off, cliché asshole jock personality intact.

Kieran tugged on the straps to his bag for something to do with his hands, and glanced between Drew and Matt. He couldn't quite read Drew's expression, but it was a mixture of imminent discomfort, guilt, and concern.

"I'm sorry," Kieran mumbled, feeling ridiculous. In fact, he suddenly felt stupid for approaching them at all. In what world would these guys want to be friends with him?

"Don't apologize for that A-hole, seriously." Matt lifted one shoulder, like it was nothing.

"Probably just forgot to have his juice this morning," Drew tried to joke, but shuffled uncomfortably.

"You know…." Matt began, pulling a bottle of water out of the duffle he had sitting at his feet. "Sometimes he's alright, and then sometimes I don't even know why we talk to him. I mean, I don't care how good his swing is, if he ever spoke to me—"

"He wasn't speaking to you," Drew interrupted impatiently, making Matt pause from taking a swig of water to frown at him.

"You forget your juice too?"

Drew cut a quick glance at Kieran and then playfully shoved Matt's shoulder. "Shut up."

Matt shook his head. "Anyway, 'sup, Kieran?" he asked before taking a gulp of water.

Kieran looked at Drew and then quickly away. "Um…."

"Is, uh, is it that art thing?" Drew stuttered quickly, both brows rising as if he was eager for Kieran to agree. "I know I was supposed to meet you to work on our art… thing. I'm sorry I left you hanging, but I don't have your cell number and…." He trailed off with a helpless shrug. "I'm sorry. I really was gonna try to find you today."

"What art thing?" Matt asked, screwing the lid back onto his water bottle before yanking his duffel back over his shoulder.

"Um, this project Trinder has us doing," Kieran supplied. "We're paired off…." He shrugged. "It's dumb but, well…."

Matt looked between the two of them, eyebrow raised as they both shuffled uncomfortably. "Well," he laughed, and slapped them each on the shoulder. "As riveting as that sounds, I gotta go." He looked at Drew. "If I don't see you before, I'll see you at practice tomorrow night, yes?"

"Yeah, cool."

"Bring your A-game."

"You got it."

"Later, Kieran." Matt held a hand up over his shoulder and was gone before Kieran could even respond.

Silence lingered between the two of them. Kieran didn't know if he should be apologizing for approaching Drew outside of the storeroom—they hadn't really discussed boundaries in that respect—but he stood there feeling hurt regardless.

"Are you okay?" Drew asked.

He shrugged, barely looking Drew in the eye. "I'm used to it."

"Just ignore Jefferson; he's a jackass, probably dropped on his head as a baby."

"If he's such a jackass then why are you friends with him?"

Drew sighed, and Kieran didn't know if he was imagining it, but it held a certain note of impatience to it. He shrugged. "He's on the team; you kind of become automatic friends with your teammates, no choice about it, really."

"That sounds kind of stupid."

"Maybe it is, but when it comes to Adam? It's just easier to be his friend than to not be his friend."

"I don't understand."

"He's an *idiot*. But he's an idiot I have to get along with because we play ball together. Plus he's… kind of dangerous."

Kieran blinked in surprise. "What? What do you mean *dangerous*?" Should he be genuinely worried?

"Not dangerous as in violent. He's mostly all talk. He's dangerous because he's ignorant and loud. And when he takes a disliking to something or someone, as you well know, he doesn't let it go." He cut a quick glance around them and lowered his voice. "He finds out I'm queer? Then the whole team'll hear about it. Scratch that, the whole school will know, and he'll have the potential to make my life hell. It's not worth it."

"So… your friendship with him is basically some 'keep your friends close, your enemies closer' bullshit?"

Drew nodded. "Basically." He tilted his head, smiling slightly. "What, you think I hang around him for the sparkling conversation?"

The corner of Kieran's mouth lifted in a reluctant smile. "I guess not."

Drew stepped a little closer. "I *am* sorry about not meeting you the other night. I really was going to come find you today to explain."

"Why didn't you? Where were you?"

Drew took a deep breath and let it out as a deep sigh, as if he'd hoped Kieran would accept his apology without question. "It's just family stuff, Kieran. I got pulled out of school and had to sort something out. I only came back today."

Kieran softened, realizing that he knew next to nothing about Drew's home life. "What kind of stuff?"

Drew regarded him unhappily, hooked his thumbs in his pockets, and hunched his shoulders as he looked away. "I don't— I don't really, uh…."

"I'm sorry," Kieran said quietly, sincerely. "You don't have to tell me."

"You believe me when I say I didn't deliberately stand you up, right?"

Kieran said nothing, just feeling him out, and then nodded. "Yeah, though… I have to say I was worried."

"About what?"

Kieran glanced around them in the now mostly empty hallway. "I was kind of worried that you might, I don't know, think badly of me or whatever."

Drew frowned. "What do you mean?"

Kieran barely shrugged, embarrassed at even having to address it. "Maybe you regretted it, maybe you thought I was like… I don't know, whatever the male equivalent of a slut is, or something." He tried to smile and pass it off as something funny, but he felt too vulnerable and exposed to carry it off.

Drew's voice instantly became softer, but no less sincere. "I had a *great* time. I don't regret it for a second and I would never think that of you. Well—" He tilted his head and bit back a smile. "I know I said the word, but… we both know it was said as a heat-of-the-moment compliment sort of thing."

Kieran did smile a little, his stomach fluttering at the appearance of Drew's dimples. "Do you want to meet tonight?" he whispered hopefully.

Drew's smile faded, his shoulders dropping. "I should probably head straight home tonight. Things aren't quite settled there yet. But we have art class tomorrow. I know it's not the same, but…." He shrugged.

"Tomorrow? I mean, *after* school?" he asked, hoping that he didn't sound as anxious as he felt and all while telling himself that he was not being brushed off.

Drew lifted one shoulder in apology. "I've got practice tomorrow night."

Kieran deflated. He knew it was true. He'd heard Matt mention it only a minute ago; he was just so afraid of whatever it was they had between them burning out. "Friday?"

Drew seemed to mull it over, and just when Kieran was becoming desperate, he finally nodded his head. "Friday should be okay."

Kieran smiled. "Great."

Drew laughed a little, probably at how infatuated he sounded, but Kieran didn't care.

"Oh, hey, give me your cell." Drew held out his hand.

"Um, okay." He pulled his cell out and handed it over. He watched Drew tap at the screen, and then took it when handed back to him.

"Now you have my number. Text me later, if you want." He shrugged in a way Kieran guessed was supposed to be flippant.

"I will," Kieran said, trying to not look as relieved and happy as he felt.

"Great. So… Friday, then."

Drew nodded, wetting his lip, and smiled in a flat-out flirtatious way. "Friday."

Kieran bit his lip and nodded. "Friday."

DREW knew he shouldn't, but he dragged his feet on the way home. It had been a bad week. Nay, it had been a fucking piss-poor week. He needed his uncle to come back home. Like, *now*. His mom just was not holding up. She called him a few days ago while he was in social studies—stressed, scared, and close to tears all because she'd burned her lunch, the mailman had posted a note through the door saying a package was waiting at a neighbor's house for them, and telemarketers had called the house three times.

He'd skipped out of class and then school the next day. It wasn't a severe brain disorder she had, she wasn't dying, and she wasn't a danger to herself or anyone else. She was just lonely and very easily unnerved. He knew that when things took such a turn, all that was required to set her back on an even keel was time and attention. Just a little time with someone she trusted, like her son or her brother, and soon enough all was well once more. Unfortunately, with his uncle away in the army, and with him attempting to finish high school, his mom sometimes faced lengthy periods of time with only the TV for company. And that made him feel guilty, it really did, but he'd hated standing Kieran up and had been at a loss as to how to get in contact with him. He was relieved that Kieran was okay now that they finally had managed to talk, but that didn't really mean anything when he wasn't even sure it wouldn't happen again.

As if all that wasn't enough, before he even got home to help his mother on Monday, his dad had called. Or rather, he called when he knew Drew would be at school and left a message. Drew was being blown off by his own dad, how pathetic was that? The anger this caused him was twofold, really. First, just hearing his father's voice had upset his mother and probably contributed a great deal to her upset two days previous. It probably took just thirty seconds of his put-out, disinterested voice, and it weakened her. She shrank, and when he got home, Drew could see so plainly the heartache and pain that was still there, even after five years. Second, he hadn't seen his dad in months, and was absolutely furious with himself for, however marginally, looking forward to this long-planned and previously postponed fishing weekend. Now it wasn't happening at all, and he felt thirteen again, waiting by the phone for his father to give a damn and call.

He dug his hands deep into his pockets and sniffed sharply. He was determined to keep his shit together. Right now, all his mom had was him, and he wouldn't let her down. Screw his dad. His uncle would be home soon, and everything would get better. Luckily, despite how potentially shitty all this had made him act toward Kieran, Kieran didn't seem to be holding it against him. That easy forgiveness with the promise of something completely spine-tingling and disassociated with the rest of his life was exactly what he needed.

Oblivious to it all, Kieran, or just the idea of being with him again soon, would see Drew through this rough patch.

CHapTer SiX.

KIERAN swallowed thickly, bitter saltiness lingering on his tongue as his lips grazed up a gorgeously toned abdomen that rose and fell with juddering breaths. Drew panted above him, coming down from an intense climax as Kieran slowly stood up before him, feeling smug and happy. He pressed his lips to Drew's neck, leaning against him and thrilling at the feel of Drew's arm loosely circling his waist.

"You're getting really, *really* good at that," Drew croaked, sounding surprised and impressed at the same time, and making Kieran feel absolutely *awesome*.

"Given the right incentive…," he murmured, continuing his spray of soft kisses against damp, salty skin.

Drew laughed. "You made your incentives pretty clear through text." He groped Kieran's butt. "Even made *me* blush."

"Kiss me," Kieran demanded, his voice quiet but confident. He pulled Drew close by the back of his neck, sighing into a much-needed kiss and winding his arms around Drew's neck. "I love kissing you," he murmured against Drew's lips. "Put your hands on my hips." He took Drew's hands and did exactly that. "I love your hands right here."

Kieran grinned as he was turned and lifted a few inches to sit on the broken desk Drew had been leaning against. Automatically he opened his legs as Drew pushed his way between them, looking to Drew for direction. His breath caught and he glanced down between them to watch Drew unbuckle his belt and unzip his jeans. Drew had come, but Kieran was still rock solid.

It was enough to have Drew's lips on his neck and his hand slowly jacking him. In fact, he didn't know if there was anything that could feel better. The sensation of being jerked off by a hand that wasn't his was still something of a novelty and utterly *amazing*. But lips pressing against the crook of his neck and behind his ear was something tender that couldn't be imagined or fantasized, only felt.

With his eyes closed and his head tilted back, lost in the most perfect feeling in the entire world, it took him a moment to realize that Drew wasn't there anymore. He opened his eyes to see Drew looking back at him as he crouched before him.

"What are you doing?" he asked, despite knowing the answer.

Drew grinned, looking nervous but self-satisfied at the same time. "What do you think?"

"What—*really*?" His breath whooshed out of him as his hands danced nervously over Drew's shoulders. "Are you sure? 'Cuz… really, w-we can just carry on with what we were doing—"

"I want you to feel this. You *have* to know what it feels like, and I'm going to be the one to show you."

Despite his brave words, Kieran saw him swallow apprehensively as he shifted to get comfortable crouching in front of him. Drew took his penis in hand, and the nervous look he cast upward, as if looking for approval, made a warm feeling swell in his chest. He reached to brush Drew's cheek, but gasped instead, his hand falling back to Drew's shoulder as a warm, wet sensation engulfed him.

"Oh my God," he breathed, closing his eyes. "Oh… *wow*." He heard Drew snort and felt him begin to pull away, and he even smiled, knowing how dorky he must have sounded, but he kept his eyes shut and dragged desperately at Drew's shoulders. "No, please, please don't—*ah*." He gasped and released a deep, agonized breath as the warm, *tight* feeling returned to his dick.

He didn't know how long that feeling of pure heaven continued— not long enough, that was for damn sure—but the second he opened his eyes, he wished he hadn't. When Drew began to scramble to his feet with a curse, it was then that he realized that they were no longer alone and Toby Bennett stood there, eyes wide with a stunned look on his face.

"Uh…," Toby said. Sounding about as intelligent as he looked.

Kieran froze and then hurriedly tucked himself back into his pants. He looked between Toby and Drew, mortified. Toby seemed embarrassed, but Drew... Drew's expression was bordering on total panic.

"Hey, look... I-I was just grabbing some supplies...." He held his hands up, showing he meant no harm.

He could practically feel Drew's desire to run away coming off of him in waves. Drew was edging away from him, his face scarlet. He tried to reach for his arm. "Drew, don't—" But the panic had set in, and Drew was out the door—pushing past Toby—in a matter of moments. Kieran stared at the door that slammed shut behind Drew, and his heart sank.

That was it, then.

Kieran straightened his clothes with a fury fueled by disappointment so acute he could barely breathe. His eyes stung and felt warm. He wanted to hit someone, he wanted to hit Toby. Clothes straight, he snagged up his backpack and turned to Toby, who was still standing by the doorway looking utterly dumbfounded. His voice, when he spoke, didn't sound like his own. It was a wounded noise he had no control over.

"Why'd you have to do that?" he shouted.

Toby blinked at him, raising his hands, palms forward once more in defense. "Hey... like I said, I was just getting—"

"I don't care, you shouldn't be here!"

"I've done nothing wrong!" Toby spluttered. "I'm staying late to try and finish my stupid art project. You guys are the ones who—"

"Just shut up!" He rubbed his hands over his face. "It's all ruined." Kieran looked up when sensing Toby close by.

"Look, I won't say anything, okay? I'm... I'm not going to *out* you, or anything."

"You won't?"

Toby seemed to study his face a moment, as if looking for something. "I always thought you might be gay too, but never in a million years would I have thought that Drew Anderson would actually—"

"'*Too*'?"

Toby grinned and lifted one shoulder in confirmation. "Guess I'm not the only gay guy in school. Hell, there's three of us, apparent—"

Kieran woke up. "You can't say anything! Not about Drew. He'd get so much shit for it, you can't—"

"Whoa, Kieran. Would you just—*hey*, calm down, alright?" He touched Kieran's arm, squeezing gently. "I'm not going to say anything."

"You won't?"

"No. That'd be kind of douchey of me, don't you think?"

Kieran didn't answer; he merely nodded miserably and shifted the strap of his backpack more comfortably on his shoulder. "I need to go catch up with him—let him know."

Toby moved out of his way. "Alright. Good luck with that." He moved past Kieran to snag up a box of acrylics.

Kieran stopped and glanced back at him. "You don't think he'll talk to me?"

Toby shrugged. "He blew out of here kind of fast, didn't he?"

"Well... I guess, but given the situation—"

"He up and left you to deal with me, didn't he." It wasn't a question.

"He was panicked."

Toby looked at him and shrugged. It came across as patronizing. "Okay."

Kieran's mouth worked as he tried to find the right thing to say, but eventually he gave up and shook his head. "I have to go."

"Alright, see you around. *Oh*," Toby said, turning to face him as Kieran was halfway out the door. "Just a thought, but use something to block the door next time, yeah?"

Kieran didn't answer and opened said door to leave, but paused when Toby spoke again.

"If there is a next time, of course."

KIERAN was at his wits' end. Drew wouldn't reply to his texts, and he hadn't picked up the one time Kieran had been brave enough to try and actually call him. He didn't come to the storage room anymore. He skipped art class. There was no mistaking that Kieran was being ignored, and the idea of it—the idea of Drew, the first person he'd kissed, the first person to try and be friends with him, trying to freeze him out—was unbearable. He didn't want to go back to just being alone all the time. Even just having someone to text was a novelty he didn't want to lose. Sure, Toby had tried to talk to him a few times. He'd even asked him if he wanted to hang out, but it didn't feel quite right to do so while his situation with Drew felt so unresolved. He'd tried to tell him through text that everything would be fine, but still there was no response.

Drew was still in school, he knew that much. He'd seen him on the field, from under the bleachers. It amazed Kieran how quickly his life had gone back to the boring slow drudge that it was. Back under the bleachers, hanging with Tony, the janitor at lunch, just reading his comics and trying to not sniffle in front of the big guy who *also* didn't speak to him.

Any attempt he made to speak to Drew had, as of yet, gone unanswered. So, out of ideas and feeling alone, he looked over his shoulder, checking again that the hallway was clear as he leaned against the locker—*Drew's* locker—and scribbled his note.

DrEw, PleAsE CalL me back, oR tExt, oR Meet ME in the S.R, aNYthIng. ToBy iSn't gOIng to Say A wOrD. CaLL me.

K x

He folded it and, after looking once more over his shoulder to check that no one was coming, fed it through the slats of Drew's locker. Voices coming down the hallway startled him; he snagged up his backpack and sprinted for the corner. Once safely out of view, he slumped against the wall, only perking up when he recognized the voices. It was Matt and Adam Jefferson.

"So we're getting hot and heavy, right? Then Tiff's sister walks in and—"

"Do I really want to hear this?" Matt asked in a bored tone.

"Trust me, you do. So Tiff's sister walks in, sees her sister half-naked with her hand down my pants and just starts screaming—"

Kieran peeked around the corner to see Matt screw his face up in distaste, a reluctant grin on his lips.

"Ah, geez, Jefferson...."

"Tiff's all freaking out, right? Because her sister's like... I don't know, thirteen or something...."

"Stop talking. Stop talking right now."

Adam shrugged, looking smug, and Kieran felt his lip curl. He hated that guy.

"The kid's gonna learn the facts of life at some point, right?"

"Stop. Talking."

Matt dropped his bag as they came to a stop where Kieran stood only seconds ago. For a horrifying moment, Kieran thought he'd screwed up and put the note in the wrong locker—knowing that Matt and Drew's lockers stood side by side—but was relieved when Matt reached for the combination padlock of the *other* locker.

"Hey, so... what's up with your boy Drew?" Adam asked, leaning against the lockers as Matt exchanged books from his backpack into his locker and vice versa. Kieran immediately perked up.

Matt shrugged. "Not sure. He might have some shit going on at home again, I don't know. He's not really in a talkative mood lately."

"Yeah, he nearly bit my head off in practice yesterday when I asked how his shit was going. Boy's got issues."

Kieran could see the heavy frown on Matt's face as he hefted his backpack back over his shoulder and closed his locker. He ground his teeth as a couple of girls walked by, chattering and making it impossible to hear what Matt said in response. As soon as they passed, he was pressed close to the wall, trying to listen closely and catching the end of a sentence.

"So he'll be there, yeah?" Adam asked.

"I guess. I don't know."

"Most of the team's going to be there."

"Look, Jefferson…," Matt said in voice that clearly indicated he was running out of patience. "I can't make him do something he doesn't want to do. He's a big boy, you know?"

"Oh come on. Thompson's parents are gone for the weekend and they have a pool. A fucking *pool*, Matt. That means bikinis."

"Sounds like a cliché eighties movie to me." He smirked. "Molly Ringwald going to be there?"

"Molly who?" Adam asked. Kieran rolled his eyes.

"Moll—never mind."

"She new here?" Adam frowned. "Is she hot?"

Matt stared at Adam. "Oh my God. Um… I'm this way." Matt tilted his head left.

"Oh, yeah, yeah. I'm heading this way." He gestured in the opposite direction. "Look, get Drew to come along, alright? He's been acting like a dick, burning bridges left and right, you know?"

"I'll see what I can do." Matt nodded. "See you later." He headed off.

"Remember, Thompson's place is on Forty-two Whiddon Avenue, nine o'clock tonight!" Adam called, and Matt held up a hand in a wave without turning around.

Kieran watched as Adam took off, and waited until he rounded the corner before slumping against the wall.

A party.

Even as the idea formed in his head, his insides churned at the mere thought of doing it. Crashing a party? Crashing a party he knew there was a good chance Drew would be at? The last time he'd been to a party was when he was... what? Five? And that had been at his dad's restaurant. The idea of going to a party now, with people from school who'd probably be drunk and that much meaner, was enough to make him break out in a sweat.

But Drew might be there.

And there was no way Drew would get mad at him in front of others, especially in front of Matt, who sounded as in the dark as he was. He wished there was something else he could do, another way to get Drew's attention without drawing attention to himself. He was holding on to the hope that if he could just somehow let Drew know that it was fine, that Toby wasn't going to say anything, then they could go back to the way things were—they could have their secret again. But as the days had passed, he was beginning to realize that perhaps all he was doing was flogging a dead horse.

His stomach grumbled. He headed off toward the janitor's closet, wondering if maybe he explained it to Tony (leaving out a few incriminating details) then perhaps the friendly janitor could grunt some sort of wisdom at him.

He rolled his eyes at himself. He was on his own in this. He heaved a heavy sigh and decided that if Drew ignored his note and didn't text or call him, then he was just going to have to grow a pair and go to the party.

DREW had no idea what the girl sitting next to him was even talking about. Her voice was nothing but an annoying buzz amidst an even louder and more annoying buzz. The house was packed, everyone was having a good time, and he felt like shit.

Kieran had texted him, called him, even left him a note in his locker, and he was too chickenshit to call him back. It was eating him up. He'd run out of that storage room like a coward and left Kieran to deal with the fallout. And even now, after the texts and the voicemail and the note telling him they were in the clear and that D-bag Toby wasn't going to breathe a word, even now he was afraid to face Kieran. It was a different ball game entirely when someone else knew. He felt exposed, and the pressure was tenfold; combine the two and it made an ugly monster inside of him. It made him afraid and isolated. Maybe worse yet, he now knew what kind of guy he was when push came to shove. He was the guy that bailed. He picked at the label on the water bottle he held. He hated himself.

"Hey, earth to Drew."

Drew looked up to see Matt looking at him funny. "What?"

The corner of Matt's mouth lifted in a bemused grin. "You totally just blew off Becky Arnold."

He looked around him. "Who's Becky Arnold?"

"Uh, the girl that was just here for the past fifteen minutes talking to you?"

He couldn't bring himself to really give a shit. "Oh."

Matt's grin fell, and he eventually glanced away with a sigh. He looked back at Drew, and Drew was unable to suppress the sliver of annoyance he felt at Matt's attention. He lifted his eyebrows and shook his head slightly in a clear "what?" gesture. He knew he was being a dick but seemed incapable of acting like anything else lately.

"What's going on with you?" Matt asked, his voice lowered enough for only the two of them to hear.

Drew let his head loll back against the couch as he rolled his eyes, then stood and walked away and toward where he was pretty sure the kitchen was. "Do you mind?" he practically barked at the couple pressed up against the counter. He didn't even know who they were, but they both frowned at him, the girl rolling her eyes and giving a catty "whatever" before they vacated the kitchen.

With them out of the way, he opened one of the kitchen cupboards, closed it again, and then opened the next until he found a bag of Doritos. He turned to lean against the counter and opened the bag, letting his shoulders slump when he realized Matt had followed him in.

"*What*?" Drew groaned.

"What?" Matt repeated. "You ignore me all week and then bite my head off when I try and talk to you and you say '*what*'?"

"Oh my God. Dude, get over yourself."

"No, I won't, you dick." He crossed his arms over his chest, making sure Drew knew he wasn't going to budge. "Tell me something, where have you been lately?"

Drew pulled back slightly. "The fuck do you mean?"

"See, the past three or four times I've dropped by your place unannounced after school, you haven't been there."

"So what, we're not joined at the goddamn hip."

"Well, your mom tells me you're at practice, but what she doesn't seem to realize is that if *you* have practice, then *I* have practice. Being on the same team and all."

Drew swallowed and glanced away guiltily.

"So I thought to myself that maybe you were hooking up with someone and didn't feel like telling me about it yet. Someone like, oh… Becky Arnold? The Becky Arnold who hangs on your every word and cheers for you at every game? But seeing as you just spent a quarter hour ignoring her, I'm guessing that's not it."

"Who are you, fucking Colombo?"

"Where were you?"

"I… I was staying late to work on my art project, alright?"

Matt blinked. "Your art project," he repeated flatly.

"Yes, the entire class's final grade is dependent on our last project, so I've been staying late trying to get the stupid thing done. Happy?"

Matt nodded. "Okay, fine."

"*Fine.*"

"Just one more thing. If you've been staying late to work on an art project all this time, then why did you tell your mom you were at practice?"

Drew floundered for a moment. "She has a hard enough time remembering when I have practice, let alone anything else. It's just easier to tell her it's practice. I don't want to confuse her." He felt shitty for using his mom as an excuse, but Matt was backing him into a corner.

One look at Matt and he could see he still seemed skeptical. He was frowning, his eyes narrowed. "Something still doesn't feel right with you."

"You're making something out of nothing."

"Something out of nothing?" Matt echoed. "I don't even know who you fucking *are* at the moment."

"Quit being dramatic."

"Uh... how about you quit being an asshole and I'll think about it."

Drew stared at him and then tossed the bag of Doritos on the kitchen counter. "Fuck you." He made to walk past Matt, sick of the stupid party and determined to go home, but Matt grabbed his arm as he walked past.

"Hey!" Matt ground out. "I don't care what you've got going on in your head; you do not talk to me like that. I'm your best friend, alright? You do not talk to *me* like that."

Drew considered yanking his arm free and putting up a fight, but instead he let his shoulders slump and he let out a deep breath. Matt had always been the one person he could talk to. "I'm sorry," he said quietly, and to his horror, he felt his cheeks grow warm and his eyes sting. Matt let go of his arm, looking over Drew's shoulder to check that no one was heading into the kitchen, and then leaning his hip against the counter as he folded his arms and dipped his head to catch Drew's gaze.

"It's okay. Just tell me what's on your mind, alright? Because something's screwing with you—you're acting like a bigger dick than usual and it's starting to piss me off."

Drew looked at Matt and was glad to see that there was a somewhat gentle, teasing smile on his lips. He shook his head, at a loss as to what to say. He hadn't only been ignoring Kieran; he'd been ignoring his best friend, too. And even though Matt deserved to know—he'd certainly never kept anything from him before—this was different. This wasn't a normal secret. This wasn't some bust-up he'd had with a girl. It was a different, *heavier* confession.

Despite not really knowing how Matt would react, and despite knowing that this was definitely not the right place to tell him, he could feel the words fighting to get out. "Matt... I've never really.... Y-you don't know—"

"Drew?"

Matt looked up as Drew turned his head to see Kieran, standing alone and looking *exactly* that: alone.

"Hi, Drew." Kieran lifted one shoulder just as one corner of his mouth lifted in a hesitant, anxious smile. "Matt," Kieran acknowledged with a nod in Matt's direction.

Matt pushed away from the counter with his hip, lifting his chin. "Hey, Kieran, what's up?"

Drew might have imagined it, but he could have sworn he heard a note of frustration in Matt's voice. Drew swallowed hard, heat slamming into his cheeks at finally being confronted by Kieran. Sweet, nervous Kieran. "Kieran," he muttered in response.

Kieran glanced between the two of them as he pulled his hands out of his pockets and crossed his arms over his chest in a way that Drew was sure was meant to look casual, but only highlighted how awkward he actually was.

"So, um... so hey, how-how's things?" Kieran asked breezily.

It was the most uncomfortable Drew had ever been. He glanced at Matt, who frowned back at him, but then offered Kieran a friendly smile when the silence lingered a little too long for comfort.

"Yeah, yeah, not bad, not bad. What about you?"

"Uh, yeah, I'm fine, thanks. How's—" He was cut off by someone who accidentally-on-purpose knocked into him as they walked past.

After saying nothing in Kieran's defense as they walked off laughing, Drew felt something curdle in his stomach. Kieran cast him a quick, wounded look before glancing back at Matt. He was suddenly all too aware of what it had cost Kieran to seek him out, and he wanted nothing more than to man up and tell those two assholes to watch where they were going. He wanted desperately to tell Matt everything, and he wanted to take that look of anxiousness and apprehension off of Kieran's face. But the words wouldn't come.

"How's Travis doing?" Kieran recovered, valiantly attempting to start up a conversation.

"He's still a butt-head." Matt nodded and then grinned when Kieran laughed, but the conversation turned quiet again and Drew had yet to say more than one word.

He started slightly when Matt nudged him in his side. "What?" he asked, annoyed.

"Cat got your tongue or something, space cadet?" Matt frowned, then looked at Kieran. "He's been like this for days, don't take it personally."

A quick look at Kieran confirmed that was *exactly* how he was taking it.

"Where the hell have you two been holing up all night— Well fuck me, who invited the spaz?"

Drew closed his eyes when hearing the familiar voice behind him. That was all he fucking needed: a drunken Jefferson. He saw the discomfort and... *fuck*, a hint of fear settle over Kieran's features, even as Matt groaned behind him.

"You know, you're not doing the rest of us any favors by living up to the jock stereotype, Adam," Matt said. "It's not your house, so why don't you just back off?"

"I'll back off when he fucks off." Adam grinned like he'd just said something utterly clever and profound.

"Just… just what is your problem with me?" Kieran asked in a voice Drew guessed was supposed to sound aloof, but came out sounding nothing but tentative and was just the kind of bait Jefferson fed off.

"My problem," Adam said with relish, pushing past both Drew and Matt toward Kieran, "is that I can't stand little *faggots* like—" He never finished the sentence.

Quiet up until that point, Drew could suddenly take no more. He darted a hand out to grip Adam's arm before he could reach Kieran, and yanked him back. He turned Adam, who stumbled slightly, and crowded him back against the wall, his face darkened with anger.

"Like what, Jefferson?" Drew asked in a low voice that was shaking, he was so furious. Furious with himself and furious with assholes like Jefferson who had the power to turn him into a coward. "Finish the *fucking* sentence," he ground out through clenched teeth, all but snarling. "I dare you. Finish the goddamn sentence and see how many teeth you have left over afterwards."

"*Whoa!*" Matt was suddenly there, pulling him back, his eyes wide with shock at the pure venom he'd heard in his usually easygoing friend's voice. "Everyone take a step back."

Jefferson all but slinked away from Drew against the wall. "Fuck, Drew. The hell is *your* problem?" He put up an annoyed and unsettled front, but it was plain as day that he was rattled by Drew's sudden show of hostility, which was so unlike him.

"Adam, just go… somewhere else, alright?" Matt bit out, still standing behind Drew, holding him lightly by both arms, just in case he made a move for him.

"Fuck this," Adam muttered, color high in his cheeks as he turned and left.

Matt let go of him, looking between Drew and an equally startled Kieran. "Um… you okay, Drew?"

"I can't stand that guy," Drew ground out as he swiped his hands over his face.

"Yeah, well, us neither." Matt gestured between himself and Kieran. "But you don't see us trying to make pâté out of the guy. This isn't like you."

"He had it coming."

"Still," Kieran said softly. "You shouldn't give him reason to—"

"Why are you here?" Drew snapped.

Kieran blinked rapidly, flushing and looking uncomfortably between Drew and Matt. "I-I thought you might... It's a party." He shrugged.

"So?"

Kieran actually jumped. "I-I can go to a party if I want."

"No one invited you!"

"Drew, what the *fuck*?" Matt hissed angrily. "Jefferson's gone, the fight's over." He reached for Drew's shoulder and glared when Drew shook him off. "What is your fucking problem? You're snapping at me, you go MIA for days on end, blanking everyone.... One second you're defending Kieran and then you're biting his head off the next! I mean what's...." He glanced at Kieran. "What's going...?" Matt looked between the two of them, his expression turning blank, as if the cogs were slowly turning and a problem was beginning to unravel in his head.

Drew's heart jumped into his throat and he felt suddenly light-headed. Had he actually considered telling Matt earlier? "I-I'm getting out of here."

"Drew, wait! Please." Kieran took a step after him but stopped when Drew held up a hand.

"Hey, no...," Matt began, looking a little shell-shocked, but his voice calmer. "Drew, it's okay, come on, just... don't, uh...." He cleared his throat. "Let's go somewhere quiet and talk, just the two of us, okay?"

"Just leave me the hell alone." Drew pushed open the door that was already ajar and strode back through the living room, where the noise instantly doubled. He made his way through the crush of people toward the front door.

"Shit," Kieran said, making to follow after him, but looked back when Matt caught his arm. He didn't look happy.

"Kieran?" Just that single word sounded accusatory. "What the *fuck*?" he whispered.

"Matt, just let me go." He pulled his arm out of Matt's grip and followed after Drew.

Drew had made it halfway down the street before he heard Kieran's breathless voice calling after him. He didn't stop exactly, just closed his eyes and tilted his head back in resignation as he slowed down. He opened his eyes and there Kieran was, standing in front of him. He glanced around, glad that there was no one around and that the music from the party was now faint and far away.

"Drew." He shook his head. "I didn't mean… I didn't mean to fuck anything up for you, I just really, *really* needed to talk to you."

"Yeah, I got that. I got your texts, I got your voice mail, and I got your fucking *note*."

"Then why didn't you text back?" Kieran shot back, hating the way Drew was being with him. "Why couldn't you just acknowledge me?"

The anger lingered with Drew for a few more seconds, then slowly bled away as his shoulders slumped and he glanced away from Kieran, across the street. "Fuck, I don't know," he said, looking back at Kieran and shrugging helplessly. "I'm a coward? Or I'm just a really shitty person who makes false promises then leaves you twisting in the wind? You pick."

Kieran swallowed, took a deep breath and then let it out quickly. "Look, Toby's not going to say anything."

"I know."

"You kn— Then why... why are you doing this, then? Am I just some guy you fooled around with and now you're done?"

"No." Drew shook his head, certain of this one thing at least. "No, I really, really like you, Kieran," he said softly.

Kieran stepped forward, his hand extended where he wanted to grip Drew's shirt, but Drew gently pushed him away, glancing around them. "Then why can't we just go back to how it was? We-we can just go back to seeing each other in secret, yeah? No one needs to know about anything."

"That guy knows."

"I told you, Toby's not going to—"

"It doesn't matter!"

Kieran's hands flew out to his sides and then went limp in a helpless gesture. "I don't understand. What can I do to—?"

"There's nothing, Kieran. It's just…. It's enough that this guy *knows*. That makes it real and…." He shook his head, letting out a deep breath.

"And what?"

"And I don't think I can deal with it just yet. I'm sorry; I know how shitty that sounds. *Fuck.*"

"But... but you're so into what we... you know, what we *do*. How can you say you're not ready to deal when you're always more than happy to have me get down on my knees and—"

"*Don't.*" Drew closed his eyes tight a second. "I know, okay? I know how fucking dumb I sound, but I can't explain it any better than that. It's just the way I feel."

"So... so that's it?"

Drew shrugged helplessly, clenching his jaw hard when Kieran's expression fell with disappointment and his eyes began to shine. "I'm sorry."

"Are you saying we're not even friends?" His voice cracked, and he cleared his throat. "You just don't want to know me at all?"

"It's not like that, Kieran."

"Yes, it is."

"No, it's *not*, Kieran."

"What… what if I moved away from you in art? And-and I won't try and talk to you in front of Matt or Adam Jefferson again, or—"

"Kieran!" Drew let out a harsh breath and swiped his hands over his face. "Do you honestly think we could be *just* friends?"

Kieran's silence was response enough.

"Me too," he said, his expression deeply unhappy.

"Maybe you just need some time and space," Kieran offered weakly.

"Kieran, we graduate in a couple of months. You said yourself, you want to leave Keys, so what are we really losing here?" He lifted one shoulder. "It's not like we were actually dating."

He watched as Kieran digested that, and hated himself when Kieran looked away and swiped at the corner of his eye with the heel of his hand.

He'd made Kieran cry. He'd made Kieran cry and he was a fucking bastard. He reached to touch Kieran's elbow. "Kieran," he said softly. "Don't."

Kieran shook his head and walked away.

ChApTer SeVeN.

"EVERYTHING alright there, Kier bear?"

Kieran winced. "Dad, you know I hate it when you call me that," he said quietly, stirring his cereal.

His dad paused from taking a sip of his coffee. "Since when?"

Since forever. Since we became strangers. Since you started treating me like nothing more than a roommate. "Don't call me that anymore."

He heard his dad sigh, and it sounded uncomfortable. "Alright. Back to my original question, though, is everything alright? You seem a little down." He gestured with his mug to Kieran's cereal bowl. "I know you like it when the milk is chocolatey, but your breakfast is turning into mush."

He lifted one shoulder, continuing to stir. "Maybe I like mush."

"Kieran," his dad said, his voice more serious.

Kieran looked up to see that his dad had lowered his mug and was actually looking straight at him for what felt like the first time in months.

"You're worrying me. What is it?"

Kieran sighed, biting his lip. Now more than ever he wished he remembered how to talk to his dad openly.

"Is it your allergies? Are you feeling sick?"

He could barely restrain himself from rolling his eyes. Of course his dad would revert back to asking what might have bothered him when he was *thirteen*. "No, Dad, I'm fine, don't worry about it," he said in monotone.

"Are you sure you don't want to take a *mental health* day?" His dad smiled at him, as if he'd just said something very funny. "Your attendance is great. One day won't hurt. I'll call you in sick if you want to have a lazy day surfing the couch, watching movies."

Kieran considered it for a moment; it was actually a nice thing to offer, but he knew it wouldn't solve anything. "No, I should go in. I've got stuff to do. In class, I mean."

"Okay." His dad shifted uncomfortably, folding and unfolding the corner of the paper he'd been skimming. "Do you want to come by the restaurant after school? We can hang out a little."

Actually, he had plans. Pathetic, loser-esque plans. He'd be under the bleachers, his very own regular, private haunt, watching Drew and doodling with markers.

Not one word. Drew had not spoken a single word or even looked his way in nearly three weeks. He'd even gone so far as to ditch art class, which not only made Kieran feel like shit, it made him feel like a leper. And when he did see Drew, he seemed fine. Quiet maybe, but fine, whereas he himself was slowly coming apart.

Drew was right, they hadn't been dating. They spent a few weeks making out in the storage room; they didn't really *know* each other. But what was apparently easy for Drew to let go of was nearly impossible for him to forget. So Drew had hooked up with someone, a *guy*, for a while. He still had friends and an easy, normal senior life to go back to. Kieran had gotten a taste of what it was like to have friends and to feel wanted. Now he was supposed to just go back to being a loner? It was eating him alive. Even Tony, the mute janitor, had glanced away from his comic books more than once to frown at him and his lack of bubbly chatter. He had nothing to do and nowhere to go and he couldn't stop missing Drew—or missing the closeness he'd *experienced* with Drew. So no, he wouldn't be going to the restaurant to hang out with his dad. He'd be under the bleachers.

"I have to stay late at school. Sorry," he mumbled. He pushed his bowl of cereal—which was indeed now nothing but mush—away and stood from the table. "See you later, or whenever."

His dad sighed. "Okay, Kier. You know where I'll be if you need me."

HE TRIED his best to ignore the empty seat next to him, but it may as well have been a swirling black hole where Drew was supposed to be. He probably looked as miserable as he felt, but he didn't much care. He could stick this out for a few more months before leaving.

And he would be leaving. The American River College had written back, accepting him. More than two thousand miles away from Keys and away from everything he'd ever known. He thought that, if anything, these gloomy past few weeks would only strengthen his resolve to take off. But it didn't. He hadn't been able to mention it to his dad—who he was pretty sure wanted him to stay local—and he wasn't sure why. And the thought of leaving the place where Drew had last spoken to him, and last touched him, filled him with misery.

He had time yet to bring it up, there was plenty of time to make arrangements and to get around his dad, and he knew he still wanted to go, but what he hadn't expected was to feel sad about leaving. He shook his head. Whatever. What will be, will be, and all that shit.

"Hey, how's it going?"

Kieran looked up, snapping out of his daydream. "Oh, hey, Toby."

Toby frowned. "You okay?"

Kieran forced a smile and nodded, but couldn't really bring himself to speak so instead went back to his open sketchbook.

"Is it alright if I sit here?"

Kieran's instinct was tell him no, it was Drew's stool, and where he sat, no one else. Then he realized how desperate and stupid that would make him sound, and lifted one shoulder instead. "If you like. You sure Trinder won't mind?"

Toby gave him an odd smile. "Your head really is in the clouds, isn't it? Mr. Trinder isn't here today. We've got a sub."

Kieran looked to the front of the class and noticed that, yes, that wasn't Mr. Trinder sitting at his desk, reading a book and ignoring the class. "Oh."

"I hope you don't mind me saying that you seem a little… out of it, just lately." Toby pulled out Drew's stool and sat himself down.

"Do I?" he asked, attempting to seem disinterested in lieu of actually having to talk about why.

"Well… *yeah*." Toby laughed humorlessly. "And I don't think I need to guess why."

Kieran glanced at him and then quickly looked away again, worrying his lip. He didn't want to talk about it with Toby. "It's nothing."

"Look…." Toby lowered his voice. "The guy's not worth it."

"*Don't*," Kieran whispered harshly, glancing around them. No one was paying attention.

"Hey, I get it, okay? He's good-looking, even I can appreciate that. Hell, I may have even carried a torch for him myself back in the day."

Kieran frowned at him, wondering just when "back in the day" was, precisely. He swallowed down his annoyance and jealousy at the thought of anyone else being with Drew. He knew he'd been Drew's first gay… whatever he'd been.

"He's athletic…." Toby continued in a low voice only for them, oblivious to Kieran's feelings. "He's cute, he's—at first glance—a nice guy, he's even academic, but he's also a total prick."

"What?" Kieran snapped. Even now, he felt loyal to Drew. It was pathetic.

"Come on. The guy freaks out and then cuts you loose like you're nothing?"

That stung, but he had no rebuttal. There was no refuting the truth.

"Surely that's not the kind of guy you want to be with?"

"Well…." He glanced around quickly and chipped off the edge of his eraser with his thumbnail. "We were never really… *together*."

"Well, there you go. Don't you want more than that?"

"I don't really know what I want." It was a lie and he knew it. He just didn't want to acknowledge it.

"What you need is perspective."

"Perspective?" he echoed dubiously.

"You need to have some *fun*. Tell you what, are you busy tonight?"

"Well, actually…." He looked at Toby, trying to read him. Why the hell not? "N-no, I guess not."

"Right, you're hanging with me, then."

The bell signaling the end of class interrupted them. Toby nudged him with his elbow as he stood.

"Meet me by the front gate when school lets out. I've got my car with me today."

"Uh… well, okay, I guess."

"Great, it's a date." He winked, looking smug, and Kieran didn't know if he was kidding around or if Toby was naturally that bullish.

Not having a chance to even respond, he slowly gathered his things together, watching as Toby took off out of the classroom with a quick glance back.

THE CD player was blaring and Kieran felt himself wince as the singer of some obscure rock band screamed at him through the speakers. This did, however, leave little space for conversation and instead allowed opportunity for Kieran to observe.

Everything about Toby exuded confidence. Kieran just wasn't sure if it was something to admire or downright annoying. Everything down to the way he dressed, the way he spoke, and the way he drove. Even his car was a little beyond what he'd expect a senior to be driving. He reasoned it had to belong to his parents; he had no idea what make it was (not having a license or being a car guy and choosing instead to mostly walk everywhere), but it was red, kind of slinky looking, and had a soft top that was thankfully *up* for the time being. It was the perfect car to be showing off in, if you ignored the faulty passenger door handle. It was with a flush that Toby had come around to the passenger side of the car and had to jimmy and yank at the handle before it would open. Aside from that, it was a proverbial chick… or dude (as the case may be) magnet.

Toby drove a little too fast, Kieran thought, but seemed very laid-back about it. He was slouched in the driver's seat with one hand on the wheel and his elbow resting on the driver's window frame. Kieran had never honestly taken a moment to observe Toby, to truly look at him, and it turned out he wasn't a bad-looking guy, really.

He had dark hair that swept across his brow and curled around his ears, and one of those tunnel things in his ear, the type of earring that stretched a hole in your earlobe and made it droopy like some kind of aboriginal tribesman. His jeans were low riding and baggy, and he wore a thin chain hooked through a belt loop and leading to his back pocket. He looked cool, way cooler than Drew. Where Drew had a straightedge, clean-cut, good-boy vibe, Toby possessed something completely different. Toby didn't quite pull off the bad-boy vibe, but he had something about him that was difficult to feel out, he was almost… indifferent, and therefore solid, *impermeable.*

Kieran could admire that, he thought. The idea of becoming like Toby—of being able to shrug off Drew or his dad or even Adam Jefferson, and just leaving them all behind with a well-placed "so fucking long, losers"—was entirely appealing to him. He looked at Toby and wondered if he'd misjudged him; perhaps he wasn't as shallow or boring as he'd first thought. Perhaps he was in fact a river that ran deep. Lost, but fucking owning it. Maybe they could be good friends, even best friends, and get lost together. He'd never have to think about Drew, his dad, or school again, and he'd finally start living his life without feeling like he was rattling around inside a birdcage with hot, sea-green bars.

Having said that, the fun Toby had promised him hadn't really materialized thus far. They'd stopped for burgers, and now they were just driving. He had no idea where to.

He turned to Toby. "Hey, Toby?"

No answer.

He attempted to raise his voice above the grungy thump of the speakers. "Hey, Toby!"

Toby glanced at him and reached to turn down the dial on his stereo. He grinned at Kieran apologetically. "Sorry."

"That's okay. Say, where are we going, anyway?"

"We're going to have a little fun and relieve some stress."

Kieran frowned at that. "Okay, so… again, where are we going?"

"You know Whiddon Avenue?"

All too well. "I'm familiar, yeah."

"Well, at the end of that street there's this little cul-de-sac, right?"

"There is?" He'd never been further than that kid Thompson's house.

"Yep."

"Okay, so… what's in this cul-de-sac?"

"The grittiest, most derelict and broken-down house you'll ever see."

That sounded unlikely. Whiddon Avenue was a decent enough looking area, and he couldn't imagine there being a shack standing amidst the run-of-the-road, middle-class houses complete with mail boxes and rose bushes. "You're sure?"

Toby glanced over at him, a grin lifting the corner of his mouth. "Oh yes." He raised his chin toward the windshield. "We're almost there. Look."

They passed the row of houses that lined either side of the road, which eventually hooked right, and just as Toby had said it would be, there was a cul-de-sac, tucked away and hiding. There were only three houses. One had a For Sale sign that looked as if it had been there for a long time. The second looked as if it might actually be occupied. The third, half-hidden amongst the overgrown lawn and trees, was a house that had been clearly abandoned and showed signs of having been damaged by a fire.

It wasn't quite the haunted house out of your typical horror film. If anything, it reminded Kieran of the scene out of *It's a Wonderful Life*, where George Bailey and Mary Hatch threw rocks at the decrepit old Granville house that would be their future home.

They pulled up outside of the burned-out house, and Kieran unbuckled his seatbelt slowly, watching as Toby climbed out of the car and closed the door behind him. He followed suit, struggling with the door handle for a second before getting out and rounding the front of the car to stand beside Toby.

"Now what?" he asked quietly.

Toby nodded up at the house, and Kieran followed him through the front gate that hung on its hinges, toward the back of the house. He watched as Toby bent at the waist and snagged up a couple of large pebbles that sat in one of the cracked clay flower pots sans flowers. A surprised laugh slipped from Kieran's lips and he smiled.

"Seriously?"

Toby put the pebbles—which were more like small rocks, now that he looked at them—in his hand. "Let's smash some shit."

Kieran laughed, his spirits lifted, and turned the rocks over in his palm. He could do this. Harmless destruction—breaking something that was already broken, he could most certainly do. "Hells yeah." He grinned. "Is this where I wish for the moon?"

Toby's nose wrinkled slightly and he looked at Kieran strangely, but his mischievous grin was still firmly in place. "What?" he laughed.

"I wish for the moon, then you throw a lasso around it and pull it down."

Toby snorted. "Oh do I, now?"

"Then I'll swallow it." He grinned and lowered his voice to whisper conspiratorially. "And it'll all dissolve, see, and the moonbeams will shoot out of my fingers and toes and the ends of my—"

"What the fuck are you talking about?" Toby laughed.

Kieran felt himself flush and laughed nervously as he looked down at his hands and the rocks he held. "Nothing, it's just a, um... never mind."

Toby raised one eyebrow in question, an expression that was something between mocking and amused on his face, and shook his head briefly before pointing up to a blacked-out window on the first floor. "How's your aim?" He glanced at Kieran, smirked, and then looked back and threw the rock. A sound of shattering glass echoed in the yard a millisecond later.

Kieran hunched his shoulders and quickly covered his smile with his hand. He'd never done anything like this before. He couldn't help but glance around to see if they'd drawn attention to themselves, expecting to be yelled at any second, but it was just the two of them. Toby laughed at him.

"Your face," he snickered.

"I can't believe you just did that."

"Why?" Toby swiped his tongue over his bottom lip and threw another rock. It was at a ground floor window this time, and was already partially broken, with black streaks ringing the frame where flames had surely once licked at the brickwork. "Your turn." Toby lifted his chin at him, taking a step behind him.

"I don't know." But even as he said it, he was turning the rock over in his palm, reluctantly excited about throwing it.

"Come on. If you break a window, then I have to buy you lunch tomorrow at school."

Kieran bit his lip. Lunch in the cafeteria, *with* someone? He felt himself nod, the idea too seductive to his inner loner, and he raised the rock shoulder high and threw it hard. The sound of breaking glass made him gasp, and then laugh a second later. He turned to Toby, who nodded with approval and raised his hand, palm up. Kieran laughed and high-fived him without hesitating.

Toby threw another, looking pleased with himself. "Feels good, doesn't it?"

Kieran grunted as he threw another rock, which missed its mark, crumbled, and bounced off of the stone wall. "Sure does."

Toby moved to stand behind him, his voice suddenly right behind Kieran's ear. "Do you know what happened to this place?"

Kieran's breath faltered slightly, feeling Toby's breath behind his ear and a hand resting at his waist. "I didn't even know these houses were here."

Toby snorted. "This part of Whiddon Avenue isn't too popular."

"I don't see why. I mean, obviously it could use a little TLC, but—"

"There was a fire." Toby pointed over Kieran's shoulder at where the black smudges outlined and licked upward around the windows on the first floor. "See?"

Kieran looked at the top half of the house. It looked pretty desolate. "Man, that had to suck; to just lose half of everything you own like that?"

"You have no idea."

Kieran frowned and glanced over his shoulder but then started as Toby took his wrist, the one that still held a rock, and raised it up. "Did-did you know the people who lived here?"

"Nah, I heard about it from my brother. It happened years ago."

Kieran allowed Toby to hold his wrist up while presumably he was scanning for an unbroken window. "The people got out okay though, didn't they?" he asked, frowning slightly. Though he knew that what they were doing didn't strictly make them good citizens, it never occurred to him that it could be inappropriate or disrespectful—that it might *matter*.

"There!" Toby spoke, excitement obvious in his voice.

Toby suddenly angled Kieran's body, putting both hands on his waist and turning him a step to the left. He pointed up over Kieran's shoulder to a window that was completely blacked out with dirt and soot, but was otherwise intact. His hands went back to lightly touching Kieran's waist, distracting him and making him swallow nervously.

"Break it," he murmured into Kieran's ear.

Kieran closed his eyes, and when he opened them again, it was to the sound of shattering glass. He'd thrown the rock without thinking, without even *looking*. He gasped quietly when Toby's arms wrapped around his waist from behind. Toby was laughing.

"A married couple lived in the house. They got out fine...." He answered Kieran's previous question. "But their baby died."

Kieran felt himself suddenly start, knocked out of whatever stupor he'd—however briefly—just been in. "What?" he whispered, something rising up the back of his throat.

Toby didn't seem to notice his sudden shift and lowered his voice as if telling a ghost story, his grin suddenly seeming unkind. "You just smashed the baby's window."

Something horrible slammed into Kieran, and he looked back up at the small window that was now broken. A sensation came over him that he hadn't felt in years: he wanted his dad. He wanted to cry and he wanted his dad.

He violently pushed Toby away, and it took him a few seconds to be able to say anything at all. "You *jerk*!"

Toby backed up a step, holding his hands up but still laughing. "Oh my God, you should see your face!"

He felt mortified. He felt as if he'd just been tricked into being someone he didn't want to be and now he was stuck. "I can't believe...." He couldn't even finish the sentence, and instead turned around and began to walk away. He was pulled to a stop, however, by a firm grip on his hand. He looked back to where Toby had a hold of him. "Let go," he ordered.

"Oh come *on*, Kieran. It was a joke."

"You mean nobody actually died in there?" he asked hopefully.

Toby let go of his hand and raised one shoulder sheepishly. "Well, no. I think a kid died, but—"

Kieran turned away with an angry shake of his head, but Toby took two large steps to stand in front of him, holding him by the shoulders.

"Hey, I lied about the window, okay? I don't know if that was the baby's window, it could be the fucking *bathroom* window for all I know."

"And that makes it better?"

Toby let go of Kieran's shoulders and dug his hands into his pockets. "You were actually having fun up until that point, weren't you?"

"Well… yes. But I didn't know—"

"And you were smiling. I got you to smile."

"Yeah, but-but that was before…."

"Then I'm sorry, okay? I'm sorry. I thought you were having a good time."

Kieran chewed the inside of his cheek. His skin felt warm and itchy, and he felt uncomfortable with the fact that he couldn't decide if he was overreacting or justified in walking away. Either way, Toby looked a little embarrassed and a lot disappointed.

He sighed. Maybe he was just being a total dork. "Can we take off?"

Toby brightened slightly. "Yeah, sure, do you want to go to the—"

"Can you just drive me home?" He could walk it no problem; it'd only take him twenty minutes or so, but he was suddenly feeling weighed down with disappointment, and he desperately wanted to wash the dirt from the rocks off of his hands.

Toby's shoulders slumped before he lifted one in a casual shrug. "Sure, whatever."

KIERAN hadn't really been paying attention to his surroundings; instead he was staring out the passenger window blindly as they drove in silence. He only came back to himself when he realized Toby was slowing to a stop. He squinted into the dark and vaguely recognized where they were. It was nowhere near his house.

Kieran looked at Toby, who was unbuckling his seat belt and turning off the stereo. Toby glanced at Kieran, that sheepish look back in place.

"I asked you to take me home."

"Yeah, I know…." Toby ran a hand over his scalp, scratching his head and ruffling his own hair before letting his hand fall to his side with a sigh. "I just wanted to…." He shrugged. "Hang? Just for a little while."

"We did. We hung out; you pissed me off, and now I want to go home."

Toby said nothing; he just bit his lip and glanced away. Kieran felt himself growing impatient. "Am I talking to myself over here?"

"You don't have to get all prissy."

Kieran's eyebrows disappeared into his hairline. "Excuse me?" He almost laughed.

"I'm trying to talk to you here, but you're—"

"Oh my God," he muttered, shaking his head.

"Can-can I just tell you something?" Toby asked.

Kieran barely refrained from rolling his eyes, and feeling tired and disappointed and no better than he had a few hours ago, he looked out of the passenger window and shrugged. "Say what you like, but then I'm walking home. Okay?"

"This was supposed to go a lot better."

"What was? What is 'this'?" He looked back at Toby, confused and irritated, the fight drained out of him. "I thought we were going to hang out like friends do or something. But then you were all...." He gestured at his own waist, feeling dumb. "With your hands, making me think something else. Next thing I know you're laughing in my face. What's that about? Are you making fun of me?"

"No! No, I guess... I guess I'm just a little messed up."

Kieran softened slightly at seeing how Toby awkwardly toyed with a loose thread in the hole over his knee in his jeans. "You're not... you're not 'messed up'. You're *confusing*."

Toby cut a glance to Kieran and offered an apologetic shrug. It wasn't actually an explanation.

"What did you want to tell me?" Kieran reminded him.

"Oh, that." Toby cleared his throat. "I ah...." He broke off, laughed a little. "No way to say this without sounding like an idiot. I... I like you." He cringed. "Fuck, that sounded juvenile."

"Well, no." Kieran frowned, trying to make sense of what he was saying. "But, I mean you like me as a friend, or...." He didn't need to finish the sentence; Toby's withering look was answer enough.

"You mean in a—in a gay way." Now who sounded stupid?

Toby's snort confirmed his previous thought. "Yeah, in a 'gay way'."

"Oh. Okay then. Uh...."

Toby winced. "Look, I know I'm not *Drew Anderson*...." There was no attempt to hide his obvious dislike of Drew.

"*Drew Anderson* isn't Drew Anderson," Kieran murmured.

"What?" Toby asked, sounding confused.

Kieran took a deep breath and shook his head. "Nothing, nothing. What were you saying?"

Toby stared at him a heartbeat and then sneered. "Jeez, that guy's got you twisted around his finger, hasn't he?" he asked, his lip curling.

"No." Kieran shifted uncomfortably, aware of the lack of authority in his voice.

"No?" Toby budged sideways, throwing his arm over the back of his seat so he could lean a little closer. "So if I tried to kiss you, you'd let me?"

Kieran's head snapped to the side to look at Toby, and unconsciously he wet his lips. Would he? "I don't know." He looked at Toby again, swallowing when seeing him leaning in. Fortunately—or unfortunately, Kieran wasn't sure—the stick shift was in his way.

Toby lifted his chin slightly. "Come here."

Kieran's mouth went dry. Something didn't sit quite right, and he had a feeling that it was his lingering feelings for Drew, or the persistent hope he had of somehow magically working things out with him, that was stopping him. He frowned. It was stupid to hold out for Drew. Drew had moved on and forgotten him. And here he was, alone, unattached, and desperate to be touched.

He shifted closer and decided to ignore the lift at the corner of Toby's mouth that wasn't so much pleased as it was smug. He didn't have to move more than a fraction; Toby took it as a green light and leaned up across the stick shift to kiss him.

It wasn't great and it wasn't bad; it just wasn't Drew. He knew he should just stop thinking. He should just let his mind float away and enjoy being kissed, maybe even try to participate a little, but Drew had been his first kiss, and there had been more than the urge to get off driving it. Their kisses had been playful, tender, and affectionate as well as hot. Toby's kiss was hot, but ironically left him feeling cold.

He jolted slightly when Toby took his hand, pulled it across the stick shift, and laid it on his groin. Toby was hard, and though the feeling of a hard dick felt right under his hand, his stomach fluttered with nerves that had nothing to do with anticipation.

Experimentally, he flexed his hand and squeezed gently. It was nothing he hadn't done before, but it became new again when it came to touching someone unfamiliar. Toby's tongue slipped from Kieran's mouth as he smiled against his lips, clearly enjoying Kieran's hand on his dick. He unzipped his pants and encouraged Kieran to slip his hand under the band of his boxers and wrap around his cock.

"I knew you'd love this," he murmured, and dragged Kieran close by the back of his neck to kiss him roughly before he could reply.

Kieran couldn't deny that while this felt different than his experiences with Drew—it being something simpler, devoid of emotion, and casual in a way that felt unimportant—he himself *was* aroused.

He could do this. There was no reason for him to not enjoy it and just go with the flow. He mustered up some courage and slowly began to jack his hand up and down, and felt a thrill at Toby's hiss, at the way he broke away from the kiss to let his head fall back and his eyes close. He was just starting get past the sense of going through the motions and starting to enjoy it when he felt Toby's hand at the back of his neck. Expecting to be pulled into a kiss, he abruptly let go of Toby's dick and shot his hand out to brace himself against Toby's thigh when the hand on his neck didn't pull him closer, but was instead trying to push him *down*.

"Whoa, uh, just-just wait a sec…." He scrambled, something inside of him rebelling against the sudden shift of making out and jacking off to something that required him to give more of himself.

"What? What's up?" Toby asked, sounding breathless.

"Nothing, nothing. That's just, um…."

"What? Was I being rough?"

Toby seemed to blink out of his pleasure-induced haze and was suddenly present. The tone of his voice, which was a fraction softer but implied confusion, abruptly made Kieran feel childish.

"Ah, no. You just— I wasn't *expecting*…."

"Oh, shit." He seemed genuinely flummoxed. "Sorry."

Kieran flushed red and shook his head, feeling pathetic. This was what guys did, right? Gay or straight, at his age he was *supposed* to be looking to hook up, right? "No, it's fine."

An awkward pause fell between them as they stalled out, though Kieran couldn't help but watch as Toby's hand strayed to his own dick, squeezing the base at first and then stroking up once. Kieran's breath caught, and his fingers itched to return to their previous activity.

Toby watched this. "Do you *want* to blow me?"

He did. And he didn't. He wanted to get off, and he wanted to suck dick, but it felt... *less* without Drew—without feeling like he was someone's boyfriend. However, actually being asked, rather than Toby assuming, took the sting out of it—made it feel normal and okay. If he couldn't have the warm, heart-pounding and breathtaking sensation he'd had with Drew, then he'd settle for the quick fix.

He nodded, and his voice sounded small and weak when he spoke. "Okay."

Toby lifted one arm, laying it along the back of Kieran's seat and watching as Kieran's head lowered into his lap. Two things happened the second Kieran took the tip of Toby's dick into his mouth. First, Toby hissed. His arm left its resting place along the back of Kieran's seat, and his hand came to settle gently on the back of Kieran's neck. And second, Kieran's eyes closed in bliss.

He was gay. He was so completely and totally fucking gay and he *loved* doing this. He loved it so much that he could forget everything else. He could forget how lonely he was, and he could forget the feeling of something close to shame and just enjoy sucking on the velvety, rock-hard flesh in his mouth.

"Shit," Toby said with no small amount of surprise and admiration. "That-that is fucking *perfection.*"

It shouldn't have, but the praise went a long way to making it easier to ignore that it was Toby—someone he couldn't say he knew or so far cared for much—he was blowing. He bobbed his head up and down, sucking and getting lost in the sensation so much that he barely noticed the hand on the back of his neck slide up into his hair. He did, however, notice when that hand balled into a fist, pulling tight on his hair, and began to guide his head.

Kieran frowned, grunted, and felt the beginnings of panic when he found himself unable to pull off the dick in his mouth. His head was pulled up enough for him to take a breath, but before he could speak he was harshly pushed back down, Toby's cock lodging almost as far as the back of his throat.

"Oh fuck *yes,*" Toby hissed. "Suck it."

Kieran grunted and felt the corners of his eyes stinging as the jarring up and down rhythm, guided by the tight grip in his hair, took away all control.

Toby pushed up with his hips and down with his hand, his eyes squeezed shut. "That's it, fucking... *bitch.*" He grunted and thrust up hard.

Any confliction left Kieran. He lifted a hand to slap at the wrist with the hand that held on so tight to his hair. He pushed against Toby's thighs, and took a deep breath as soon as he was able. To Toby's credit, he let go immediately.

He liked to go down on a guy; sure, he knew that without a doubt. But not when it was being used as some sort of domination over him. It had worked with Drew, and he still wasn't sure why, but with Toby, it didn't feel—or no longer felt—like just getting off.

Toby wet his lips, oblivious to Kieran's conflicted feelings. "Get in the back."

"The back?" Kieran coughed, his voice rough. He blinked hard and wiped at his mouth. One look at Toby and his stomach dropped. The whole "I like you" bit? Bullshit.

Toby leaned close and ran his fingers through the hair at the back of Kieran's head, tugging slightly. His smile that had always seemed to be a mish-mash of forced confidence and something smug looked nothing but cocky now. "I've got lube and condoms," he said in a low voice.

Shocked, he shifted away from Toby as something inside of him slammed on the brakes. "Whoa, *no.* No way."

"Why not?" Toby frowned at him. "You were up for it a second ago."

"No, I wasn't!" Kieran spluttered.

"So that wasn't you sucking my dick like a Singapore whore?"

Kieran was left speechless for a moment, just staring and shaking his head. "That was… I was only—"

"Look, you need a little tit for tat?" He looked down to Kieran's lap and then met his eyes again, lifting his chin slightly. "Unzip. I can get you in the mood."

"Uh. *No*, you couldn't."

Toby blanched slightly, looking for just a second as unsure of himself and as lost as Kieran. "What, you're… you're not into me?"

Kieran let out a harsh breath, looking at him in disbelief. "I don't like having my head screwed down on someone's *dick*," he ground out.

Toby glared and gestured down to Kieran's lap, or more pointedly, down to his erection. "Yeah, well that says otherwise."

"This hard-on isn't for you," he snapped.

Toby frowned, but then an emotion Kieran couldn't quite pinpoint—jealousy?—shuttered across Toby's face. "Fucking *Anderson*?" He spat out the name.

Kieran really hadn't meant to bring Drew into it. He'd meant that Toby hadn't been a part of it, he'd been looking to get off—to see if he *could* just get off with someone that wasn't Drew. He supposed he had his answer.

"What, are you in fucking *love* with the guy?"

"No!"

"Because I know you're not frigid. Fuck, how long before you rolled over for Anderson, huh?" He sneered. "How long before you were down on your elbows and knees?"

Heat slammed into his face. "That's… I-I've never—!"

"What," Toby scoffed. "You're a virgin? Yeah, sure you are."

Kieran spluttered, enraged. "Just because you saw me with Drew *once* does not mean I'm going to willingly let you—a guy I barely *know*—fuck me in the back of a car!"

Toby swallowed hard, looking utterly rejected as he zipped himself back up. He shook his head. "Whatever, man. Thought we could be friends with benefits or something. I'm over you. I don't care." His mouth scrunched up in distaste. "Fucking *Anderson*."

Something connected so instantly that it took Kieran a moment to speak. "Oh my God. This has got nothing to do with me, does it?" He only felt surer of himself when Toby cut him a startled glance. "You're into Drew, aren't you?"

"W-what? Fuck off."

"'I may have carried a torch for him back in the day', that's what you said. You're totally into Drew." He shook his head, shocked at himself for not seeing it sooner. "You weren't talking to me in art class; you were just too scared to talk to Drew." As quickly as it came, the anger drained from him.

"Oh that is just—you know what? You're not worth my time, you fucking faggot."

And it was back again.

"You don't have a goddamn clue what you're talking about." Toby gripped the steering wheel, his knuckles turning white. "I was talking to *you*, I felt sorry for *you*. Everyone knows how weird you are and that you hang out with the janitor because you don't have any friends, you fucking *freak*."

His every insecurity, thrown at him in such a small space and by someone who'd just been using his mouth, was enough to make Kieran want to cower. Instead, he turned to the passenger door and tried to open it. The handle was stuck.

Toby cursed. "Kieran... Kier—ah *shit*, I-I didn't mean to say that." His voice wavered, as if he were close to tears himself. "Kieran, I'm sorry, okay? *I'm* the asshole. Look, would you just—" He craned his neck to try and see what Kieran was doing. "Just stop for a second!"

"Open the door," Kieran ground out through clenched teeth, ignoring the hot, damp streak he felt against his cheek.

"Kieran, I'm sorry, okay? Just let me drive you home."

"Open the fucking door!"

"Look, just… just get out of the way!" He leaned across Kieran, practically pushing him back against the stick shift. "You have to jimmy it." He pulled up and back, his elbow jutting backward just as Kieran was leaning back up.

Kieran let out a gasp as Toby's elbow came into sharp contact with the corner of his eye. Toby instantly turned, his mouth falling open in shock at what he'd inadvertently done.

"Shit! Are you okay? Kieran? Oh man, I'm so sorry!"

Kieran, both shocked and dazed, pushed Toby's hands away. He reached blindly for the door handle, found the door ajar, and lurched out of the car. He stumbled away, feeling dizzy. He touched the heel of his hand gently to the corner of his eye, which already felt sore and puffy. He looked behind him to see that Toby had climbed out of the car, and took off at a slow, disorientated jog away from him.

"Kieran! Kier—for fuck's *sake*, let me drive you home. I'm sorry!"

Kieran ignored him, and only glanced back when hearing a car door slam closed. He watched as Toby—who had evidently given up on him—did a quick three-point turn and took off in the opposite direction. His shoulders sagged with relief, and it was only then that he let out a miserable, choked-off sob. He wasn't crying because his eye hurt, and he wasn't crying because Toby had only been using him because of his previous connection to Drew. He was crying because apparently, it was common knowledge just how much of a freak he was.

A friendless freak. A stupid faggot. And no one was ever going to want him.

When he got home, the house was empty. His dad wasn't there, just as he'd said he wouldn't be. Kieran was for once relieved. It bought him a few hours at least to try and explain what he was sure was turning out to be a black eye. He looked in the bathroom mirror and was shocked to see that his eye was swollen and already a dark shade of purple around the socket.

He jumped when he heard the front door open and his dad call out to him. He glanced back at his reflection and then toward the open bathroom door.

"Kieran?" his dad called.

Kieran craned his neck out of the bathroom door, and, seeing the kitchen light flip on, he made a quick dash for his bedroom. Once his bedroom door was closed behind him, he called out to his dad.

"I'm just going to bed, Dad." He winced when he heard his dad stride down the hallway toward his room.

"Can I come in?"

"Uh… I'm just—I'm just getting changed." He whipped his T-shirt over his head and reached for the scrunched up T-shirt with the logo to his dad's restaurant on it, which he kept under his pillow, and pulled it on.

"I thought I'd come home early tonight so… so we could hang out for a little bit."

Kieran blinked in surprise, and only felt even more upset that his dad had chosen tonight of all nights to try and reconnect with him.

"What do you say?"

"I'm—" He winced when his voice cracked, and cleared his throat. "I'm kind of tired, Dad."

"Kieran, is everything alright?"

Before he could tell his dad not to, his father was opening his bedroom door, and stopped stock still after spotting his black eye.

"Kieran, what's going on—what the *hell*?" He rushed over to examine Kieran's eye, taking Kieran's chin in his hand and turning it to see the extent of bruising. "Who hit you?" he demanded.

"*No* one. God." He yanked his chin free and stepped back. He was distantly aware of how pathetic he must look with his hair all mussed, a black eye, and standing there in nothing but his socks, boxers, and his dad's ratty old T-shirt that was three sizes too big.

"Why didn't I get a call from the school? Are you being bullied?"

"Dad, *Jesus*, drop it, I told you no one hit me!"

"Then how did you get a black eye, Kieran?"

"Look, it was after school, I was horsing around with some friends and I *accidentally* got an elbow to the eye. I'm fine." It was at least partially true.

His dad seemed only slightly mollified as he stood with one hand on his hip, the other swiping over his mouth. "You're telling me the truth?"

"Yes." He wrapped his arms around his middle, not quite able to meet his father's gaze.

"Would you even tell me if it wasn't the truth?"

Kieran looked up at him, unable to speak or even hide what it was he was feeling. His father's head tilted to one side as he let out a heavy sigh, and he stepped toward him, one hand extended toward Kieran's elbow. "Kier…," he said softly.

But it was too much. He was too raw and too tired. He was tired from the constant hot and cold, back and forth with Toby that evening. Tired of missing Drew, and tired of not knowing how to talk to his dad—the one person in the world who was supposed to know him, inside and out. He couldn't talk to his dad because there was too much to explain, and they were now so estranged from each other that instead of feeling reassured by his father's presence, he felt vulnerable. When his dad reached for him, he snatched his arm away.

"Would you just leave it be? I mean, that's what you're good at, right? Leaving shit be and taking off to do your own thing that doesn't involve me."

"Kieran, come on. I know I'm not around as much as I should be, but—"

"Just leave me alone! I don't want to fucking talk to you!"

His father balked, his eyes widening slightly with shock. He opened his mouth to say something and closed it again. He shook his head minutely, turned, and closed the bedroom door behind him as he left.

Kieran automatically took a step after him but stopped. He'd never sworn directly at his father before. He'd made snide comments about his absence, but he'd never intentionally said anything cruel to him.

The one time his dad reached out to him and the one time when he truly needed it, and what had he done? He'd pushed him away.

He sat on the edge of his bed and put his head in his hands after hearing the front door open and then close. He was alone in the house.

He was completely and utterly alone.

CHApter EiGhT.

DREW sat at the kitchen table with his head in his hands and with only one thought running through his head: *keep it together, keep it together*. She was cleaning again, and there was nothing he could do about it. To an outsider, a mother keeping a tidy home may not seem like much to fret over, but his mother was not your average stay-at-home mom.

One two-minute phone call from his father, and the house now stank of bleach. When his mother cleaned, it was usually an early indication that her fragile sense of wellbeing was circling the drain. She didn't just run a vacuum over the carpets; she shampooed them. More than once. She didn't just clean the cupboards, she washed and rewashed every plate and mug, she scrubbed the insides of the cupboards with every foul-smelling cleaning product known to man, and then repeated the entire process. It was pointless trying to keep up a normal conversation; when she spoke it was mostly disjointed, and she'd constantly start the next sentence before finishing the last. It was exhausting, and it was lonely to be the only observer and be unable to walk away.

Though feeling lonely was quickly becoming less of a novelty to him. He hadn't seen or spoken to Kieran in three weeks, and it was a horrible thing he was doing, avoiding him—he knew that. But at the time, it had seemed the smart thing to do. *Now*? Now he kind of hated himself. He hated himself for the way he treated Kieran, just cutting him off like that, and he hated himself for not being as brave as he wanted to be. Problem was, there was no other person he could point at to lay the blame on, not even Jefferson.

Since that Toby guy walked in on them, nothing had happened. No one else knew, and the world hadn't ended. And not only that, but since hearing Adam let rip the F-word at that stupid fucking party, he'd even shown to himself that he could handle the kind of ignorant aggression he would expect from others. He and he alone was responsible for how miserable he felt now. He couldn't talk to his uncle, his mother was already going through a rough time, he'd been a dick to Matt and had flat out refused to discuss anything to do with what happened at the party, and he'd cut Kieran out of his life—which was ironic really, because the one person he wanted to talk to right now was him.

The past three weeks had brought him nothing but regret and guilt. He missed Kieran. As new as their undefined relationship had been, he missed his friend. He missed the person who knew and shared his secret. Despite realizing that he and Kieran hadn't taken the time to really get to know one another and had instead ploughed straight into necking, he missed him. He caught himself thinking about that quiet, nice laugh he had. How shy and self-conscious he got when talking about what turned him on. The way Kieran looked at him—like he was the guy who was the exception in an otherwise harsh, boring world. Mostly, he missed having the opportunity to know Kieran better, because they could have been something amazing.

He thought perhaps his greatest realization had been that he hadn't prevented trouble by dismissing Kieran. He'd instead cut off the one person who had—or could have—truly known him. He didn't have that now. No one honestly knew him, and the resulting feeling of disconnection was crushing him.

He looked up at his mother, who was muttering to herself as she scrubbed the granite kitchen counter with more force than necessary. It was just the two of them in the house, but he may as well have been sitting there by himself. He didn't want to be alone right then, and not for the first time he wished he had a normal mother, or at least a mom who wasn't so fragile. He splayed his hands across the table cloth, and he swallowed thickly. "Mom?"

"Honey, I'm going to need some Pledge. Could you run out and get me a can, one of the big ones?"

"Mom, I'm gay."

"There's money in the cookie jar."

His sigh was more of a shuddering breath as he pushed away from the kitchen table, his chair scraping against the squeaky clean linoleum floor. "'Kay."

He unscrewed the lid to the cookie jar where his mom kept the cash. It was looking a little empty. He looked forward to the day when he'd be working and able to help out. As it was, they got by with his father's alimony payments, help from his uncle, and the occasional washing and mending his mother did for a few regulars who would bring their clothing over to the house for her.

"And you get yourself something, sweetie. Are you running low on anything?"

"I could use some new socks," he muttered. He'd never really missed out on anything as a kid. When he wanted a new bike, his mom and uncle made it happen, and whenever he needed new clothes or school supplies, he always got them, but that didn't mean he liked to ask. He took a ten-dollar bill, folded it, and slid it into his back pocket. "I'll be back soon."

"Alright, honey. Be care—"

He looked back at his mom when she suddenly fell quiet midsentence. She stood up from where she'd been crouched under the sink, still wearing her yellow rubber gloves and clutching her plastic spray bottle of disinfectant.

"Mom?"

"What did you say?" she asked softly, her eyes a little wider than usual.

He felt his heart begin to hammer. "I… socks?"

"No, no, honey. You said something else."

What had he been thinking? Blurting it out like that when she was already frazzled. He swallowed hard, figuring that she had to know some time. "I-I said I'm gay, Mom."

She gasped, one yellow rubber glove coming up to cover her mouth. He knew she was shocked, but he couldn't tell if she was upset or… he didn't know. If his mom was to shout at him or hate him, he knew he'd crack, right there and then.

"Mom," he spoke, his voice thick. "Are… are you okay?"

"You're gay?" she asked. Her eyes were glassy, but she was still mostly unreadable.

He nodded. "Yes."

"How do you… are-are you sure, Drew?"

He nodded again. "I'm sure."

"But how do you know?"

He felt himself flush, and he was unable hold her gaze. "I just know, Mom."

Her answer was a breathy "oh," realization dawning. "You… you have a, ah, a special friend?"

He was confused. Though there was a hesitant and shaky smile beginning at one corner of her mouth, there were also tears shining in her eyes.

"Sort of. Are you mad?" He felt as if he was five and he'd just broken her favorite crystal rather than having told his mother his biggest secret.

"Oh, *no*, baby," she breathed, taking a few steps closer but seeming hesitant to touch him, as if she thought *he* was the one who might bolt.

"But you're crying," he said with a hitch in his voice. "If you're not mad then why are you crying?"

Her mouth turned downward. "I'm crying because you look so scared, Drew. You just told me you're gay and you look like you're expecting me to scream at you. That's why I'm crying, baby."

She pulled off a glove and quickly wiped away a tear with a dainty sniff. She stepped forward and then cupped his cheek with her bare—and now damp—hand. "Why on earth would you ever be afraid of me?"

"Mom," he whispered, and fell into her thin arms, which she automatically opened for him. He sighed when she stroked his hair, and the relief he felt was a balm of sort to the jagged edges of all the complicated details. "I've been having kind of a rough time with it."

"Honey," she crooned. "It's alright, everything is going to be alright, I promise."

"You don't know that. I screwed up."

"Okay, come on...." She led him back to the kitchen table and encouraged him to sit down. She took a glass out of the cabinet to pour him a glass of water from the faucet, and he thought distantly that at least she'd stopped cleaning.

She handed him the glass, and it was only when seeing that his hands shook that he realized how much his mom's approval meant to him. He took a sip of the water and looked at her when she pulled another kitchen chair close, right beside him so she could stroke his arm.

"This would have been so much easier for you if I had just asked you the question."

"You mean you suspected?" he asked hopefully. For some reason, the thought of her having suspicions made actually telling her feel less exposing for himself, and less like a burden for her to acknowledge.

She pressed her lips together and shook her head. "No. I know you never really talked about girls or ever brought any home, but to be honest I... I just thought that maybe you were too embarrassed to." She tilted her head. "Too embarrassed to bring anyone home because of me," she added gently.

He frowned. "You don't embarrass me, mom. I just worry about you, that's all."

She squeezed his arm. "You shouldn't have to." She took a deep breath. "I didn't suspect, but your uncle...."

His eyes went wide. "Un-Uncle Rich *knows*?"

"No, no, he *suspected*." She lifted one shoulder in an almost apologetic shrug. "He said that if you'd wanted a girlfriend by now, you'd have one, no problem, and that you were never unkind. Not like how most boys can be sometimes, not even when joking around. And before you panic, no, he did not care either way, he just worried about you. He didn't want you to be carrying around such a big secret—if there *was* a secret—like some kind of burden."

His opened and closed his mouth, too stunned for the moment to speak. "Why *didn't* he say anything?" he managed eventually.

"Well, I didn't think it was the case—because evidently I'm a *moron*—and… well, if there was a chance, we agreed that it would be best for you to approach us." She looked at him remorsefully. "Honey, if I knew I could have made this easier for you by listening to your uncle, I never would have just waited to see what happened. I'm so sorry, sweetie."

He shook his head slowly, still digesting. "It doesn't matter, I guess. I'm just glad you're not throwing me out or something."

She slapped his arm, and just as quickly she pulled him into a hug, making him crack a tremulous smile. "Don't you dare say such a thing. I'm agoraphobic, not one of those religious nut-bags off the television."

He managed a garbled laugh and let her squeeze him for a minute.

"I like this," she said quietly.

"What?"

She rubbed his back. "When you let me be your mom. Seems like it's always you taking care of me lately. It shouldn't be like that."

"Mom," he said gently. "I'll always take care of you. You know that."

She let out a watery little laugh and kissed the top of his head before letting him go. "What on earth did I do to deserve you, hmm?"

The relief he felt was overwhelming. He finally told someone, and he was still standing. His mom loved him, his uncle already knew, and while he was sure Matt suspected something, his friend was still trying to get through to him rather than pushing him away. Though he knew he didn't have the balls to tell Matt yet, not by a long shot, he still felt a world of relief now that someone else knew. Someone as important as his mother.

She patted his leg. "So… you've 'sort of' met someone?" she asked carefully, looking nervous.

His happy glow dimmed slightly. "I did, yeah."

"Did?"

"I screwed up. I… I got jittery. I got scared about people finding out and just… just *dumped* him."

"Oh," she said softly, and when he looked at her, he was glad to see there was no disapproval in her eyes, only sympathy.

"'Oh'? I was horrible, mom. He was so nice to me and I just cut him loose. I hurt him."

"Drew, honey, you're *eighteen*, and this was—I'm guessing—your first relationship?"

He nodded, feeling himself begin to blush at discussing with his mother his first ever foray into the dating world.

"Well then, we all make blunders, sweetie. It's not like you were married."

Drew snapped his head up from where he'd been studying the pattern of the tablecloth to look at her, and it dawned on him why he was so utterly wracked with guilt. "I'm just like Dad."

"*What?*" His mother actually laughed at him. "Drew, what on earth are you talking about? You couldn't be any different from your father if you tried."

"But… but I just *abandoned* him, Mom. I left him all alone." And that was really why it didn't sit well with him. Not only because of the fact that he missed Kieran, but because of the way he'd ended things.

"Oh Drew, honey, *no*. That is not what I meant. I wasn't comparing you to your father and me!"

"But—"

"Drew, everyone gets skittish, particularly when it's to do with something so new and frightening."

"You don't understand, I was such an ass. I…." he sighed. "I made him cry, mom." He admitted, cringing and with no small amount of shame.

Something in her eyes softened. "Let me ask you this, is he a nice boy?"

Drew laughed sadly, rubbing the back of his neck. It was such a motherly thing to ask. "Yeah, yeah he's real nice, mom."

"And do you want to fix things between you?"

Drew flinched. Now that the emotional admissions and words of acceptance had been voiced, actually talking about his would-be love life—with another dude—with his mother, was weirding him out. Evidently this was written all over his face, because his mother was laughing softly.

"Is this getting a little strange?"

"Yeah, it really is," he admitted with a sheepish smile.

"Okay, we can leave it be if you prefer, but just tell me, do you want to fix things with…?"

"Kieran," he supplied quietly, flushing—yet again, goddammit—at actually saying his name out loud to his mother. "And yes, I think so," he said with a hint of surprise. Surprise that was immediately followed by anxiety at the very real and valid thought of what he wanted now being irrelevant.

She smiled gently. "Then if he's as nice as you say, he'll understand if you just explain to him why you acted the way you did."

His brow puckered in thought as he frowned. "I don't know."

She squeezed his arm and leaned forward to kiss his cheek. "Just think about it, then, and if you ever need to talk to me about it again—no matter how awkward—just know that you *can*."

He nodded. "Thank you."

She smiled, stood, and then pulled off her one remaining rubber glove as she surveyed the kitchen. Drew followed her gaze.

"Do you still want me to go get your Pledge?"

She let out a heavy sigh. "No. I think it's out of my system." She reached behind to untie her apron. "Tell you what, how about we use that money to order a pizza for supper?"

He smiled. "Sounds good to me."

KIERAN thought he'd have to sneak out of the house quietly this morning so his dad wouldn't notice, but that hadn't been the case. Rather than feeling relieved, he was instead upset that his father wasn't attempting to make stilted, awkward conversation with him. Where he wanted to feel angry and hold on to his resentment, his insides felt shaky, and he was worried about his father actually not caring about him anymore.

It bothered him all morning, through first and second period. It bothered him so much that he'd barely thought of Drew or Toby at all, despite the shiner he was sporting. He had no doubt that it'd drawn him some attention, but for once, he didn't care. Hell, maybe it would work in his favor and encourage others to leave him the fuck alone, because at that moment, that was all he really wanted. He wanted to throw in the towel and be left alone.

He struggled to pull his notebook out of his backpack, which was settled between his feet. With a muttered curse, he knelt down to unzip the pack properly and yanked out the notebook. When he stood back up, his locker door—with a squeaky hinge that pissed him off every time he opened it—had swung partially closed. The corner of the door glanced off his temple and he quickly ducked back down with a hiss, lifting a hand to touch the sore spot.

"For fuck *sake*." He hissed, prodding his temple softly to check he wasn't bleeding.

"Are you okay?" came a hesitant question from beside him.

He looked up and nearly groaned, seeing Toby there with his hands deep in his pockets and looking uneasy. He stood, taking care to not hit his head again, and tried his best to act uncaring as he swapped books over in his locker. "I'm fine."

"Okay, I just wanted to—holy *shit*, your eye!"

Kieran instinctively pulled away with an annoyed frown when Toby stepped closer, dipping his head to get a better look at his black eye. "I'm fine," Kieran snapped.

"You have a black eye," he said numbly. "Shit, I gave you a black eye."

"Your elbow gave me a black eye, and it was an accident."

"I'm so sorry."

He really didn't give a shit if Toby was sorry. He was already giving Toby an out, but he just stood there, continuing to stare. "I said it was fine. It was an accident."

"But… but I was still a total dick to you."

"Yep. You were." He hadn't forgotten Toby's harsh words, not at all. In fact, he'd rather have two black eyes than have to think about that conversation again.

"I guess… I guess there's no real way to be friends after this."

Kieran slammed his locker door closed and shot him an *are you fucking kidding me* look.

"Would you just… I don't know, give me a minute to apologize properly? Then you won't have to talk to me again."

Kieran sighed, turned to lean against his locker, and despite his better judgment, nodded his head. "You have one minute."

DREW spied Matt in the courtyard talking to one of their teammates, Garrison, and waited until Garrison took off before approaching Matt. He knew the second Matt spotted him because Matt's back went straight and he crossed his arms over his chest. Never one to shy away, Matt watched him approach, resettling his duffle bag over one shoulder. Drew knew he was in trouble; he'd been a shitty friend, he hadn't been able to face him, and he'd avoided all text messages and phone calls. Matt probably wouldn't want to talk now, but Drew wanted to at least apologize, and if possible, begin to explain.

"Long time no see," Matt said without a smile.

"Hey." He was more than a little sheepish. "How's things?"

Matt shrugged. "I'm alright, but don't worry, I know better than to ask you that question."

"Matt, I'm sorry I've been MIA, alright?"

Matt shrugged. "Whatever. I've got somewhere to be. See ya."

Drew sighed and grabbed Matt's arm, stopping him from taking off. "Okay, okay. I'm an asshole. Better?"

Matt squinted, head tilted. "You're getting there."

"I'm a douche bag?"

Matt nodded. "*Yes*. And…?"

Drew felt a small smile lift the corner of his mouth despite himself. "I'm sorry." He ticked off on his fingers. "I'm an asshole, I'm a douche bag, *and* I don't deserve a friend like you."

"No truer words have ever been spoken."

"Are you going to forgive me and start talking to me again?"

"I guess, though if you'll remember, I wasn't the one who stopped talking."

Drew ducked his head, nodding. "Yeah, I know," he said quietly, and looked up to meet his friend's eyes when Matt stepped closer.

"Look, you've got some shit going on in your life right now, yeah?"

He nodded. "Yes."

"And some of it you're… you're clearly not ready to talk to me about, right?"

Drew swallowed and looked away.

"But you know that you can, if you need to, understand?"

Drew took a deep breath and nodded again. "I know. I'm sorry."

"Alright. Stop apologizing, it's weird."

Drew laughed quietly, lifting one shoulder. "Can't help it. I feel kind of like shit."

Matt looked at him, pressed his lips tight together as if undecided on what he wanted to say next, and then spoke in a quiet voice. "I'm guessing this is Kieran-related?"

Drew looked up to meet Matt's gaze and then just as quickly looked away. For some reason he couldn't do it. Matt was his closest friend, but for whatever bullshit, cowardly reason, he couldn't just nod or admit to what was really going on.

He told his mom, yes. But it was different with Matt. It was a different relationship, and he'd hazard a guess that he would feel differing, conflicting feelings when broaching the subject of being gay with anyone he was close to, depending on his relationship with them.

His mother was something else. She was his flesh and blood and he'd worried about disappointing her, about laying more on her shoulders than she could handle, but she'd been great. Matt was his best friend; there were no blood ties, but he was as good as a brother. While his mother was the person who perhaps had the closest relationship with him because she'd seen him grow and change, Matt was his equal, his partner in crime. He wanted acceptance from Matt so badly and thought perhaps he'd get it, if he'd only man up and talk to him, but just the idea of Matt looking at him differently was enough for him to shy away from it.

Oblivious to Drew's inner ramblings and insecurities, Matt continued. "Does your feeling shitty have anything to do with that fucked-up party a month ago, or the black eye he's walking around with now?"

Drew swallowed hard, his skin prickling and nerves twisting in his stomach at the mention of that dumb fucking party. Unable to give an honest answer just yet, he attempted to form some sort of regretful lie when Matt's words actually penetrated. "What? A black eye?"

"Yeah, saw him earlier today; he's got a hell of a shiner." Matt watched him carefully. "You've got nothing to do with it?"

Drew's head snapped back. "'To do with it'?" he repeated. "The hell does that mean?"

Matt's shoulders fell, and Drew wasn't sure, but he looked relieved. "Sorry, just... the last I saw you talk to him... well, you were kind of a dick."

"I'd never hit Kieran!" If he could take back the outraged snap in his tone of voice, he would have. Matt was watching him closely again, and there was a distinct feeling of awkwardness between them.

"Okay," Matt said. "Glad to hear it, but you don't know anything about it?"

"No. I don't." He was seeing red. He could feel anger as he'd never truly felt before building up in him. "I, um... I have to go."

Matt frowned. "What, why? Where are you going?"

"I just—" he snapped, closed his eyes, and then started again in a calmer voice. "I have to go do something."

Matt's hands flew out to his sides. "Well, see ya, then. I guess we'll catch up in another few weeks."

Drew was already walking away. He'd apologize later, *again*. But right now he had to find Kieran and find out what the fuck was going on.

KIERAN was well and truly running out of patience. He didn't doubt Toby's sincerity, because he did genuinely look and sound remorseful, problem was Kieran didn't really care. He was done. He was running on empty.

"I've always thought that-that you and I were kind of the same, like we could be good friends or something."

"I don't think so, Toby," he said quietly.

Toby nodded. "I get that it's not going to happen *now*, but I still need to apologize for pushing. You're cool and everything, but I don't really know why I tried to make it into something more than just hanging out." He shrugged. "I guess I was just bummed or lonely, and I could tell you were too—"

"Toby," he sort of groaned. He'd kept his eyes trained on the floor this entire time, but looked up at Toby, and then past him when he saw Drew approach, looking right *at* them. "Uh…."

"Look, I'll walk away and leave you alone, but I just needed to apologize for last night. *All* of it, not just the black eye."

Kieran was only half listening, but saw the moment Drew heard Toby's words. Drew's steps faltered, he stopped, and then a look of stunned fury passed over his usually handsome face as he reached for Toby's shoulders, took the guy completely by surprise, and then yanked him backward and slammed him up against the lockers.

Kieran winced at the loud clatter Toby's body made against the lockers, and he could only watch, eyes wide as Drew began to snarl into Toby's face, not even an inch apart. Toby's eyes were wide and his hands were on Drew's wrists, trying to make him loosen his grip. It took a few seconds, but Kieran moved—ignoring the stares of the few who'd been passing and were now standing still, watching—and tried to pull Drew back. Drew had never looked so big to him before.

"You hit him?" Drew snarled.

"I-I—" Toby stuttered.

"Drew, let *go* of him!" Kieran hissed, pulling at his arm.

Drew pulled Toby forward and then slammed him back against the lockers again. "Did it make you feel good hitting someone weaker than you? *Huh?*"

Affronted, Kieran yanked at Drew's arm, managing to pull him off of Toby, and pushed him back a step. "Hey!" He growled. "I am not *weaker* than anyone!"

Drew managed to look contrite. "No, no you're not. But he is bigger than you." He looked back at Toby, who was pulling his T-shirt straight. "In fact, you're a damn sight closer to my size than his, wouldn't you say?"

Toby's hands went up, palms forward. "Hey, hey look… it-it was an accident."

Drew barked out an ugly laugh and then took a quick step closer to him, but was stopped by Kieran, who stood between them and pushed back at Drew, hands against his chest, as hard as he could. Drew actually stumbled back a step, looking both surprised and aggravated. Kieran looked back at Toby. "Toby, apology accepted. We're done, got it?"

Toby muttered something in the affirmative, ran a shaky looking hand over his hair, and took off, throwing a few quick glances behind him. Kieran turned to Drew, who was watching Toby leave with a look of hate. He shoved Drew in the chest again.

"What the *hell*?" he snapped, and when he heard laughter behind him, he whirled around. "Get the fuck out of here!" he yelled, and the three girls who'd been watching curled their lips up at him and took off. He turned back to Drew, out of breath, his face warm, and completely lost. He shook his head. "What were you doing? You don't threaten people; you don't start fights. That's not you!"

"That is me when some guy goes around punching you!"

"I'm not any of your concern, remember?"

Drew flinched, his gaze falling to the floor for a second. "I… I'm not…."

"You're not what?"

Drew looked at him, gentler now. "I'm not just going to stand by and let someone get away with hitting you, Kieran."

"It's really none of your business."

"*Yes*, it is."

"*No*, it's not. Not anymore. Not since you cut me off and decided you didn't want to know me anymore."

"Of course I want to know you."

"Well, you have a stupid fucking way of showing it."

Drew reached for his arm, but Kieran took a step backward. "No. You don't get to drop me one second and then pick me up the next."

"I know I fucked up," Drew pleaded softly. "I'm sorry, I—"

"I don't care." Kieran swallowed, simultaneously hating himself and taking pleasure in watching Drew flinch. "It's none of your business who I hang out with, and it's none of your business who I *date*."

Drew pulled back, blinking quickly. "Date?" he asked quietly.

Kieran scoffed, just as something inside of him curled up tight in misery. "What, you didn't think I could get anyone else?"

Drew swallowed, opened his mouth to answer, and then closed it again.

Kieran felt his throat grow thick. He hated what he was doing. He hated that look of hurt on Drew's face, but he was also feeding off it. It was kindling all the wretchedness he'd been through the past few weeks. "Yes, date." He swallowed, unwilling to take back the half-truth, even though he kind of wanted to.

"But-but I thought—"

"You thought what?" Kieran snapped. "Like you said, it's not like *we're* dating."

Drew seemed to absorb that, his throat working and his jaw clenching. "Okay, but he hit you; you can't be around people like that, Kieran."

"It was an accident. We were making out in his car...." He stopped when Drew flinched and looked away, but forced himself to continue. "And then the date was over. I couldn't work the door handle, he reached over to open it for me, and I got his elbow to my eye. That's. It."

"Oh," Drew almost whispered, looking away from Kieran.

"Yeah. Oh."

Drew looked around them, and Kieran noted that they were thankfully—for the moment at least—alone.

"I'm sorry for the way I treated you," Drew offered, his voice subdued.

"I'm hearing that a lot lately."

"Are you… are you going to see him again?" Drew shuffled on the spot, his eyes to the ground and his hands in his pockets.

Kieran wanted to snap at him—until he saw the brightness in Drew's eyes. Kieran swallowed hard. "No. No, you heard me tell him we're done."

Drew nodded. "I wanted to talk to you today, but…." He looked at Kieran, pressed his lips together. "But you don't—you don't actually even *like* me anymore, do you?"

Kieran felt like crying, but he wouldn't. "I don't know what to say to you, Drew. I don't think we ever actually got to know each other, so how do I answer that?"

Drew stared at him and then nodded. "I'm sorry." He turned and walked away without a glance back.

Kieran watched him walk away, feeling betrayed by himself for implying what he had to Drew, and angry at Drew for walking away— again—so easily. He turned and slammed his fist into his locker.

ChApTeR NiNe.

FRIDAY night with nothing to do and nowhere to go. Kieran sat in the kitchen, pushing the food around on his plate. His dad was actually home for once, but seemed to keeping a safe, quiet distance, rather than attempting to talk to him. It made him a little sad.

He looked down at the squares of pasta that had long since gone cold on his plate. His dad had been home but hadn't waited to eat with him—his plate had been already resting in the sink when Kieran got in late from school after spending nearly two hours making some sort of sense of the—now dreaded—art storage room. He'd found a prepared plate for him in the microwave.

If he craned his neck he could see his dad sitting in his office, slumped over a laptop and completely absorbed. At least he'd left the door open like usual, and it wasn't as if his dad was giving him the cold shoulder; he was just leaving him alone like Kieran had asked him to. Why he'd started to listen to him *now* Kieran didn't know, and wished it was otherwise.

He pushed his plate away, unable to eat. His appetite was gone and regret was eating at him. Regret for the awkwardness that lay between his father and himself, and regret from the upsetting and frustrating confrontation with Drew earlier that day. He knew the situation with Drew was over with. It had been as wonderful as it was brief, but it was done now and he had to deal with it.

His dad wasn't going anywhere. Not only that, but Kieran only had so much time before he had to broach the subject of college, and then if all went well he'd be gone for at least three years. Nothing felt resolved, but despite how unimportant he felt sometimes, it hurt when his father wouldn't even look at him.

"Dad?" he called weakly, suddenly feeling very young and very vulnerable.

His dad glanced over his shoulder and then saved the document he was working on before closing his laptop and strolling into the kitchen. He rested his hip against the kitchen island in a casual stance and crossed his arms.

"What's up?" he asked.

The vaguely guarded set to his father's shoulders was difficult to look at. "Um, I'm... I'm sorry for how I was yesterday." He worried his lip. "I didn't mean what I said."

His dad's posture became more genuine and relaxed as his shoulders dropped, and the expression in his eyes softened into something less cagey. "Alright," he said gently.

Kieran's heart sank. That didn't exactly sound like forgiveness. "I-I'd had a bad day."

His dad nodded toward his black eye. "I could see that."

Kieran gestured at his eye. "This really was an accident; I was standing too close and caught someone's elbow to the eye." He lifted his shoulders, feeling helpless. "That's all."

His dad sighed. "That's all?" He had that penetrating stare only a parent could use—one eyebrow lifted in question and a *don't you dare lie to me* set of the jaw.

"That's all. I wasn't being bullied." *That time.*

"Would you tell me if you were being bullied?"

He was trying to be contrite, he really was, but the question prickled. "I'm nearly eighteen, dad."

"I don't care how old you are, Kieran, you're my boy!"

Something inside of Kieran dissolved. "I am?" he asked softly, a hint of accusation in his voice as he glanced away, unable to hold his father's stare.

His dad's hands flew out to his sides as he looked around the kitchen in exasperation. When he peered back at Kieran, his lips were set tight together and he leaned against the kitchen island with one hand, the other resting on his hip. "What the hell do you think?"

Kieran lifted one shoulder up in a sullen shrug. "I don't know. You don't talk to me anymore." He hated how, just recently, the more hurt he felt, the more difficult it was to convey this without sounding like a spoiled, bratty child.

His dad closed his eyes and sighed, as if he were searching for that extra bit of patience sometimes required. "Kieran...." He sighed, his voice softer. "I... I know we're... we're not—"

An AC/DC ringtone—his father's cell phone—interrupted them. His dad cursed, pulled the cell out of his pocket, and checked the screen. Kieran's eyes narrowed slightly at the hesitation written on his father's face. It was *her*. He was relieved when, after a moment's hesitation, his dad sent the caller to voicemail and set the phone down on the counter.

His father pinched the bridge of his nose. "Where were we?"

"You not being around. Me feeling neglected." Now he *knew* he was being a brat. What the hell was wrong with him?

"Kieran," his dad groaned, and Kieran realized that they were getting onto snappy, uneven ground again.

"Who was calling?" Screw it. He didn't care if his dad didn't want to talk about it or involve him in that part of his life; they were getting into it.

The indecisive, hesitant look in his father's eyes, as if he were weighing his options, gave Kieran one small ounce of hope. But the flippant shrug and blatant lie that came next set his teeth on edge. "Just the restaurant. It can wait."

Kieran's jaw clenched. "Sure about that?" His knee began to jump up and down as that familiar pang of disappointment and distance stretched out between them. "Could be important."

"I'm talking to you right now. They can wait."

"Really? Because usually you take one look at your phone and answer on the second ring."

"That's not—"

"Then you walk into another room, looking all flustered and happy, and you close the door behind you."

His dad blinked owlishly, looking cornered. "I don't do that."

Kieran sighed. It was a sad sound. "Do you think I'm stupid or something?"

"What—*no*! Kieran, I don't appreciate—" The chirpy interpretation of "Back in Black" came from the countertop, and the phone lit up and vibrated against the granite once more. "Dammit," his father grumbled, and snatched the phone up. "Just give me one second," he said to Kieran, and turned and hunched his shoulders as he answered the phone, speaking in a hushed voice.

"Hey," he heard his dad murmur. "No, I'm sorry it's a bad time… no, it's okay, I'm talking to Kieran, is it urgent… *what*? But that fish was fresh."

Kieran sighed to himself and slid off the stool to walk past his dad and to his room. He'd apologized, that was all that really mattered. He didn't want to get into another argument, and it was clear that he'd gotten about as far as he was going to when it came to his dad's personal life, which evidently no longer involved him.

"Wait," his dad called out, cell pressed to his chest, before hastily bringing it back to his ear. "Can you hang on a second, honey?"

Kieran almost spluttered and lifted one eyebrow victoriously. *Got you.* "Honey?"

His father's face went blank, and the panic that set in only served to upset Kieran. Why couldn't his father talk to him about this? What, was he embarrassed of the weird, loner kid he had for a son? Did he think Kieran would come between him and his new girlfriend?

"Ah… well, Kieran, I need you to understand—"

A loud knock at the front door interrupted them, and having had enough, Kieran took the opportunity to walk away, shaking his head when his dad called after him. His focus was on his father, who was hastily hanging up the phone, so when he opened the door, he wasn't prepared to see Drew standing there.

He was pissed at his dad for keeping his personal life a secret, and here stood the boy he had a big gay crush on, making him a hypocrite. Drew was quick to stop fussing with imaginary lint on his button-down shirt. His eyes snapped up to meet Kieran's, and he smiled hesitantly, about to speak, but then was looking over Kieran's shoulder.

"Kieran, we're still talking here. Whoever that is...." His dad stopped short, looking at Drew. As if seeing another kid Kieran's age stumped him. Kieran turned away from his father and looked at Drew. They both stared at Drew, and no one spoke.

"Um. Hi," Drew offered weakly.

"Hi," Kieran said.

"Hi," his dad said.

Drew shifted uneasily, glancing between them. "So... so is this your dad?"

Kieran sucked in a quick breath and shook himself slightly. He glanced back at his dad and then to Drew, nodding absently. "Uh, yeah, yeah. Dad?" He moved his body to one side out of politeness, allowing his father to step forward. "This is Drew. We go to school together."

Drew smiled and then held his hand forward. "Hello, Mr. Appleby, nice to meet you."

His dad nodded and they shook hands. "Nice to meet you too, Drew. Do you two have classes together?"

"Art," they both chimed, and then shot each other a nervous look.

His father nodded. "Oh. Well. That's good. Kieran doesn't usually introduce me to many of his friends."

Kieran shot his dad a glance that all but screamed *hypocrite*, and his father had the good grace to shift uncomfortably.

"Yeah, well," Drew spoke haltingly. "Um, well I was just wondering... I-I mean I was driving past, so I thought maybe you'd like to hang out? Go see a movie or something?"

Kieran stared at Drew, blinking dazedly and—he was sure—looking stupid. Had he imagined their argument earlier that day?

"Well, I'm sorry, but we were actually in the middle of something," his dad said, and Kieran bristled.

"No, we weren't." Perhaps, had he not been arguing with his dad, he would have maintained his previous frosty front with Drew after their last encounter, but at that moment? He was pleased to see Drew on his doorstep, and he was eager to walk away from his dad. If his dad lied to him now, he was sure their relationship would take a knock too hard to get over with just a simple apology.

"We can talk later," he tried, knowing that later would probably be put off as his dad was dragged back to the restaurant, and eventually the conversation would be avoided altogether.

Earlier he'd been eager to make amends, and then keen for a confrontation. Now he just wanted to walk away. He wanted something familiar and comforting. He looked at Drew. That was what he wanted. He'd wanted it all along.

His dad sighed behind him, but Kieran slipped into the combat boots he kept near the front door and pulled a jacket off a coat hook, ready to go.

"Kieran, I'd rather talk now."

"I'm sorry," Drew said. "You're busy...." He took a step backward, clearly reluctant to leave.

Kieran shook his head. "No, it's okay," he said to Drew. And then to his dad, "I'll come by the restaurant tomorrow." He lied. He wouldn't go, and his dad wouldn't remember.

His father sighed again. "Kieran... fine. Fine, be back by eleven."

"It's Friday, weekend tomorrow."

"Alright, be in no later than eleven thirty. And we *will* talk," he said pointedly. "Tomorrow."

Kieran nodded. "Tomorrow," he agreed, knowing no such conversation would take place. He glanced at Drew, who took the cue and stepped back so Kieran could step onto the porch and give a brief, halfhearted wave at his dad before closing the door.

Having escaped the conversation he didn't relish having with his father and now alone with Drew, he was suddenly assaulted with nerves and uncertainty. Why was Drew here?

"Why are you here?"

Drew's already tentative smile quavered slightly, but he was nodding, and Kieran was at least glad to see that Drew wasn't going to play dumb and would at least acknowledge the peculiarity of his presence at Kieran's home.

"We didn't so much as talk as yell, earlier today."

"To be fair, I'm pretty sure it was me doing the yelling," Kieran conceded as he pulled his jacket on. "You don't think we said everything that needed to be said?"

Drew nodded up the drive toward where he was parked, and they walked toward the rusty Buick sat at the sidewalk. "Are you telling me you're happy to leave things with us as they are?" he asked softly.

Kieran swallowed. "No, I'm not. But you gave me the impression there wasn't an 'us', remember?"

They came to a stop beside the driver's side door, and Drew toyed with his car keys. He nodded to himself, and then glanced up at Kieran, looking him square in the eye. "I got scared. I got scared, and I let it make a coward out of me. But...." His gaze went from intense to almost... pleading? "But you were my first boyfriend, my first anything. I made a mistake and I'm sorry. I just want the chance for you to get to know me better, and to know that I'm better than that."

Kieran was stuck on one word. "Boyfriend?" he whispered.

Drew's cheeks flooded with heat and he ducked his head in an uneasy way that was completely disarming. "You were really important to me; I just didn't show you that."

"Well," Kieran murmured, feeling shaky and nervous. "We kind of just…." He tried a hesitant smile. "Just jumped into the physical stuff, I guess. We didn't really get to know each other. Properly, I mean."

Drew lifted one shoulder, looking hopeful. "There's nothing stopping us from getting to know each other now, is there?"

Kieran swallowed. Nothing to stop them? No. There was only the fact that they were both still relatively inexperienced in the scheme of things, leaving plenty of space for further blunders and, more to the point, plenty of opportunities to get hurt again. Not to mention Kieran's absolute determination to leave Keys in a few months without looking back.

But he looked at Drew. He looked at the first person who, in a long time, had been kind to him, had sought out his company, and who actually on some level *got* him. He missed the physical stuff, sure, but he missed the butterflies too. He missed the beginnings of a friendship and time spent in the company of someone who was, to a degree, like him.

Drew seemed to panic slightly at Kieran's lack of response, wet his lips, took a step closer, and lowered his voice. "Let's just… let's just hang out, maybe? It doesn't have to be anything else."

For some reason Kieran found his gaze focused on Drew's shoes. He was wearing a newish pair of Converse that Kieran hadn't seen before. He looked upward. Drew wore a pair of khakis, pressed and clean. A button-down shirt and his team's jacket. His hair had gel in it, and he smelled good. He felt the beginnings of a smile and quickly smothered it. He looked at the car. It was a Buick that had to be nearly as old as he was. It was hard to tell if it was red or a dark orange because of the amount of rust, but it struck him as odd that Drew would be driving when he knew Drew usually walked everywhere. It certainly wasn't as flashy as Toby's red car with the bum door handle, but for some reason that was reassuring.

"Kieran?" Drew asked. "I'm just trying to be a friend. I mean I'll always kind of be hot for you," he said with a nervous smile. "But if you don't want that, then we can just be friends, right?"

Kieran bit his lip, looking up at Drew. He felt his insides soften.

Drew's throat worked as he swallowed. "If you just want to hang out or… whatever, then let's go, let's get in the car. But if you just want me to leave, it's okay, I won't bother you again."

He thought perhaps he should think about that, but he was sick of thinking everything through and overanalyzing every little thing. He wasn't entirely sure what he wanted, or more to the point, what was good for him, but despite the past few weeks of feeling worthless and thoroughly upset, right there and then, there was no hesitation. He got in the car.

THE feeling of relief when Kieran opened the passenger door and got into the car was quickly replaced by flat-out panic. Kieran was in his car. Conversation was a struggle at first and spattered with awkward pauses, but by the time they made it to Subway, they'd managed to fall into an easy banter that Drew had missed.

They had a table at the back which awarded them some privacy, but to any onlooker, Drew would think they'd seem to be nothing but two friends getting their grub on. He knew Kieran wasn't totally chilled yet, but he expected that. The company alone was enough for him.

"I'll pay you back next time I see you," Kieran said with a shy smile as he unwrapped his meatball sub.

"Don't worry about it, it's cool." He'd wanted to pay anyway, not to make amends, but because he wanted to. So when Kieran had patted his back pocket, blushing when realizing he'd left his wallet at home, Drew was only too happy to foot the bill. "Actually, I'm kind of thirsty, you want a soda?"

"Uh, no thanks, I'm fine." Which clearly meant *yes, but I don't want to impose.*

So of course he brought two sodas back with him. He slid back into his seat, setting a can in front of Kieran without a word, and went straight for his sandwich, missing the warm smile offered to him. "So, go back to this job interview...." He made a rewind motion with his finger as he chewed.

Kieran groaned, swallowed his mouthful, and set his sub down back in its open wrapper. "Okay, so my dad's always wanted me to help out at the restaurant, and I've always said no."

Drew frowned. That sounded kind of cool to him. "How come?"

Kieran sighed. "I guess because that restaurant is his whole life and it kind of pisses me off. I know how childish that sounds but...." He shrugged. "It's just complicated. Anyway, he comes out and tells me that he'd like me to get a little work experience *somewhere*, just on the weekends, so he sets this interview up with a friend...."

"Where at?" Drew asked before taking another big bite.

"The hardware store on Jameson Street. My dad's pals with Mr. O'Brien, the owner."

"Okay, so, how did you—in your own words—'pown' your dad?"

Kieran hesitated, biting the inside of his cheek. "You know, when I say this stuff out loud, I sound dumb. Dumb and spoiled."

"What happened?" he asked and took a gulp of his soda.

"I wore a tuxedo."

Drew snorted soda and began to cough. Kieran reluctantly laughed.

"You wore a tuxedo to a job interview at a hardware store?" Drew asked when his snort-giggling was under control.

"I can't really take credit; I saw it in a movie. Thought it was funny as hell."

"Where did you even get a tuxedo?"

"It was my dad's; I rolled up the pants and sleeves and then stapled the hems."

He rested his elbows on the table and pressed the heels of his hands into his eyes as he chuckled. "Oh my God, Kieran."

"I thought it was funny back then. Seems kind of stupid now."

"Why'd you do it?"

"To screw up the interview. I didn't like that he just set it up without mentioning it to me. Like I'm *special*," he said with air quotes, "and can't do that stuff on my own."

"Are you sure you just didn't want to work in a hardware store?"

"There's that too."

"It's going to happen eventually, you know. You might as well get the experience while you can."

Kieran nodded. "I know. I got myself a job a few weeks later."

"What did you do?"

"I worked at Walgreens for a while, but then the SATs came along and my dad—ironically—told me to quit so I could study more."

"Sounds familiar, though I'd take Walgreens over McDonald's any day."

Kieran hissed. "Ouch."

"Tell me about it. I would not have turned down a job at your dad's restaurant, put it that way."

"You don't know my dad."

"He seemed cool," Drew offered, focusing on his sub for a moment, growing quiet. "I mean, seems like he cares about you."

"Appearances are deceptive, trust me," Kieran mumbled.

Drew let it go; he didn't know enough about Kieran's home life to judge, and to pry would only invite questions about his own dad that he wasn't prepared to answer.

"Did you quit too when exam time came around?"

"I did, but it was mainly because my uncle got shipped out and I didn't want to leave my mom alone at home so much."

"He's a marine, right?"

"Yep. He's overseas right now, doing his thing."

"Do you miss him?" Kieran asked softly.

Drew looked at Kieran, nodded, and then went back to his sub.

A comfortable silence settled between them for a few minutes. When Drew finished his sub, he crumpled up the wrapper and wiped his mouth with the back of his hand. "You want to make a move?"

Kieran, who had been slowly turning his soda can around in his hands, looked up and blinked in surprise. "Uh, yeah sure. Are you taking off?"

"What? No. I thought…." He cleared his throat. "I thought you might like to see the new *Avengers* movie? We should head off if we want to catch the eight o'clock showing. It's a comic book kind of movie, right? That's your kind of thing, isn't it?"

"Oh! Uh, yeah, I want see it. But, well, I don't have any cash, so…." He rose when Drew did to get rid of his trash, and then stood there somewhat awkwardly, hands in pockets and rocking from heel to toe.

"That's okay, I got it." Drew lifted his chin toward the front doors and began to walk that way.

Kieran followed, taking two quick steps to catch up outside and then lightly touching Drew's arm when he reached for the car door. "Wait, uh, you've 'got it'?"

Drew shrugged, trying to play casual. "Yeah, is that a problem?"

Kieran stared at him for a moment, still mildly confused. "Okay then, I'll pay you back."

"How about this one just be on me and you get the tickets next time?" Without waiting for an answer, he opened the car door and sat, but didn't close the door straight away. Instead he looked back at Kieran and smiled. "You need to get in the car, though," he said playfully.

Waking up, Kieran rounded the car to the other side and let himself in. He watched Drew start the engine and pull away from the curb. "You look good."

Drew shot him a quick look and then peered back out the windshield. He shifted in his seat and cleared his throat. "Thanks."

"I mean you look kind of *dressed up* good."

"Oh, well...." He kept his eyes on the road but lifted one shoulder, all casual-like. "Just-just what I had clean."

Kieran turned to look out the passenger window. He could see his own smile reflecting back at him. "You're still you," he said quietly.

"What do you mean?"

Kieran shook his head. "Nothing."

IT HAD been oddly sweet, standing aside and waiting for Drew to buy their tickets, his smile shy as he handed Kieran his ticket, the way he'd stuttered when asking if he wanted popcorn. It had been fun, slouched down in their seats, whispering to each other about which trailers looked good and which ones looked like crap. And it was comfortable, sitting now in Drew's car, which was idling against the curb a little way away from his house, laughing quietly and shooting each other nervous glances as they both attempted to prolong saying goodnight.

Kieran leaned forward in his seat to look upward out the windshield. "Look." He lifted his chin. "It's so clear out tonight."

Drew turned the ignition off, unbuckled, and with one hand on the steering wheel, dipped his head to take a look. "Wow, yeah, look at it. Pretty."

"That's one thing I'll miss if I leave Keys, I suppose; clear nights like this, the smell of the sea...."

"You're always complaining that Keys smells like fish." Drew laughed.

"Well, yes." He grinned. "But sometimes you can just smell the water."

"So you're definitely going?"

He was quiet a moment. "I think so. You?"

"Community college. I'm still going to be a fireman."

Kieran smiled. "And I still think that's cool."

"Hmm." Drew tapped his thumb against the steering wheel. "I don't want to think about it just now."

Kieran nodded, and silence stretched out between them. He looked at the dash—it was eleven twenty. He knew he needed to get going, but for the moment he just did not want to move. He was happy, sitting in the dark with Drew.

"I told my mom I'm gay."

Kieran snapped his head to the side to look at him. "You—? Holy *crap*. Are you okay?"

Drew nodded. "Yeah, I'm...." He sounded almost mystified as he spoke. "I'm fine, actually."

"But, but your mom...."

"She wasn't expecting it." He nodded, following Kieran's trail of thought. "But she's okay with it." His brow puckered. "Actually, I think she's happy that I told her. She saw that I needed her and she...." He shook his head, searching for the word. "She regrouped, she gathered herself. I think she remembered what it was like to feel needed." He looked at Kieran; it was dark in the car with only a fine, silvery light peeking through. "I feel bad that she'd forgotten what that feels like."

"Hey." Kieran spoke gently. "You shouldn't feel bad about anything; sounds to me like you're both better off for it."

"Do you think you're any closer to telling your dad?"

Kieran thought about it a moment and slumped back in his seat. "I don't know. I don't think so. He doesn't... we're not really...."

"He seemed like an okay guy. It looked like he really wanted to talk to you before we took off."

"You met him for like two minutes."

"True. But that's two minutes more than I've spent with my own dad in the past few years."

Kieran was immediately contrite. "I'm sorry."

Drew shook his head, eyes briefly squeezed closed. "Uh, crap. No, no don't be. In fact, forget I said that."

Kieran swallowed. He reached to toy with the fraying edge of the duct tape that held the glove compartment together. "I don't think I'll tell him, at least not yet," he answered.

"Why not?" Drew asked softly, and then snorted at himself. "I mean besides the obvious terror that comes along with telling your parents you're gay."

"It's going to make me sound petty."

"Don't worry about how you sound around me."

Kieran looked at him, worried his lip. "He has a girlfriend."

It was dark in the car, but not too dark to see Drew's expression turn to one of confusion.

"Okay," he encouraged.

"He's been seeing someone for a long time, and I think he's actually super happy about it."

Drew frowned. "Okay, so… so that's a good thing, surely?"

"Well, *yeah*. Thing is… it's been going on for more than a year, I think, and he still hasn't mentioned it to me, even though it's more or less obvious at times."

"Do you think he might be trying to protect you? Like… like maybe you'd think he was trying to replace your mom or something?"

Kieran shook his head. "No. I could forgive that—in a heartbeat, actually. I don't even remember my mom, so she's got nothing to do with it. He just doesn't want to involve me." He shrugged, unable to hide the hurt it caused him.

"How'd you mean?"

"We barely cross paths. We never really talk anymore—or at least not how we used to." He glanced out the window. "I haven't been able to talk to him. He's either never there or he's just too preoccupied. In fact, yesterday was the first time in I don't know how long that he actually asked me what was going on with me." He sighed. "It took a black eye for that to happen. And you know what? I wouldn't be complaining or acting like such a girl if it wasn't for the fact that...." He let out a sharp breath. "I've had the shittiest time for the past two years...." He looked at Drew. "You know that. I needed him. I needed my dad."

Drew hesitated at first, but then he stretched out a hand, reaching behind Kieran's head to let it rest against the nape of his neck, his thumb moving in soft circles under his hairline. "I understand that."

Kieran offered him a shaky smile. "Yeah, I think you do."

Drew's jaw clenched, and Kieran could see him swallow hard. "Does your eye still hurt?" he murmured.

"Not really."

Kieran watched almost warily as Drew shifted closer, his arm sliding behind Kieran's shoulders. He was reminded of Toby—of Toby making a move on him in his flashy red car. He closed his eyes and felt Drew near, but when the kiss didn't come he opened them just as Drew lifted his chin, and then closed them again an instant later when Drew's lips brushed softly against his bruised eye.

He kept his eyes closed and took a shuddering breath when Drew touched his brow against Kieran's temple.

"Kieran," Drew whispered. "Everything's going to be okay."

Kieran swallowed, opened his eyes, and pulled back a fraction to look at Drew through the silvery darkness.

"You're going to be okay, I promise."

Kieran let out a juddering breath he hadn't realized he'd been holding. He swallowed and nodded. He knew Drew had no way of knowing how things would pan out for either of them, but for just now? It felt true. He was comforted.

He reached a hand to touch Drew's cheek, and instead of waiting to be kissed, he looked at Drew's lips and leaned forward to press his own against them.

He'd missed this feeling. When he'd been with Toby, he told himself that a kiss was a kiss. It simply wasn't true. Toby's kiss had managed to get him hot, without a doubt, but it went no further than that. Toby's kiss was an aggressive invitation; Drew's kiss was a gentle request. When Drew kissed him, it felt to him as if Drew was reaching for him. Wanting every bit of him.

Toby had cornered and mauled him in his expensive car with the broken handle. In Drew's car, which was ninety percent rust and duct tape and where it was dark as night, he was kissed as if he was something to be cherished. He *felt* cherished. And when Drew pulled away and he opened his eyes, he thought maybe Drew was right, and everything could—*would* be alright.

"Okay?" Drew whispered.

A smile slowly spread across Kieran's face, and he nodded once. "Okay."

Drew craned his head back—unwilling to actually move away— to look at the digital clock on the dash. Kieran couldn't help but notice the definition in Drew's neck and admire how he was lean but muscular at the same time. He was so annoyingly gorgeous, but Kieran felt like he was still his Drew. The thought gave him pause. It worried him. He didn't want to think of Drew as his again, only to have that right ripped away from him once more.

"It's after eleven thirty. Are you in trouble?"

Kieran bit the inside of his cheek and answered with a question of his own. "Is this how you thought the night would end?"

Drew blinked in surprise. "What, with a kiss?"

"Did you think, or hope, that everything would be back to normal between us?"

"I-I hoped that we'd be something close to friends, but am I happy that there was a kiss? Well, yeah." He laughed softly and then sobered. "You're still mad at me, then?"

Kieran thought about it. He didn't think he was mad. He was just wary. "No. But I don't want you to think that a movie and a kiss erases what happened in my head, you know? I'm not flighty." He touched Drew's hand and rubbed his thumb over his knuckles. "You said 'sorry' and I accept your apology... just don't think that I'm easily changeable, alright?"

"I don't think that. I promise."

Kieran nodded, to himself, mostly. "Okay." He looked at Drew and felt himself begin to grin. "So...." He bit the corner of his lip, and Drew grinned.

"So...." Drew repeated.

"School?"

"At school we're just you and me, fuck what anyone else thinks."

Kieran's eyes widened in alarm. "Uh... I-I don't think I'm quite ready to be—"

Drew laughed again, reached for nape of Kieran's neck, and kissed him. "Sorry, no I didn't mean that." He snorted when Kieran visibly sagged in relief. "I'm not ready for people to know *that* about me; in fact, I was hoping to finish high school without anyone finding out. I meant that as far as school goes and as far as anyone else is concerned, we're friends and we hang out because that's what friends do."

Kieran nodded, relieved. "Okay, good. What about Matt?"

Drew's smile dimmed slightly. "He knows something, or he suspects something, but I can't... I just can't say anything just yet. That's a different kettle of fish all together."

Kieran nodded. "Okay, then. Can I ask one thing?"

Drew blinked in surprise. "Uh, sure, of course you can."

"No meeting up in the storage room?"

Drew tilted his head. "If that's what you want, but how come?"

Kieran thought about it a moment, worrying his lower lip. "I guess because that was before, and that was where it all went wrong.

This is…." He shot Drew a hesitant look. "This is different now. I'm not your secret, despite the fact that neither of us wants people to actually know."

Drew nodded. "That makes sense to me. There are a million other things we can do, loads of places we can be."

Kieran smiled, pleased. "Okay, then."

Drew wet his lips, looking suddenly nervous. "Now I ask something."

"Okay…."

Drew's voice dropped to a near whisper, and despite the darkness, Kieran thought he could see a blush spreading across his cheeks. "Are you—are you my boyfriend now?" He let out a small groan. "Oh man, that sounded dumb."

A smile split Kieran's face, and he leaned in and took Drew by surprise by pressing a firm kiss to his lips. He let out a small, breathy laugh when he pulled away a fraction. "Not dumb. And yeah, we're boyfriends."

Drew smiled, his voice gone soft. "Yeah? There's… there's no one else?"

Kieran knew what Drew meant, and he shook his head no. "No one else. There never was."

Drew's smile was slow and intimate. He lifted his chin in invitation for Kieran to kiss him, which he did, ever so softly. "Just us."

Kieran smiled against his lips. "Just us."

CHaPtEr TeN.

"ALRIGHT, so remember, feel for your friction point—that's it, feel it? Now gently lift off the clutch while giving it a little gas. That's it."

Kieran bit back a smile. He was driving. Okay, he was driving in an empty parking lot and only in second gear, but he was *driving*!

"Okay, now try a tighter turn—good job, Kier."

Kieran glanced at Drew and couldn't help but laugh a little. That pleased, proud look on Drew's face made him feel kind of giddy.

"Okay, go around that dumpster and—whoa, whoa, brake! *Brake*!"

Kieran panicked for a second before slamming onto the brakes, his knuckles white where he gripped the steering wheel. "I'm not very good at this," he admitted, and offered Drew an apologetic smile, but he was warmed by how unruffled his boyfriend seemed and by the gentle hand rubbing his thigh.

"No, no it's, um… you're doing real good."

Kieran snorted and raised a disbelieving eyebrow.

"Okay, you suck a *little*." Drew grinned. "But everyone does when they're learning."

"Why did it speed off like that?"

"It was my fault, but first things first. Pull on your parking brake. That's it, now shift it into neutral and relax your feet."

Kieran relaxed into his seat. He'd always thought driving looked so easy, and he jumped at the opportunity when Drew offered to teach him. If he could learn how to drive before heading off to college, it'd probably make his life a lot easier when he got there. "How was that your fault? I was driving."

"Yeah, but I should have told you to change down to first gear. If you're moving too slowly in second, then you'll either stall out or the car might try to run away from you—if you're an inexperienced driver, anyway."

"Oh."

"Don't be discouraged, you're doing great. My first few times behind the wheel, I used to bunny hop."

"Bunny hop?" Kieran laughed.

"I couldn't get that leverage between clutch and gas to move off smoothly so I'd keep going back onto the clutch. Then I'd try again and the same thing would happen because I was worried about stalling out, so the car would jolt back and forth." He shrugged. "Bunny hop."

Kieran grinned and leaned close to kiss Drew, drawing it out a little and loving how Drew leaned forward to prolong the kiss when he attempted to pull away.

"What was that for?" Drew asked, his voice smoother, almost sleepy as he looked at Kieran's lips.

"I was just imagining a nervous, sixteen-year-old Drew behind the steering wheel for the first time. It's sweet."

"Super nervous, more like."

"You're a good driver."

"Yeah, *now*." He laughed. "I think my uncle was pretty terrified, sitting in the passenger seat those first few times. I should point out he's a marine."

Kieran laughed out loud, something he found he did a lot lately. For thirty days now he'd been someone's boyfriend—secret boyfriend, but boyfriend nonetheless—and Drew had been his. A month of waking up and having something to look forward to. A month of school being bearable and a month of feeling idyllically, blissfully *normal*. And he had the person sitting beside him in a crapped-out Buick to thank for it.

He turned the key in the ignition, and the engine eventually rattled and rumbled into silence.

"Enough for one day?" Drew asked.

"I think so." He unbuckled and turned slightly in his seat to face Drew. "Did you learn to drive in this car?"

"Yeah, it's the family car." He patted the dash affectionately.

"Wouldn't it have been easier to learn in an automatic? In fact, aren't most cars automatics nowadays?"

"I guess." He lifted one shoulder. "But this is what we had. Automatics are easy, no gear box, two pedals... if you learn to drive with a stick, then you'll be better off for it, I think."

"What do you mean?"

"Well, when *you* buy a car, for instance, you'll be buying whatever's available and a good price, right? I mean, unless your dad splurges on you and gets you something pretty."

Kieran snorted. "I've got around eight hundred dollars saved from when I worked at the hardware store. I figure I could get myself a decent runner with that, right?"

"Maybe." Drew picked at the duct tape. "I don't really have any savings; I gave all my earnings from my part-time job to my mom." He shrugged. "To help out, you know?"

Kieran didn't know, not really. As much as he bitched about his father, he'd never wanted for anything. When he needed new clothes, he got them without asking. When he wanted a new bike, he got one. A new computer? He mentioned it once and his father bought him the best he could find. His dad owned a restaurant and, now that Kieran was older, worked sixty-plus hours a week. He knew he was lucky, but given the choice, he would have traded the computer for a little more of his dad's time.

"I'll probably be driving this thing when I'm old and gray," Drew joked.

"What's your dream car, a Ferrari?"

"No, I've kind of always wanted a Chevy truck."

"A truck? Really?"

"Why sound so surprised?"

Kieran thought about it. "I don't know, I guess I was expecting you to want something more... flashy, like most guys."

"Chevys can be flashy. Sort of."

"Flashy like a Jag?"

"No, more... *working class* flashy."

Kieran grinned at him. "Okay, so why a truck?"

"Ah, well, if I had a truck, then my dog could ride in the back when we went to the beach."

"You want a Chevy truck so your dog can sit in the back," he repeated. "Okay. How big is your dog that it requires a truck to get to the beach?"

"The truck is just because I like them. And not very big. I want a beagle."

Kieran laughed, surprised. "A beagle?"

"Yeah, and?" Drew feigned being affronted. "Beagles are cool and loyal and... they're just super cute, okay?"

Kieran chuckled, looking at him. "Speaking of super cute." He leaned forward and pulled Drew into a hard kiss. When they pulled apart, Kieran couldn't help but reach out to touch Drew's flushed cheek, cupping it almost. His thumb stroked over the light stubble on Drew's cheek, and he pressed a soft kiss to his lips. "You are so adorable," he murmured quietly.

"I thought I was totally hot?"

"Well, *yes*," Kieran said. "But it's recently come to my attention that you're also quite adorable."

"No, I'm not," Drew griped halfheartedly.

Kieran tugged at the front of his T-shirt, pulling Drew back. "Uh, yes, you kind of are." He sighed into the kiss, loving the fact that they slid into it with such familiarity and ease. He loved kissing Drew, he always had, but now that they were together, legitimately together, it was with a sense of ownership that never failed to turn Kieran on.

This had become *their* place. Not the storage cupboard, but this car. Intimately, they hadn't moved much past what they'd experimented with in the art storage room, and Kieran knew he would be reluctant to do so in a car—as was Drew, he was sure. This was something, however, that he wanted to change. High school was coming to an end, and though he couldn't really bear to think about it, so would his relationship with Drew. But this was something both he and Drew knew and had discussed before getting so tangled up in each other, and so he knew they'd deal with it when the time came. For now, he wanted Drew. He wanted his every first, his every new experience to be with Drew.

He was ready to all but climb into Drew's lap when the headlights from a passing car spilled through the windshield, causing them to pull apart. He shot Drew a sheepish glance and settled back in his seat. "I didn't realize it was getting dark already."

"It's not, it's just dusky. In fact"—he gestured between them—"let's switch over."

They swapped seats and buckled up, and Kieran watched as Drew slung one arm over the back of his seat—his hand brushing the back of Kieran's neck while he reversed—then turned and drove out of the vacant car lot.

"Where are we headed?" Kieran asked finally.

Drew leaned forward, dipping his head to look up at the sky. "I wanted to show you somewhere before it got too dark. It's, um… it's my favorite place. I go there all the time with my uncle when he's home, and we throw a ball about sometimes." He looked at Kieran. "It's just a park, but it's always kind of quiet and deserted—just a few dog walkers, you know?"

"Where's it at?"

"It's not far from school, actually. But I always go there when I want to be alone or need to think." He winced slightly. "That sounded kind of douchey."

Kieran smiled softly, thinking of how the bleachers had been his place to go for the longest time. "No, no, it's not; I'd love to see it."

The sudden relaxed drop of Drew's shoulders and the pleased look he shot him did all sorts of things to Kieran. He realized that it was important to him and suddenly felt touched that Drew wanted to share his little hideaway with him. "Are we going to play ball?" he asked, only half serious.

Drew nodded over his shoulder. "My mitt's in the back."

HE'D never been any good at sports. Not football, baseball, basketball, none of them. He didn't have a favorite team and he didn't understand the rules, but *this* he liked. It seemed like a pointless pastime, but he had to admit there was something satisfying about throwing a ball and then catching it in return.

Drew brought along two mitts, his own and a spare, and a baseball. They stood in a near empty clearing surrounded by a copse of trees at the back end of the park—which was indeed surprisingly close to school—tossing the ball back and forth. He never would have guessed how satisfying the simple activity would be. The *thwap* of catching the ball in his mitt, of pitching it back and of smacking his fist into his mitt, just like a guy's guy, just like he'd watched Drew do a million times.

He had a few embarrassing false starts of dropping the ball or missing it altogether, and his throw had at first been... well, for *shit*. But Drew hadn't made fun of him, and he supposed it was just something that eventually came naturally with practice, because here he was, playing catch not quite like a pro but no longer like a ten-year-old girl, either.

"Man, check me out," he called teasingly. "I'm playing catch with the Squids' pitcher!"

Drew caught the ball and groaned. He rolled his eyes before throwing it back. "Seriously, I get the sea theme, but the Squids?" He shook his head. "Our team name is so fucking lame."

Kieran laughed. "Yes. Yes it is."

"I mean, why couldn't we have been the Sharks, or the Stingrays, or even the Jellyfish?"

"Aww, squids are cute."

"Not they're not. They're gross."

"Well, then maybe you should have gone in for football."

Drew caught the ball, taking a few steps to the left and sticking out his arm to catch a crappy throw with absolute ease. He shook his head and threw the ball back. "Nah, I don't relish the thought of getting pummeled, thanks."

"Well then, quit complaining." Kieran smirked, loving to tease him.

Drew caught the ball, but didn't throw it back immediately. He grinned, his eyes narrowing, and threw the ball to him before slowly approaching Kieran. "Complaining, hmm?"

Kieran raised his fist to throw the ball and then warily lowered it again, seeing Drew approach with a look of pure mischief. "I don't like that look." Despite his words, he was smiling. "What are you doing?"

"Just seeing if I'd be any good at football. I mean, I'm no expert, but if this was a football game and you had the ball, I'm pretty sure I should be...." He frowned and clicked his fingers. "Oh yeah." He left it at that and charged.

Kieran let out a squawk that was a mixture of panic and laughter. He took two stumbling steps backward, his hands held out in defense. "Here!" He quickly threw the ball away and watched it bounce into the tree line. He looked back just in time to brace himself as Drew took him down.

They both grunted and landed in a heap of breathless laughter. They lay that way for a few moments, getting their breath back, but eventually Drew lifted himself up on his arms, keeping Kieran trapped where he was.

"I kind of like this. Maybe I *should* have gone out for football."

Kieran snorted and then ineffectually and halfheartedly pushed the back of his hand against Drew's chest. "You're heavy."

"Dude, you calling me fat?"

"I'm calling you heavy, jerk." He laughed.

Drew grinned, cast a look around them, and then dipped his head for a quick kiss before lifting up off of him. Kieran instantly missed his weight but took the hand offered to him. He was pulled up so abruptly he more or less fell into Drew's arms, and didn't bother to check they were alone before pulling Drew close by the opening of his team jacket and kissing him. "You can tackle me any day," he murmured against Drew's lips, his own pulling up into a grin.

Drew bit his lip, trying not to smile, and playfully moved in for a kiss but then pushed Kieran away. He pointed toward the trees. "Go get my ball."

"Spoilsport," Kieran grumped, and took off in a light jog toward the trees. He scanned the floor, kicking at the leaves. He rubbed his arms, feeling goose bumps. His jacket was at home and the temperature dropping slightly now that it was getting dark.

Spotting the ball, he crouched and tried to reach underneath a rickety-looking old fence that was in the way. He supposed it must have been from the previous layout of the park, years ago, and could see the ball settled on a walking path that was now overgrown. Unable to reach the ball, he stood, planted one hand on the gate, and hopped over. Immediately he hissed and brought the soft flesh of his hand, just beneath his middle finger, up to his mouth. Inspecting it closer, he saw what he thought might be a splinter. He shook his hand, bent to snatch up the ball, and took extra care when climbing back over the fence.

"I was about to send a search party. What took so long?"

He studied his palm, squinting in the low light. "I think I got a splinter. Ouch." He hissed, shaking his hand again.

"Let me see." Not waiting for a response, Drew took Kieran's hand, bringing it close and then farther away to try and see better. "I think you're right. Want me to squeeze that sucker out?"

Kieran snatched his hand away. "What? *No.*"

Drew grinned, reaching for his hand again and laughing when Kieran evaded him. "You know what happens if a splinter's left in there to fester, right?"

"Nothing. Nothing happens. Stop it."

"You could lose the whole hand."

"Oh my God," Kieran laughed, snatching his hand away again when Drew made to grab it. "You are such a dick."

"I'm kidding."

"I know that. I'm not retarded."

"But you should still get a drawing pin or something. Poke it out."

Kieran pulled a face of distaste. "Ugh, no thanks."

"No, Kier, that could get infected. Let's go back to the car; it's getting dark now anyway." Drew took his wrist to pull him along but stopped when he met resistance. Kieran was pouting at him. "You are such a baby," he said softly, almost fondly.

Kieran brought his hand up to his mouth again. "Am not," he muttered and then shivered.

"Are you cold?"

"A little. Stay away from my hand."

Drew bit the inside of his cheek. "You want my jacket?"

Kieran lowered his hand and a bemused, almost shy smile tugged at his lips. "Your jacket? How very eighties of you." He felt something warm curl up in his stomach when Drew actually flushed.

"Let's just get going. You're all goosepimply."

"Okay." Kieran bit the corner of his lip. "I do want your jacket," he admitted quietly, and looked up at Drew through his lashes, feeling kind of shy and dumb.

Drew watched him for a second, and then shimmied his Squids jacket off of his shoulders. "Here you go."

"You won't be cold?"

"Nah. Got more muscle than you, don't I?"

Kieran took the jacket and pulled it on. A smile split his lips and he spoke before thinking. "It smells like you."

Drew tucked his hands into his jeans pockets and dipped his head as his shoulders lifted; he nodded toward where his car was parked. "Let's go. I'll take you home."

Kieran fell in step beside him. "I thought you mostly walked everywhere."

"I do."

"Then why do you always come pick me up in your car now?"

"It's my mom's car, really. And... uh," he laughed uncomfortably, glancing at Kieran. "Well, privacy." He tilted his head. "For us."

Kieran felt himself flush and hunched into the jacket both for warmth and to hide his pleased grin. There was that. Drew's car had certainly seen more action—still virgin-like action but action nonetheless—in the last month than it probably had in the last ten years.

He heard Drew clear his throat. "So let me ask you this, how come you haven't learned how to drive yet?"

His good mood very nearly evaporated. "My dad said he wanted to teach me, but he's always busy, so…."

"Why didn't you just ask for an instructor?"

Kieran shrugged. "He seemed determined to do it himself; he just tends to not follow through with stuff like that." Or much of anything else. They hadn't really spoken since their last argument, and he was pretty sure it had slipped his dad's mind altogether. He felt more resigned than anything. "Honestly, that's just kind of the way he is." He frowned, knowing he'd usually be unwilling to admit this to himself, but for some reason he felt comfortable to admit it to Drew. "I think his intentions are always good, he just lets us both down a lot."

"Have you guys talked any more about... you know, his girlfriend?"

Kieran shook his head, eyes trained on his shoes. "No. But I guess that's okay. I mean, I think that's the way he wants things between us now so…." He shrugged. "It's a shame, but it isn't like I'm not keeping a few secrets of my own, you know?"

Drew snorted. "Uh, yeah. He doesn't suspect?"

"Not a bit. He's not around enough to suspect anything, I think." He toyed with the sleeves of Drew's jacket. "I haven't even told him about Sacramento."

Drew shot him a glance. "Sacramento?"

He nodded. "American River College. I got accepted."

Drew stopped walking. "But—but that's so far away."

"A long, long way away, yeah."

"And you really don't want to go anywhere more… local?"

Growing uncomfortable and not even sure about what he wanted anymore, Kieran simply shook his head.

Drew swallowed. "There's nothing really keeping you here, then, is there?"

Suddenly desperate to avoid Drew's gaze and the doubts it filled him with, he shrugged and looked away. "At the time it seemed perfect. Now… I was thinking that it might even do Dad and me some good. Maybe it'll make him miss me."

He started to walk again and a moment later Drew was at his side, eyes on the ground and quiet. Kieran nodded to the baseball Drew palmed between his hands. "You know, I don't even remember the last time I played catch with the old man."

"Yeah, me neither," Drew muttered.

Kieran looked at him. "You're not close with your dad either?" he asked carefully.

Drew was quiet for a few moments, glancing away, scratching the back of his head and letting out a deep breath. He was quiet for so long that Kieran thought he wasn't going to answer at all. "My dad… he's, uh, he has this other family now." He looked at Kieran. "Other kids. He doesn't really call me all that much anymore. And when I call him he's too busy to come to the phone."

Kieran frowned sadly, but he couldn't think of a thing to say. He thought distantly that this should make him feel closer to Drew, and in sharing these small, painful details, he did, but it wasn't because of their similar situations. He wasn't quite sure how to put it into words, but then Drew went ahead and did it for him.

"I don't mean this to be a pissing contest over who has the crappiest dad," he said softly, "but I think, from what you've told me, that your dad's heart may be in the right place. He's just screwing up a lot." He shrugged in a way that Kieran was sure was supposed to look casual, but Drew looked young, and he looked vulnerable. "My dad doesn't think about me, Kieran. I don't exist anymore."

"That's... y-you don't know that," Kieran all but whispered, his chest aching with the need to take away that wounded look in Drew's eyes.

Drew sighed and glanced away. "No phone calls, no money for my mom, no nothing anymore." He shrugged again. "I don't know. All I'm saying is that I think you still exist, Kieran." He reached out and briefly ran his hand up and down Kieran's back before putting his hand back into his pocket. "You're still in his peripheral vision; he's just being an idiot."

"Drew," Kieran said almost breathlessly. "I like you so much it's ridiculous." He was beyond relieved at the quick glance, and then pleased, wide smile his words earned him. "And... and maybe you're right. He's an idiot, but it's not like I'm a kid anymore. I guess I could try to make more of an effort instead of just waiting for him to suddenly become dad of the year."

Drew nodded, pleased. "That's up to you, but that sounds good to me."

Kieran worried his lower lip. "I'm sorry about your dad," he said quietly.

"Thanks. I've got my mom and uncle, though."

"Your uncle comes home soon, doesn't he?"

A genuine smile crossed Drew's lips, and his shoulders slumped in what seemed premature relief. "Yeah. We haven't heard from him recently, but that's because he's due home soon. I can't wait to see him."

"Is it tough when it's just you and your mom? I know it can feel that way between my dad and me sometimes."

Their feet crunched across gravel, and when they reached the car, Kieran hesitated beside Drew as he leaned against the driver's side door, his hands toying with the keys. Kieran stayed silent, pulling up his hands into the sleeves of Drew's jacket, and he leaned against the car next to him, waiting patiently.

"My mom, she's um, she's agoraphobic." He looked at Kieran. "You know what that means?"

Kieran frowned and nodded slowly. "I think so. Is it the fear of wide open spaces?"

"More or less. She can't leave the house."

Kieran looked at him in surprise. "Oh man, Drew, I had no idea," he said softly, things suddenly falling into place. He shook his head; a dad that didn't want to know him, an uncle away fighting wars, and a mother who couldn't leave the house? Damn. He reached out to rub a hand over Drew's arm, squeezing gently. "That's tough."

Drew pressed his lips into a tight line. "Yeah, yeah, it can be. Sometimes she's not so bad, like, when my uncle's home, she'll go into the yard and stuff. But when he's gone...." He shook his head. "Sometimes she won't even answer the door. She's kind of reliant on me." He looked at Kieran. "That's why I can't go any further than the local community college." He looked at Kieran. "I can't leave. No matter how much I may want to, I couldn't leave my mom alone."

"I see," Kieran murmured. "Not even with your uncle home?"

"No," He said quietly with absolute conviction. "She has no one else."

"Do you mind me asking how...?" He hesitated, unsure if he had the right to ask what he wanted to.

"What? It's okay, you can ask me."

"How did she get like that?"

Something shuttered closed in Drew's expression and he closed his fist, thumping it gently on the roof of his car a few times before he answered. "She was always agoraphobic, but no way near as bad when I was younger—when my dad was around," he clarified, and then wet his lip. "He just... he took off and left her in pieces, really, and she just got steadily worse from there on, and then my uncle moved in. That's when I realized that people could really suck. Well, that and when *Johnny 5* got beat up in *Short Circuit II*."

Kieran smiled weakly at the attempt at humor. "That's really harsh," he said softly.

"Yeah, but she's not like... she's not scary or anything. She's just got this... *thing* that stops her from going anywhere. Other than that she's a regular mom." He tilted his head. "She knows about you."

Kieran's eyes widened. "Me? You mean she knows you're gay and... *being* gay with someone."

Drew laughed. "You have such a way with words. No, she knows I'm 'being gay' with someone called Kieran."

A hesitant smile hovered over Kieran's lips, and it was on the tip of his tongue to ask if he'd ever meet his mom, perhaps go over to his house. But considering what he'd said only minutes ago about college, it seemed pointless to ask. He settled for a quiet "oh." "So, you're going to local?" he asked, meaning local community college. "I mean, I know that's what you want, but have you had confirmation?"

Drew nodded and then chewed on his thumbnail, avoiding Kieran's gaze. "I got the letter a few days ago, actually."

"That's great. How come you didn't say anything?"

Drew sighed softly, plastered on what looked like a suspiciously false smile and shrugged. "I guess I don't want to think about that stuff yet."

"But you're on your way." He gently pushed his fist that was covered by the sleeve of Drew's jacket into Drew's chest, playfully pushing him back a step. "You're on your way, Mr. Fireman."

Drew's smile seemed to become more genuine as he batted his hand away. "I guess. I think my uncle's going to get a real kick out of it. He wanted to be a fireman when he was my age; he just ended up enlisting instead."

"So what exactly does it take to be a fireman? I'm assuming it's not straightforward, otherwise you'd be applying and skipping college, right?"

"Well, you can actually apply if you're a high school graduate or have a GED and clean driving license, but that's not to say it's an easy job to land. I have to earn my Certificate of Compliance for Firefighter Minimum Standards at college, but if I can go for the Emergency Medical Technician or Paramedic Certification, then I'm hoping my chances at landing a job might be better."

Kieran blinked. Here he was, not really sure of what to study or do with his life, and Drew had the next ten years mapped out. He suddenly felt worried about his lack of ambition for anything other than *leaving*. "That sounds… wow."

"Yeah, it's not going to be easy and I've got a lot of studying ahead."

"You can do it. In fact, I'm certain you'd just nail it." He swallowed, feeling inexplicably sad. "You can do anything."

Drew's smile was intimate and lingering without feeling awkward or pressing. When Drew looked at him like that, he just wanted to sink into him. He wanted to grab Drew, take hold of him and stay that way.

"Come on," Drew said softly, nodding over to the passenger side of the car. "Let's go."

Kieran got in the car, but he knew he wasn't letting Drew go home, not yet, and not when he had an empty house at his disposal.

ChApTeR EleVen.

DREW pulled up to the sidewalk outside of Kieran's house. He didn't let the engine idle this time, but turned the ignition off. He craned his neck to look past Kieran and at the house. He was used to dropping Kieran off and seeing at least one light on somewhere in the house, but tonight it was completely dark.

"Is your dad still at work or something?" He looked at the clock on the dash. "It's kind of late."

It was impossible to miss the flush in Kieran's cheeks or how he suddenly fidgeted. Drew frowned, perplexed by his sudden discomfort.

"No, um. Well actually he's uh… he's away for the night."

It took only a split second for him to fathom why it was Kieran suddenly seemed so nervy. His mouth went a little dry, his pulse sped up, and he tapped his thumb nervously against the steering wheel. "Oh?" he said in an attempt at casual interest, but his voice came out at a near squeak. "So where's he at?"

"He's over at Piney Point. He's looking into opening a second restaurant near the airport and took one of his chefs to go check it out." He picked at the frayed rip in the knee of his jeans. "He's staying over there for the night—has a meeting or something the next morning."

"So…," Drew began uncertainly.

Kieran looked at him. "So… you want to come in for a bit? Hang out?"

"For a bit?" he asked softly, now near enough certain of his intentions, even if Kieran was too shy to come right out and ask.

Kieran visibly swallowed. "For a bit, or... longer."

Drew offered a shaky smile, his stomach doing somersaults. He nodded. "Yeah, okay."

Drew followed Kieran up the drive to the front door, stood there silently with his hands deep in his jeans pockets with his shoulders hunched anxiously as Kieran unlocked it, and then followed him inside. Standing in the entryway of Kieran's house, he was instantly flooded with anxiety. They'd hung out plenty in the past month, sure, but this was something new and entirely different.

It felt almost like they'd spent every spare and waking moment they had with each other, either in his car or at the movies or anywhere else he'd go with any other friend, in what felt like an attempt to soak each other up while they still could. It was to the point where he'd begun to alienate himself from Matt (something he knew he would have to remedy quick-smart lest he piss Matt off for the last time) and neglect school and even practice on a few occasions. He knew Kieran would be leaving soon—in a matter of months, actually. This evening was the closest he'd come to being brave enough to touch on the subject of what came after graduation, and part of him hoped, perhaps naively, that Kieran might still change his mind.

"So, this is my house," Kieran said and smiled nervously.

Drew nodded, feeling like a moron. "Cool. Uh... should I take my shoes off?"

"No, you're fine. You want a quick tour? Or a drink? Food? Are you hungry?"

"Whoa, steady on, there," he teased gently. "The first one."

"Right. Sorry. Okay, well, this...." He motioned with his head for Drew to follow him. "This is the kitchen. Um... through there is the living room." He gestured and then walked through.

Drew followed through the spacious kitchen with shiny counters and a large island with a cool net-thing of pans hanging above, into a spacious living area that was *awesome*. "Um. Wow."

What didn't seem like much to Kieran almost had Drew's jaw hitting the soft, plush carpet. There were two love seats and a large, L-shaped sofa against one wall and a plasma screen attached to the other. Two bookcases packed with books and a sizable oak coffee table in the center. It was sparse, but in the way an art gallery looks: pristine and expensive. He was afraid to move in case he touched something and it shattered—because sofas were known to do that, of course.

"This is really... dude, are you rich or something?" He laughed, only half joking.

Kieran shifted uncomfortably, scratching the back of his head as he looked back at the living room, as if trying to see what Drew saw. "My dad does quite well for himself, I guess."

"Right. Owning a restaurant and being his own boss and all...."

Kieran studied him for a second. "Does all this make you uncomfortable?"

Drew glanced once more at his surroundings and then shrugged. "No. You're just never coming to *my* house." He laughed.

Kieran grinned and then shoved him playfully. "Come on, I'll show you my room."

"Ah, the Batcave?"

Kieran shot him a surprised look and then laughed. "Funny you should say that. I do have *Batman* memorabilia."

Drew snorted. "What, really?"

Kieran stopped where he stood, facing him with a look of legitimate apprehension. "Oh God. Okay, you might want to prepare yourself for just how big of a geek you're dating."

"Now I have to see. Move it."

Kieran made a noise close to a whimper and took his hand, leading him up a carpeted staircase and toward a closed door that had a sticker which read "You Shall Not Pass!" on the front. Drew barked out a laugh and then quickly smothered it behind his fist. "Sorry, got a... uh, cough."

"Okay, we're not doing this."

Kieran turned, taking Drew's hand to drag him away, clearly forgetting that despite Drew's gentle nature, he had a good twenty or so pounds and two or three inches on him and could not be dragged anywhere if he didn't want to be. Drew tugged on Kieran's hand, shot him a shit-eating grin and happily opened the door, then dragged a protesting Kieran in behind him.

"Whoa." Drew laughed, letting go of Kieran's hand and taking a few steps into the room. "Your room is... cool?" He looked back at Kieran, who was visibly wincing, and melted. "Would you stop it?" he said gently and pulled Kieran close by the hips.

"You're not freaked out? You don't think I'm a geek?"

"Well... yeah."

Kieran groaned and squeezed his eyes shut, making Drew laugh.

"Hey, quit it. I obviously have a thing for sci-fi and comic book—"

"Graphic novels."

Drew nodded, corrected. "—graphic-novel-obsessed geeks."

Kieran thumped his arm. "That's still an insult."

"Geeks are hot. *You're* hot."

Kieran pursed his lips to suppress a smile. "Okay, shut up now."

Drew shook Kieran's hips slightly before pushing him away a step so he could explore the room. "You were honestly worried that I'd be put off just because...." He looked around and snagged up a figurine. "Just because you have a... a red monkey-man doll-thingy?"

Kieran spluttered, snatching it out of his hands and holding it close to his chest. "This is a Hellboy figurine from the Golden Army series, complete with Big Baby shotgun and signature cigar."

"Kieran." Drew plucked it out of his hands and put it back. "I'm fucking with you."

"Jerk."

Drew grinned at him over his shoulder and went back to snooping. He spotted an open textbook on Kieran's desk; there were notes and doodles scribbled all over it. He couldn't help but bite back a grin when he remembered the doodle of their initials that had kick-started their relationship all those months ago. "Can I ask you something?"

"Um, sure?"

"What's with the random capitalization thing?" he asked, not looking back at Kieran but continuing to pick random comic-bookish figures up, studying them before placing them back where he found them. "I mean, don't get me wrong, it's cute and a total Kieran thing to do, but why?"

"Um, well, I-I just thought it looked better when I was a kid— more fun. And I don't like being told what to do or how to do it, so...."

"So it's a nonconformist thing? Like the suspenders and bowties and stuff?"

"I wouldn't say nonconformist. That makes me sound like I'm trying to make a point. It's just something dumb that I did when I was younger and still do. People always labeled me as weird, so I just... I don't know. I don't like to stick out, but at the same time I'm my own worst enemy, because if someone's going to call me a freak, then to hell with it, why even try to be the same as everyone else when they won't let me?"

Drew glanced back at him and shook his head. "You are made of awesomeness, you know that?"

Kieran's sudden interest in the carpet and his dismissive snort would suggest that he thought Drew was being stupid, but his lips pressed together to smother a smile that indicated how pleased Drew's comments made him.

"You know, Matt's brother—you remember Travis, right?"

Kieran nodded and Drew carried on. "Travis would lose his shit if he could see all this." He spotted something propped up in the corner of his room against a bookcase. He bit the inside of his cheek to keep from smiling as it dawned on him what it was. "So ah, what's that...." He lifted his chin. "Over there?"

Kieran shifted uncomfortably. "That, um, that may or may not be a lightsaber."

Drew raised an eyebrow, enjoying the blush in Kieran's cheeks and making him squirm.

"I'm like... at a hardcore level of nerd-dom."

"Stop that," Drew admonished. "Hey, is that a Middle Earth poster?"

Kieran looked over his shoulder. "It's a map; it's a thicker material than paper." He shrugged. "I'm not sure what it's made of, but my dad framed it for me when I was a kid."

"I may not be into this stuff as much as you, but I did love *Lord of the Rings* when it came out. It was the first film that ever grabbed me, you know? That and *The Prophecy*." He continued to look around the room as he spoke, and stopped when his eyes fell on Kieran's computer desk. "Nice setup."

"Oh, thanks. I got that laptop for my birthday. It's pretty nifty."

Drew shot him a look that clearly showed he doubted Kieran's sanity at calling an Apple MacBook with printer, scanner, and surround-sound speakers *nifty*. "I would never leave this room, if it was mine."

"Believe me, for a couple of years, I didn't."

"So... top-of-the-line stuff to make up for...?"

Kieran nodded, glancing away. "Pretty much." He shrugged off Drew's jacket and folded it over his arm. "Don't forget your jacket later."

Drew tilted his head. "Hang on to it."

Kieran's head snapped up, and Drew nodded before Kieran could ask if he was sure. A small, quietly delighted smile touched Kieran's lips, and he folded the jacket over the back of his computer chair.

"Could be worse, Kieran," Drew said softly. "Your dad could ignore you completely."

Kieran gave him a remorseful look. "I know. I'm sorry."

Drew shook his head, dismissing the needless apology. "No, forget it. Doesn't make how you feel any less legit."

Kieran took a breath and then moved to take a seat in his large leather computer chair. Drew squawked in surprise when Kieran yanked him close by the wrist so that he more or less fell into Kieran's lap.

"What are you doing?" Drew laughed. "I'll squish you."

"What, you too butch to sit on my lap?"

"Fine." He'd been trying to stand, pulling his weight off of Kieran, but then sat fully in Kieran's lap, smirking.

"Oh *crap*, get off! Get off!" Kieran laughed, pushing at him.

Drew tilted his head back and laughed. As he stood he yanked Kieran from the chair and then pulled him back into his own lap. "That's better."

Kieran held the pretense of being put out, but it was obvious to Drew that Kieran enjoyed it as much as he did. "That's a super-duper, fancy-shmancy computer." He tickled at Kieran's sides and he grinned when Kieran began to squirm and chuckle.

"Argh! Stop it!"

"Um, no. Not when you're squirming in my lap like that."

"Perv. Quit it!" Kieran choked. He made a quick grab for Drew's wrists and held them tight. "You're evil," he laughed breathlessly.

"How much porn do you have on that computer, just out of interest?"

"More than you can imagine," Kieran freely admitted with a smirk.

Drew snorted. "I was trying to make you blush."

"Well, it didn't work."

"No, it didn't. You're not all that shy talking about sex. No, if I want to make you blush, all I have to do is compliment you."

"That's not true."

"You have the cutest little butt."

Kieran let out a flustered breath, rolling his eyes and looking away with a shy smile. "Shut up."

"And voila! Blushing!"

"You cheated."

"No I didn't, you do have a great butt; it fits right into my hands."

"Stop talking about my butt!" Kieran laughed.

"What should I talk about, then? Your gorgeous blue eyes? The way your brow puckers when you concentrate…?"

"Stop it," Kieran murmured.

"That one, shy smile you have that makes me so damn nervous?"

Kieran gently took hold of his face and kissed him with a nervous energy that made his hands shake and his breath unsteady. He sighed into the kiss when Drew's hands moved up along his back to cup the nape of his neck, and he melted against Drew's solid form as if it was the most natural thing in the world.

"Kier," Drew murmured, running his hand along Kieran's spine and nuzzling his nose along his cheek. "Are—are we leading up to something, here?"

Kieran let out a deep breath that wavered, betraying his nerves. He ran his fingers through the hair at the back of Drew's head and swallowed hard. He opened his mouth to try and say something, anything, but instead climbed out of Drew's lap, Drew's hand following the lines of his body as he pulled away. He stood there, uncertain, and nerves got the better of him. He bit his lip, glanced toward his bed and back at Drew beseechingly, hoping that he wouldn't have to say the words out loud, because he wasn't sure he could.

A smile in equal parts tenderness and something else intimate spread across Drew's lips. "There's that smile I was talking about," he murmured.

He crowded up close to Kieran, Drew's hands going to his hips and then dipping his head to catch a kiss as he walked Kieran backward. They stopped when the bed touched the back of Kieran's knees, and Kieran ran his hands nervously along Drew's arms, not knowing what to do with them.

"I don't know what I'm doing after... after a certain point."

"Me neither. It's fine, though. Isn't it?"

Kieran's face changed and something slid into place in his expression, a realization. "You're totally terrified." Despite his words he sounded relieved.

"Uh, well maybe... just a little bit? I'm mostly really happy about hopefully having sex for the first time, though."

Kieran snorted and dipped his head to press his forehead against Drew's chest as he laughed. "I like that we're... people always remember their firsts, don't they?" He looked up at Drew and fisted his hand in the front of his T-shirt. "They remember always, even when they're long gone and it was forever ago."

Drew's chest heaved as he took a deep breath. He hunched both his shoulders and dipped his head to pull Kieran forward by gently cupping his face into a kiss so hot and deep that it was felt from head to toe.

"Take off your clothes," Drew murmured, his voice low and his hands already tugging at the hem of Kieran's T-shirt.

"We're really doing this?"

Drew nodded hastily and whipped his own shirt up and over his head. "We're doing this."

Kieran watched as Drew quickly stripped, his heart thundering in his ears. When Drew stood only in his boxer briefs and socks, he paused to look at Kieran and his smile disappeared. "You look scared."

His hand reached for Kieran's cheek. "Have you changed your mind? It's okay if—"

"I haven't changed my mind. I'm just... I-I don't think I ever actually thought this would happen for me. And it's not only happening, it's happening with you. That's just... whoa."

"O-okay, but... just to clarify, you still want to do it, right?"

"Oh yeah." He nodded straight away. "I don't even know why I'm still talking."

Drew grinned widely and then wet his lip. He gently guided Kieran, touching his elbows, to sit on the side of the bed, and then reached for his belt buckle. He glanced up to meet Kieran's eyes, to check that what he was doing was okay, and Kieran lifted his hips in answer. He pulled at the waistline of Kieran's jeans, taking the underwear with them, and pulled them down his legs. "I'm so glad you wore somewhat normal clothes today, otherwise this could have been embarrassing," he joked.

Kieran smiled, letting out a short, breathy laugh, but realizing he was completely naked, he curled his body slightly, sitting back further on the bed. "Now you," he whispered.

Drew bit his lip, hooked his thumbs into the sides of his boxers and slid them down. He stepped out of them and quickly toed off his socks, and when standing there, completely naked in front of Kieran, he thought he could perhaps understand Kieran's reticence. They'd fooled around plenty together, first in the storage room and then in the back of his Buick. They'd seen all the good stuff, so nothing came as a shock to either one of them, but they'd always been at least partially clothed, and it was only when completely stripped down in front of one another that they realized they could still be scared of this. Watching Kieran now, Drew thought he seemed flushed and vulnerable.

"Lay back," Drew whispered, and followed—not entirely gracefully—as Kieran reclined.

It took a moment to arrange themselves, but as soon as they were reclined, skin to skin, their heat pooling into each other's bodies, they let out simultaneous gasps of both surprise and understanding.

"Oh my God," Drew breathed. "I had no idea that just *this* would feel so good."

"Skin to skin," Kieran whispered with dawning wonderment. He dragged his hand up Drew's bare back. "Drew, we're in a bed." His voice was conspiratorial, as if they were sharing a secret or discovering something incredible that no one else was privy to.

Drew let out a quiet laugh. "*Naked.* In a bed *naked.* God, come here." He covered Kieran's mouth with his own, his kiss hot and demanding. "It feels so good to be spread out like this. I love being on top of you."

"You really like this?" Kieran asked, rolling his hips upward as his teeth tugged at his bottom lip. "Because I sure do."

A noise left Drew that wasn't so much a groan as it was a garbled moan, grunt, and whimper. "Oh crap."

"Oh crap?" Kieran laughed.

"I wanted to be amazing our first time—I wanted to… you know, blow your mind or whatever, but this is going to be pathetically unimpressive."

They rolled their hips together, and Kieran dragged his hand up and along Drew's sides, his fingers leaving red trails. "I had no idea doing this naked and *horizontal* would be ten times hotter." He clamped his hands down on Drew's sides, a gasp leaving his lips as they thrust together just dead-on at the same time.

"Kieran… we-we should stop a sec—*ah!*" He hissed, clenching his jaw.

Kieran pressed his lips to the side of Drew's throat where the skin was already damp and salty. "When you shudder like that? I can feel it in your shoulders, makes me feel amazing. Turns me on…."

"Okay." Drew pushed up on his arms; his body nestled intimately within the juncture of Kieran's thighs, hips pressing into hips. "Okay, I need a second to-to…." He took a deep breath and let it out quickly. "God, I thought I'd be so much cooler than this." He laughed self-consciously.

Kieran looked up at Drew, at his wide shoulders and strong arms. And he realized with relief that it didn't matter that he was smaller than Drew, or that he was underneath him. Watching Drew from the exposed position he was in, he could see so plainly that Drew was as affected as he was. He was as vulnerable, eager, and as *in this* as Kieran. There was no top or bottom, not really, because Drew was as afraid as he was. "I have… I have what we need in the drawer—" He lifted his chin toward his bedside table. "There."

Drew looked at the drawer and touched his tongue briefly to his upper lip. "We're doing this?" he whispered.

Kieran nodded. His chest rose and fell more quickly as his breathing became shallow.

"And you're okay with-with it being like this?"

"Like this?" Even his voice shook.

"With me… on top of you and—"

"That's what you want, isn't it?"

Drew let out a sputtering laugh. "*Yes*," he said, as if it were a ridiculous question.

"Okay, well, me too."

Drew nodded once. "Okay."

"Okay…." Kieran snorted. "I feel… given your athletic background, that I should be making some sort of catcher-pitcher, baseball-themed joke here."

Drew laughed a little, but his throat bobbed nervously as he cut a quick glance to the bedside table, then back to Kieran.

Kieran leaned up on one hand to stretch to the drawer, and he rummaged for a second before pulling out a condom and a small tube of what could only be lube. Looking back at Drew, it seemed unfair to just hand them over when he looked so daunted—horny as hell, but daunted. He left them on the comforter beside his hip and brought his hands to stroke Drew's forearms, which braced either side of his shoulders. "It's just us," he soothed.

Drew's arms slowly folded, and his stomach pressed to Kieran's. Kieran ran his hands up along his arms and threaded his fingers through his hair. They didn't kiss; they simply took a second to look at one another and take in the feeling of allowing themselves to be so intimate and open to another person for the first time. It was Kieran who lifted his chin a fraction, an invitation, and then they were kissing, slow and easy and shaky and natural.

There was no awkwardness when it came to Drew using the lube. It was something they'd done countless times, but of course there'd always been a stopping point before. The only point where nerves threatened to overwhelm was when Drew guided his cock to Kieran's entrance. There was a brief flash of green eyes, seeking reassurance from Kieran, and Kieran nodded, holding himself as open as he could.

Drew nearly stalled out, heat slamming into his cheeks, when he could not find the right angle to penetrate. But then Kieran pulled a pillow from behind his head and Drew instantly understood. He urgently looped an arm under Kieran's waist and lifted him to place the pillow underneath. The slight shift in position did it, and the next time Drew pushed against Kieran there was a yielding, followed by quiet gasps as he slid home without even meaning to.

"'M sorry," Drew breathed. "I didn't mean to… a-are you okay?" He put his weight on his knees and one forearm and lifted a hand to brush against Kieran's flushed cheek, a tremor in his fingers noticeable to both of them.

Kieran's mouth hung open slightly, his eyes dilated and lids fluttering as he looked at Drew. A smile that was small and slightly afraid lifted the corner of his mouth as he turned his head toward Drew's gentle touch. He looked back at Drew and wet his lips. "Hey." His voice was nothing but a whisper but still cracked. "C'mere."

Drew leaned down to kiss him and even that one small movement shifted his cock inside of Kieran. He grunted into the kiss, his brow puckered in pleasure so good it hurt. He kept his brow to Kieran's. He closed his eyes tight in a grimace as he thrust cautiously forward, arching his back. It felt so good he cried out loud, pulling out only a fraction and pushing forward again. His head fell to Kieran's shoulder and he pressed his face to his neck. "Alright?" he asked, his voice garbled and strained.

Kieran stroked his hands over Drew's shoulders and he nodded as he experimentally lifted his hips, trying to meet Drew somewhere in the middle. "Yeah, yeah, go. Go, it's okay."

Drew let out a noise that sounded helpless and agonized. He slid his arms under Kieran's back, his hands hooking over his shoulders. He looked down at Kieran as he began to move. There was no pausing or awkward first slide and pull, and they soon found a gentle rhythm and moved together for the first time.

"I want to see you!" Kieran gasped, pushing up against Drew with his torso until Drew slid his hands from underneath him and he rose. Kieran groaned and slid his hands down Drew's abdomen. Drew's body carried the kind of muscle only achieved by being eighteen and playing a lot of sports. It drove Kieran crazy

Drew tipped his head back as his hips shifted, circled and then went back to that first, newly discovered rhythm that felt as natural as breathing. Drew looked down to where he disappeared into Kieran, and then up to his flushed face. He leaned forward, moving gently so he could pant against Kieran's lips. "I'm fucking you." It wasn't crude or meant to inflame, it was only a statement of wonder. "I'm fucking you, Kier," he gasped.

Kieran pressed his head back into the mattress, his back arching. He no longer had to concentrate on lifting his hips to meet Drew's movements. It came naturally. And it felt good but it wasn't quite right; he lifted his hips higher, instinctively trying to find the right angle, but Drew had his lower half pinned.

"What—what do you need?" Drew gasped, slowing his movements. "Tell me, I'll do it."

"Higher, I need to be higher."

Drew eased back onto his heels, shifting carefully so his thighs rested beneath Kieran's back and Kieran's thighs pressed against Drew's sides. He encouraged Kieran to wrap his legs tightly around him, and gripped his hips in both hands. He delivered a careful thrust, watching Kieran closely. Kieran cried out helplessly, speared and unable to shift. He threw one hand out to his side to clutch at the comforter and threw his other arm over his face as he let out a sound close to a sob.

Drew's movements stuttered slightly. "Kier, are you—?"

The hand that covered his face shifted. "Don't! Don't stop!"

Drew moved his hips at a faster pace. There was a delicious sensation coiling in his groin in equal parts from the snug warmth pulling him into Kieran's body and the picture of Kieran desperately clutching at the comforter with his head moving against the sheets as he rocked his body back and forth. "Oh God," he ground out, "I don't want to come yet!"

Kieran grunted at a particularly hard thrust and curved his body, his back lifting from the mattress, which only served to impale him further on Drew's cock.

"Ah! Kier! Y-you can't do that, it's too much, you can't—"

Kieran did it again and Drew let out something that sent a bolt of excitement through Kieran. Drew was suddenly over him, curling Kieran's body to a point that would have been uncomfortable were it not for the fact that it opened him up even more to Drew's cock. Kieran clutched at him desperately as Drew began to piston into him, completely out of control and unable to stop or slow down.

"'M coming," Drew panted against his cheek.

Kieran waited until Drew tensed, his movements becoming uncoordinated and juddering. He let go of his grasp on the sheets and snaked a hand between their bodies to stroke himself. So revved up he could scream, it took only one touch to his dick and he was coming, even as he could feel himself sliding to the edge of the bed under the force of Drew's movements. Nothing could have prepared him for this feeling. He'd been oblivious to how incredible an orgasm brought on by anything other than his own hand could actually be.

As soon as he'd come, Drew was toppling over that peak after him. He wound his fingers into the back of Drew's hair tightly, mesmerized as Drew's eyes screwed shut in a look of pained pleasure. He grunted softly at the pulsing he could feel inside of him as Drew came, and thought he'd never seen anything as incredible as Drew, bunched and tensed and buried deep inside of him.

Drew let out a deep breath, more or less collapsing into Kieran's arms and resting his forehead on Kieran's shoulder. He groaned as he sank into him, their chests slick and rising and falling together. "My bones," he muttered weakly.

"Hmm?"

Drew stretched his neck and practically purred at the feel of Kieran running his fingers through his damp hair. "My bones are all gone."

Kieran laughed—as much as he could when breathless and pressed under Drew's weight—and kissed his temple. "Drew?" he murmured. "We're kind of hanging off the edge of the bed."

Drew—with what looked like monumental effort—lifted his head to take a look, and huffed an exhausted laugh. He slowly pushed up on his hands and carefully pulled out of Kieran. Drew kneeled up and pulled off the condom and tied a knot in it. He touched Kieran's flushed cheek, running his thumb along his lower lip. "You're okay?"

Kieran took a breath, and as he let it out a silly smile spread across his lips. He covered his face with his hands and laughed, feeling oddly shy but content. He looked at Drew, bit his lip and nodded. Drew grinned at him, and leaned forward to kiss him softly before climbing off the bed.

"Do you have a…." He gestured around him, and Kieran pointed to the corner of his room where there was a wastepaper basket.

Kieran reached for the tissues he had in his bedside table, and wiped quickly over his stomach before lying back, utterly spent. "Come back here."

Drew took the tissues Kieran had used and put them in the basket before climbing onto the bed. Kieran shifted over for him, and they lay naked together, both a little stunned and dazed. Kieran bit his lip and rolled against Drew's side, resting his head against his shoulder.

"So, that was—"

"Fucking incredible?" Drew breathed, looking up at the ceiling.

"Uh huh."

Drew nuzzled close for a second, his voice growing husky. "Next time? I'd really like if-if you were on your stomach. Or if I could do you on your hands and knees." He swallowed thickly. "I've kind of fantasized about that—about having sex with you like that."

Kieran let out a deep, shuddering breath and nodded. "Oh yeah." He wet his lips. "How do people... I don't get how...."

"Oh man, did I make you forget how to speak? Is my dick made of magic?"

Kieran snorted and poked him in the ribs. Drew captured his hand, keeping him from poking him again and then just held it in his own. "I was just wondering how anybody gets anything else done. Ever."

"When they could be doing it instead?"

"Sounds dumb, doesn't it? I sound like a total sex fiend."

"No, not really. You're laying here all amazed and stuff, whereas I'm already wondering when we can do it again."

Kieran laughed, curling up close and pressing his face against Drew's neck, just under his jaw.

"I am not even joking," Drew murmured intimately, a smile in his voice. "I'm ready to go again when you are."

This made Kieran laugh harder, and he tried to pull his hand away so he could jab it into Drew's ribs, but Drew wouldn't let go.

"Oh no, you don't," he sniggered quietly, rolling over Kieran and pinning him. "Try and poke *me*, will you...."

"You poked me," Kieran giggled. Actually *giggled*.

"Was that a filthy double entendre?" Drew skimmed one hand down over Kieran's ribs in an obvious tickle threat as he used the other to hold Kieran's wrists together. "You filthy, filthy bastard."

Kieran chuckled and managed to pull one hand free but then hissed, automatically bringing his hand up to his mouth. "Ouch."

"What's up?" Drew frowned, pulling Kieran's hand away from his mouth. "Your splinter again?"

"It's fine."

"You said 'ouch'."

"I'm still fine."

"I think that splinter needs to come out."

"I think you need to stop looking at my hand."

"D'aww, afraid of your big, bad boyfriend?"

"No." He brought his hand back up his lips. "Yes."

"Alright." He sat up and swung his legs over the side of the bed, and after a quick search, pulled on his boxers. "I need a safety pin."

Kieran scooted back on the bed, up against the wall. "No way."

"Do you *want* your hand to fall off?"

"Stop it." Kieran laughed. "Eventually it'll just fall out by itself."

"What moron told you that?"

"Uh, excuse me, Dakota Fanning in *War of the Worlds*, that's who."

"Though I applaud your extensive—and baffling—memory for film dialogue, that splinter is coming out. You have a safety pin, or what?"

"Nope. No safety pins. Aw, what a shame."

"No, it's fine," Drew muttered, looking around him. "I'm sure there's something that I can... ah hah!" Drew could barely keep a straight face as he pulled what looked like a samurai sword off of a mounted plaque on the wall. "This should do nicely."

"What the—put that back!" Kieran laughed, plastering his back against the wall, sheets twisted around him.

"Seems your nerd paraphernalia has come back to bite you in the ass." He held the blade in both arms, holding it out and squinting as he looked down the blade.

"You're insane."

"I'm not the one with pointy things mounted on my bedroom walls."

"*Poin*—? I'll have you know that is a *Hattori Hanzo* samurai sword. Very dangerous and very cool."

"It's pretty."

"That is Japanese steel designed to kill vermin."

Drew lowered the sword. Raised an eyebrow.

"Okay, it's a cheap replica I got off of eBay, but you could still poke an eye out with that thing."

"Not an eye, a splinter."

"Put it back. Now."

Drew grinned and relented, putting it back on the plaque. "Okay, serious time. This is my serious face." He pointed at his face. "Safety pins, where are they?"

Kieran whimpered.

Drew went back to the bedside table, pulled open the drawer, and rifled through the contents. "Got one!"

"You suck."

"You weren't saying that fifteen minutes ago. In fact, fifteen minutes ago you were pretty damn happy with me."

Kieran pressed his lips together to smother his smile. "Stop being so pleased with yourself and stop trying to make me blush. Be serious."

Drew nodded. "I'm sorry. Serious it is. Now... show me the booboo."

"*Drew!*"

Drew grinned and sat back down on the bed, holding his hand out for Kieran's. "Come on, give it." He waited until Kieran hesitantly put his hand in Drew's palm. He took a moment to look at Kieran, so close and so genuine with his little frown as he worried over his splinter. "You are stupidly cute," he muttered fondly.

Kieran looked at him, blue eyes seeming all the bluer for being so close. "Did you just call me stupid?"

Drew grinned widely, looking back at Kieran's hand in his and shaking his head slightly. "Okay, just hold still a second, alright?"

Kieran sighed and turned his head away, resting his ear against Drew's shoulder. "Ow. Ow. *Ow!*"

"All done."

"I guess that wasn't so bad," he said begrudgingly.

Drew shook his head. "You're such a baby."

"No, I'm not. Splinters are evil." Kieran heard a familiar chirping noise and looked down at the floor. "I think your phone is ringing."

Drew grumbled and snagged up his jeans, then pulled his phone out of the pocket. He looked at the screen, hesitated, and then put the phone back in the pocket and the jeans back on the bedroom floor.

Kieran raised an eyebrow in question. "Avoiding someone?"

"Not avoiding," Drew answered quickly. "Just… not sure what to say to them yet."

Kieran noticed Drew's slight frown and the way he worried his lip, and decided not to push him on the matter. For now, at least. Instead, he lay back on the bed, pulling Drew with him. "Lay with me."

Drew followed, rolling onto his stomach so that he could rest his head on Kieran's shoulder. He closed his eyes as Kieran began to brush his fingers through Drew's hair; it felt amazing. "You know how I said the park was my favorite place?" he asked quietly.

"Yes?"

"I changed my mind." He ran a hand up along Kieran's side, moving his head to a more comfortable position on Kieran's shoulder. "It's right here."

Kieran was glad Drew couldn't see his face, because such a statement had him blinking hard. What he'd been hesitating to ask Drew about now came out without hesitation. "You want to stay over?"

Drew lifted his head to look at Kieran. "Stay the night?"

Kieran nodded. "My dad won't be back until tomorrow afternoon."

Drew smiled slowly and then lifted his chin in his way that meant *yeah, okay*. "Cool. I'll call home in a few, check that my mom's doing okay and tell her I'm staying at Matt's."

Kieran frowned. "Why at Matt's?"

"It's just easier."

"Okay," Kieran whispered, then looked at his now splinter-free hand. "Thank you for getting rid of my splinter."

Drew took hold of his hand and placed a kiss on his palm. "Welcome."

ChaPter TweLve.

CLOTHES were never something Kieran deliberated over. In fact, usually it was a case of picking up what looked relatively clean from his bedroom floor and which clashed the most. Today was different. Drew said they were going somewhere, and he didn't know where because it was a surprise, but that meant he had no idea if his usual wardrobe would be appropriate. He didn't expect to be going anywhere fancy, but he wasn't used to having expectations. Period.

His gaze fell over Drew's jacket hanging over the back of his computer chair. He didn't know if Drew was aware that maybe it was strange to give his *boyfriend* his jacket, instead of a girlfriend, but it went without saying that it wasn't for him to wear around school. It wasn't fair, but he didn't want the attention either. He looked at the Hawaiian shirt he held in his hands and thought about how often he contradicted himself; he didn't want to be bothered by people, but he liked to dress kind of goofy. But then he nodded resolutely. He would wear what the hell he wanted, when he wanted, and nobody had the right to bother him about it. Except when it came to the jacket, which had to be the one exception for now. He sighed. He may not be able to wear it, but he loved having it.

"Kieran?" his dad called through the door, knocking twice. "Do you think we could have a chat?"

He barely refrained from groaning out loud. "I'm going out." He dropped the shirt and snagged up a thin sweater, figuring clean jeans and combat boots were pretty neutral.

"I'd really like to talk, Kieran. Can I come in?"

"Yeah, whatever," he called distractedly as he sat on the edge of his bed to tie his laces. He looked up when his dad came in and did that thing where he looked around his bedroom, pretending to be familiar with it. "What's up, Dad?" To his horror, his father turned the computer chair to face opposite him, and took a seat.

"We never really caught up from last time we had a chat."

"I've been right here." He held his hands out, palms upward.

"I know. I know it's my fault. I've been run off my feet and distracted with this new restaurant, but I wanted to talk to you about that and some other things...."

"I already told you, I'm going out."

"Where are you headed to?"

He shrugged. "I'm just going out with Drew."

"Is Drew the guy who was here a few weeks ago?"

"Yes," he muttered, standing to look for his wallet. He started slightly when his dad grasped his wrist. When was the last time they'd actually touched?

"Please sit."

Reluctantly he sat back on the bed. For what seemed like forever he'd craved just a little bit of his dad's attention, but now that he had it, he wanted nothing more than to escape it and any delicate questions he may have.

"We've been out of sync for quite a while and I think it's about time about time we address it."

Kieran shifted on the mattress and lifted one shoulder in indifference. "Alright," he said.

"Alright," his father agreed with a nod. "So um, why don't you tell me what's been going on with you lately." He reached forward and squeezed Kieran's knee.

Kieran stared. He'd expected to talk about the girlfriend. "Um... not much."

"How's school?"

Kieran barked out a laugh before he could stop himself. He quickly recovered and shook his head.

"What?" his dad asked, a hesitant smile forming as he waited to be let in on the joke.

"Dad. School's been hell."

The smile slipped away. "What do you mean?"

"You're seriously going to sit me down now, with only a few weeks left of high school, and ask me 'how's school'? Seriously?"

"Kieran, what do you mean '*hell*'?" His voice was pained and his face pinched as he scooted to perch on the edge of the chair. "I asked you if you were being bullied!"

Kieran swallowed, suddenly desperate for Drew to knock on the door. "Forget it."

"No, Kieran, we're not forgetting it. What the hell has been going on with you?"

"Oh, don't do that. Don't pretend like *I've* been the absent one."

"I know the restaurant keeps me busy, but you knew you could always come to me with—"

"Come to you with my problems? Are you shitting me?"

"Kieran, you do not talk to me like that."

"You don't talk to me at all!" He stood quickly, feeling stupid and cornered. "How do I tell you about anything when I know you have absolutely no interest in hearing it?"

His dad stood and held out a placating hand. "Kier, that's not... that's not even remotely true," he said softly.

"You won't introduce me to your girlfriend because I embarrass you." There, he'd said it. He looked up at his dad, his eyes begging to be contradicted, but when he saw nothing but his father's panicked expression, he felt something inside him curl up at knowing he was right. "You think I'm a freak, just like everyone else." He made to move past his dad, not wanting him to see him upset, but was caught by the arm.

"Hey! You are *not* a freak! You're quirky and unique and a good kid and I love that about you, I always have!"

Kieran shook the grip off of his arm. "I don't know why we're even talking about this, there's no point now." He looked at his dad and summoned up enough courage to yank open his dresser to pull out a brown envelope, already torn open. "I'm leaving Keys." He handed it to his father, who took it and stared at it blankly before pulling out the paperwork.

"What is this?"

"An acceptance letter from the American River College. I got in."

"Kieran, that's... well, that's great." For what felt like the first time in a long time, he thought he saw some pride in his father's face. He almost hated to say what he had to say next.

"It's in Sacramento."

His dad's head snapped up. "What? But that's... that's so far away."

He nodded. "Yes, it is."

"That's ridiculous, you're not moving that far away, don't be ridiculous, Kieran!"

"I thought you'd be relieved."

"Relieved? My only child hates me so much that he wants to move two thousand miles away and you thought I'd be *relieved*?"

To Kieran's shock, he thought he could see glassiness to his father's eyes. He swallowed hard, feeling utterly lost. "I don't hate you. I'm just over being unimportant to you."

His dad turned around to face the wall, one hand covering his forehead. When he turned to face Kieran, he looked just as lost. "You think you're unimportant to me? You are *everything* to me." He suddenly screwed up the acceptance letter and lobbed it across the room. "How in the hell did we get to this point?"

"You stopped seeing me."

"You stopped talking! And you are *not* moving to Sacramento, young man."

"Yes. I. *Am!*"

"And just who is going to pay for it, tell me that?"

Kieran clenched his jaw and attempted a casual lift of one shoulder. "I'll get a job; I'll pay for it myself."

"You're going to work *and* study; you think that'll pan out, do you?"

"I'll make do!"

"Kieran," his father sighed, pinching the bridge of his nose. "It doesn't need to be this difficult. I've wanted to talk to you about your future for a while, but I needed to see if I could make things official before I made any offers I couldn't keep."

Kieran frowned. "What do you mean?"

His father stared at him, and then sat back in the chair with a heavy sigh. "I wanted this to be a happy thing. I wanted it to be a gift."

"I have no idea what you're talking about—"

"The restaurant is yours."

Kieran blinked, hearing the words but making no sense of them. "What?"

"The restaurant? Our restaurant? It's now your restaurant."

"I-I don't... *what?*" he asked again.

Kieran's father rubbed his hands over his face tiredly. "I wanted to give you something special. Not a car, not cash, but something that'd last, something that could give you financial security." He looked at Kieran. "I know it isn't exciting, but I wanted to sit down and talk to you about college and about your life. I want to know what you want out of life and be able to tell you to go for it because you will always have the restaurant to fall back on."

"I-I've never wanted—"

"You never wanted anything to do with it? Yes, I know. And to be honest that's always hurt me a little. But this isn't me trying to trap you into a family business."

Kieran's breath was shallow and there was a buzzing in his ears. That restaurant was his father's pride and joy. It meant everything to him, and now it was his? "Then... what?"

"I was hoping you would want to go to college locally or at least in the same state, but then afterward you would have a choice. That's your graduation gift."

"A choice? My gift from you is a choice?"

He nodded. "You can come back and run your restaurant. *Your* restaurant. Or you could remain the owner and hire a manager. Either way it would be yours and you would have a substantial income from it."

"So if I didn't want to run a restaurant...?" he asked quietly.

"Then you do whatever the hell makes you happy, Kieran. Go be an artist, a teacher, anything, and don't worry about paying your rent or not having something to fall back on. There will be two Appleby restaurants in Keys; mine—the new one I'm looking into opening—and yours. Even if you wanted to sell it, you'll be able to buy a house from the proceeds, you won't have to worry about rent or a mortgage." His shoulders slumped. "Maybe it's a stupid gift, but it would keep us connected, wouldn't it?"

Kieran had no idea what to say. He was absolutely speechless. On the one hand, he thought it sounded like a financial dream. On the other, the untrusting, lonely, and hurt part of him was telling him it was something to keep him quiet and busy, something to make them square after his father's sheer lack of presence in his life. "And if I don't want it at all?"

He father looked up from where he'd been studying the carpet, a look of hurt and confusion crossing his features. "Why wouldn't you want it? I worked myself half to death making that restaurant what it is today. It could set you up for life. I *want* you to have it!"

"And *I* want out of Keys!"

His father shook his head. "I don't understand you."

"Believe me, you've made that very obvious." Part of him knew that he was being petty, childish, and ridiculous, but there were simply too many unresolved issues between them for a gift, even a gift of this magnitude, to solve everything.

"I'm offering you something I worked very hard on making happen, Kieran. Do you have any idea how long I've been looking into this second restaurant so I could give you the other one in time for your graduation? I've legally put the restaurant in your name; I've arranged to move half the old staff over to Piney Point and hired new staff for the first! I've—"

"Oh my God," Kieran said, then laughed as it dawned on him. "I know what this is. You've opened a new restaurant and split the staff just so you can keep your girlfriend a secret from me. Oh my *God!*"

"Kieran, that's not—"

"Are you that ashamed of me that you're literally moving whoever she is—I'm guessing a waitress, or something—just so you don't have to include me in your life? Wow, Dad."

"You could not be more wrong!"

"Then why, huh? Why haven't I met her?"

His dad visibly swallowed but said nothing.

"Okay, let's start with something easier. Do you at least admit that you have a relationship with someone at the restaurant?"

He was sure his father wouldn't answer, but eventually he did. "Yes, yes, fine, there is someone."

Actually hearing his dad say it hurt him more than he'd expected. "And how long has it been going on?" he asked.

He sighed. "Nearly three years."

Kieran's eyes widened. He hadn't expected it to be that long. "So… so you're serious about her then?"

His dad hesitated, and there was something in his expression he couldn't read. "It's serious."

"Are you in love?"

He watched his dad's throat bob as he swallowed, and he watched him nod before he whispered: "Yes."

All of his fight was gone. He was no closer to understanding his relationship with his father than he'd been ten minutes ago. Once, they'd been close. His dad had been his hero and the guy to go to whenever something was wrong. But he didn't feel like his dad could be that person to him anymore. He felt confused and alone and tired.

There was a knock at the front door.

Neither of them moved for a few seconds, and they continued to look at one another until Kieran left without a word, heading to where he knew Drew stood, waiting to surprise him. He heard his dad call out behind him—a tired and sad tone in his voice—but he ignored him. He went straight to the front door and whipped it open without hesitation.

Drew was there, hand still poised in the air to knock again, and before he could even say anything, Kieran took Drew's wrist and dragged him down the drive to where he was parked at the curb.

"Kier, what's going on? Are you okay?"

"Just drive."

"DID you get into it with your old man again?"

Kieran cut a glance to Drew. He was watching the road, but his concern was obvious. After gaining an insight into Drew's relationship with his father, it felt selfish and juvenile to bitch and moan about his own, who—while far from being the perfect parent—at least lived in the same house. Despite the lingering feeling of frustration and inadequacy he felt and had been feeling the past two years, this was no longer something he could discuss with Drew. It felt unfair to.

Looking at the facts, he knew he was a brat. His father had given him a restaurant, and he'd stormed out of the house. Who did that? But things between them were not so black and white, and though he felt that if he were to be put on the spot and asked exactly why it was he was so angry he would probably fuck it up and just sound dumb, he knew the feelings he felt were just and not so easily erased with such a grand gesture.

Explain that to a guy whose uncle, who he rarely saw, was a more prominent father figure than his own father, though. There was no doing it.

"It's nothing," he answered, and felt the tension inside of him wind all the tighter for not being able to share his feelings with Drew, of all people.

"You sure?"

"Yeah, I'm fine." He shot Drew a smile that he hoped seemed genuine. "It's nothing worth mentioning."

"Okay, well, if you're sure." He tapped his thumb against the steering wheel.

"So, um." Kieran cleared his throat, desperate to lighten the mood for what was supposed to be a surprise for him and a fun day out. "Are you going to tell me where we're going?" He was glad to see Drew's excited grin return.

"Alright, so first off, you need to know that my own enthusiasm for surprising you may have actually hyped up where it is we're going."

Right then Kieran couldn't have cared less—he was just happy to be alone with Drew—but Drew's earnestness was infectious and he found himself grinning. "Are you going to tell me where we're going?"

Drew didn't answer; instead he stopped and put the car into park. "I don't have to, we're here."

Kieran frowned and looked out the passenger window and windshield. Nothing seemed out of the ordinary. There was the Subway, the comic book store—which looked unusually busy—and the movie house down the street. "I don't get it."

"We're going to the comic book store."

Kieran stared at him blankly and then snorted. "Okay, well I am *surprised*."

"No, no, no." Drew unbuckled and then reached into his back jeans pocket to pull out a very wrinkled and slightly torn flyer. "Check it out." He handed it over.

Kieran read the flyer, letting out a quiet gasp when he realized what it said. "Mike Haven is doing a comic book signing? *Here*?"

"Yep!" Drew beamed, pleased as hell with himself. "He's doing some sort of tour thing, even visiting small towns. Maybe there's another movie coming out?" He shrugged.

"How did I not know about this?"

"You never get involved with anything going on in Keys. *Ever*. I'm not astonished you missed it, but I'm real glad you did, because now I get to be the badass boyfriend who surprised you."

"B-but how did *you* know about it?"

"You remember when we came here ages ago, that first time? I saw the flyer then. I swiped it and googled the guy's name. He's one of the artists for those graphic novels you like, right?"

"Oh my God." It was by far the coolest surprise he ever had, and he'd had a few of those lately. He unbuckled at the speed of light and flung himself at Drew in a bear hug. "You are so awesome!"

Drew laughed, giving him a squeeze. "Cool. I'm glad I could put a smile on your face, even if I didn't really do anything."

"This is so amazing—oh!" he gasped, realizing that he was empty-handed, which was no way for a fan to meet one of his idols.

"What?"

"Do we have time to swing back by my house? I have nothing for him to sign."

"See, this is where I really *am* the shit." Drew leaned back over his seat, reaching for his backpack. "The last time I was over, I swiped a load of your comic—I mean *graphic novels* with this dude's name on them."

"You fucking sneak." He grinned affectionately, taking the books in hand.

"Did I do good?"

"You did awesome, just wait until I get you alone later, I'm not even kidding. That's how psyched I am."

"Score."

"In every sense of the word."

Drew laughed, tipping his head back slightly. "Let's get going. I think there's quite a line forming inside."

HE'D expected Kieran to be happy, but not *this* happy. He thought it was due mostly to him genuinely being excited to meet the artist of one of his favorite graphic novels, and then perhaps in part to his crappy morning. He didn't know what had gone on between Kieran and his dad, and to be honest, there was a strange truce of sorts between them when it came to discussing it.

He'd never quite opened up about his dad to anyone the way he had to Kieran, and he thought the case may be the same for Kieran, but all the same, there was a hesitance between them now to discuss it any further. He thought it had to be that Kieran felt it unfair to discuss the issues he had with his father in front of him, whose father was more or less completely absent from his life. And though that wasn't how he wanted it to be, it was for now probably easier that way. He didn't want to be jealous, and he certainly didn't want to make Kieran think his issues with his dad were smaller or held less significance, but there wasn't really any common ground when it came to this one thing.

Looking at Kieran now, however, Drew thought he seemed happy. Happy because of where he was and what he was doing, even though it wasn't anything Drew would consider life-altering. But happy was good. Being happy is being distracted and that was the best possible departure from whatever was bothering Kieran. Or so he told himself.

Kieran had his signed comic book and stood with his hand raised, waiting to ask a question in an impromptu Q and A. He always thought Kieran was good-looking, but he was especially cute when he was as eager and engaged in something as he was now. Drew was ruminating on this as he leaned against the counter at the back of the store, behind all the other people with their hands raised, when Kieran glanced back, looking for him. He was pretty well hidden where he was, so he lifted a hand in a wave to get his attention. Kieran saw him and discreetly wove through the modest crowd toward him.

"Hey, what are you doing at the back on your own?" Kieran asked quietly.

"I was watching."

"Aww. Creepy."

He grinned, and after casting a quick look around the room and at the back of people's heads, he pressed a kiss to Kieran's cheek, resting his hand at the small of Kieran's back.

"That was brave." Kieran looked at him and blinked rapidly for a second. "And nice."

"No one was looking."

He had only a second to consider what Kieran's mischievous grin was about before Kieran—much as he had—glanced around them and then pushed him behind an empty comic book rack. He pressed his body flush against Drew's and reached for his face to bring him down for a hard kiss.

It felt secretive and wonderful, and he held Kieran close, enjoying the feel of his smaller frame against him. It didn't feel like anything could ever be less than perfect—until suddenly it was.

"Drew."

They pulled apart with quick intakes of breath to see Matt standing off to their left, his expression completely blank. Drew felt his stomach drop, and he took a single step away from Kieran. A quick look at Kieran and he could see how his shoulders rolled forward and that his cheeks were flushed with heat and anticipation of something unpleasant.

"Matt. What... what are you—?"

"What am I doing here?" Matt asked, his words clipped. He lifted his chin over to where Travis was sifting through a sales bin of merchandise. "I brought Travis here to get an autograph from that artist guy. But you'd know that if you weren't such a shit friend. You would know this if you hadn't ignored me for the past few weeks, wouldn't you?"

"Do you two want to talk alone?" Kieran began, looking between the exit of the store and the small crowd oblivious to the awkward and hushed discussion going on behind them.

"No," Drew answered, almost urgently.

"Yes," Matt practically spat, surprising them both. "Yeah, maybe get lost for like… five minutes? Give me just a little time with the guy who used to be my best friend until you arrived?"

Kieran blinked in hurt, stunned silence. He looked between Drew and Matt, that old feeling of being the outsider sneaking back in. "I never—I never stopped him from—"

"I was nice to you," Matt said, his face twisting slightly. "You know? I was nice to you even when your *boyfriend* here wasn't."

"Matt, shut it," Drew hissed, already seeing that familiar expression of discomfort shutter across Kieran's face. He took Kieran's hand in his own but was dismayed when Kieran slowly pulled it free. "Kier, it's okay—"

"Do you honestly have to hold his hand through everything? It's not enough that he's come between us, but he can't even speak for himself?"

Kieran shook his head when Drew reached for him again. "I'll be outside by the car." He didn't spare a glance backward as he wove his way through the crowd to the front of the store.

Drew turned back to Matt, furious. "The fuck is your problem?" he hissed.

Matt took two quick steps forward and shoved him none too gently in the chest so that he took a staggering step backward. "My problem? My problem is that you completely blanked me for *weeks*."

"I-I was…."

"Busy? With your *boyfriend*?"

Drew winced at how Matt used the word in an effort to wound him. "I didn't know what to say," he offered lamely.

"What, you thought I'd call you a fag and never speak to you again?"

Drew could only shrug, but this just seemed to piss him off further.

"You're unbelievable. You dickhead. You absolute dickhead."

"Well, look at the way you're being! Look at the way you spoke to Kieran!"

"I'm pissed at Kieran because I was nothing but nice to him and he paid me back by stealing my best friend, by making me fucking invisible to you."

"Do you have any idea how pathetic that sounds?"

Matt started to say something, stopped, and then stepped forward, crowding Drew back against a bookcase. "Do you have any idea what it's like to have the guy who you thought was your closest friend not only ignore you, but think so little of you as to not share the most intimate, important, and fucking *obvious* of secrets?"

Drew blinked. "Ob-obvious?"

Matt's shoulders slumped and he stepped back, his head tilting sadly to one side. "I should have been the very *first* person you told. I would have had your back in a second flat."

"Crap," he whispered. "Crap, Matt... I was scared shitless of you... of—"

"Don't you dare say you thought I'd hate you."

"Or that you'd be uncomfortable. Like you'd think I was in love with you or some shit. Or I wouldn't feel like your brother anymore."

"So instead you cut me off completely," he said. "That makes *perfect* sense."

Drew nodded. "It sounds so dumb saying it to your face like this."

"It sounds *retarded*."

Drew shook his head. "You don't get it, Matt. You don't get the fear of maybe... of potentially losing—"

"Let me make this easier for you." Matt cut him off with a shake of his head. "You're gay. And I don't give a fuck."

A quiet, almost hysterical, and brief laugh burst out of him and a weight he hadn't even realized he was carrying lifted off his chest. "That means a lot."

"I'm still pissed, Drew. I'm pissed at the pair of you for not giving me a second thought and leaving me out in the cold."

Drew worried the corner of his mouth. "You don't really hate Kieran, do you?"

Matt rolled his eyes. "Of course I don't. He's just as big of a selfish dick as you are, that's all."

Drew shook his head. "No, he's not."

Matt looked at him for a few seconds and then sighed. "No, he's not," he admitted quietly, then scratched his cheek. "I guess I was having a bitch fit at losing my favorite toy to him."

"Did you really just refer to me as your *favorite toy*?" Drew grinned hesitantly.

"Shut up," he muttered and then looked at Drew seriously. "At the risk of sounding completely self-centered, you cutting me out the way you did really didn't feel too great, Drew."

Drew studied him, realizing—now that he was finally speaking frankly with him—just how much he'd missed his best friend. "I have one more big secret."

Matt raised an eyebrow, saying nothing.

"I love Kieran," he said in a rush, and let out a deep breath. "I'm completely in love with Kieran." He laughed breathlessly.

Both of Matt's eyebrows disappeared somewhere near his hairline. "Um. O-okay?"

He refrained from rolling his eyes. "The significance of this being that I'm telling you before I've even told him—before admitting it to myself, even."

"So this is you throwing me a bone?"

Drew nodded. "Something like that."

Matt deliberated. "Okay, I'll take it."

"We're friends again?"

"I'm no longer going to beat you," Matt said and crossed his arms over his chest, glancing back to check on his brother. "I'm still pissed at you, though."

"A true friend would forgive me," Drew teased with a hesitant but weak smile.

Matt narrowed his eyes and let out an agitated breath. "Dammit."

"I'm sorry." Which was really what he should have begun with.

Matt nodded. "Yeah, okay, I guess."

"I'll be better."

"Damn straight you will."

Drew groaned. "Am I going to have to stand outside your bedroom window holding a fucking boom box to get you to forgive me?"

"You're making jokes? *Really*?"

Drew bit back a smile, but then looked down to where he scuffed a shoe nervously, his hands in his pockets. "Matt, you are going to apologize to Kieran, right?" The quiet stretched on for so long that Drew glanced up. Matt wasn't smiling.

"I suppose I should, seeing that I was sort of but not really out of line. And because you're all in love, and stuff."

"He's really important, Matt."

Matt watched him, and then nodded. "Okay. Just. Just don't forget that I'm important too, okay?"

Drew pulled Matt into a brotherly hug, murmuring his apologies again. It was only after a brief moment of hesitation that Matt patted his back. "We're good?" he asked.

"We will be."

ChapTER ThIrTeEn.

HE DIDN'T wait by the car. In fact, he didn't even hesitate and walked right past the car and toward home. Matt had seemed like such a good guy before, but just seeing his glare and hearing those words spat out at him was like taking ice water to his face. It was a familiarity he'd wanted to forget about and a reminder that Drew was the exception—the one guy who did actually like him. And Kieran just cost him his best friend.

He knew he'd done nothing wrong and wasn't about to play the martyr, but he felt so fucking *raw*. He could see his father's dejected, disappointed, *frustrated* face. He could hear every acid-like comment hurled at him, every withering glance ever thrown his way. And again, the exception was Drew. His day had started out upsetting. Then Drew had come, and everything had been good for a while. Now this. Now this feeling of having nowhere to be and of not fitting in with whatever "normal" was.

He dug his hands into his jacket pockets, his head down as he walked along the sidewalk. Feeling good for only a while just wasn't going to cut it. It never was. Drew had quickly become that one good thing. His one thing to look forward to and a reason not to dread going to school, but he wasn't enough to keep the rest of his life from pressing down on him, and Kieran knew that if he didn't leave, he'd suffocate. He couldn't be the disappointing son anymore; he couldn't be the school loner.

He knew then that no matter what, he was going.

He pulled his hand up into his sleeve and swiped it over his eyes before shoving it back in his pocket. He'd been selfish. He'd known all along that he wanted to leave, and he'd known all along that Drew didn't want him to. What was worse was that he'd said nothing. He hadn't budged either way. Instead he'd remained silent, unable to do the kind thing and tell Drew with absolute conviction that he would be leaving. And he'd told himself this was fine, because Drew knew his intentions. But deep down, the truth was that his silence and being vague had given Drew false hope. So he wasn't just weird and infuriating, he was cruel, too. He was being cruel to the most wonderful person he'd ever met.

He couldn't be angry with Matt, because he knew Matt; he knew he was a nice guy. He'd been kind enough to include him, to talk to him and even defend him. He was Drew's best friend, and you didn't get to be Drew Anderson's best friend by being an asshole. No, Matt was a good guy who now hated him, which to him was just proof that he was a fuckup from head to toe.

He ignored the honk of a car horn from behind, hoping it was anyone other than Drew, trying to get the attention of anyone but him, but a familiar rust bucket pulled up to the curb just in front of him. He considered ignoring him and walking away for just a second and then dismissed it as immature and unkind. It was time to man up.

"Kieran?" Drew called even before he was all the way out of the car. "Kier, you said you'd be by the car."

He looked anywhere but at Drew for a minute, then swallowed and nodded. "I know. Changed my mind."

Drew stood before him, looking uncertain and worried. Kieran couldn't look him in the eye and wished furtively that he wouldn't speak—that he would not say a single word because Kieran had no idea how to say what he needed to.

"So. Um. Matt's okay now. He's sorry for the way he acted, so don't worry about that."

He nodded and muttered quietly, "Okay."

"Are you going to tell me why you took off?"

Kieran forced himself to meet Drew's eyes and instantly wished he hadn't. There was wariness there, as if he sensed what was coming but didn't want to believe it. "I just needed to get out of there—needed to leave." He looked Drew straight in the eye. No more being vague, no more false hope. "I *am* leaving, Drew."

Drew looked away quickly, glancing around them. "That's cool; we can go hang somewhere else—"

"That's not what I meant."

"Matt's going to apologize, Kier, he told me he would."

"It's not because of him, it really isn't."

"School is nearly over, Kier; you don't have to worry about Jefferson or that Toby asshole or anyone else—"

"I'm leaving Keys, Drew, and I'm sorry, because you really are amazing and quite easily my favorite person in the whole world, but my feelings for you don't change the fact that I'm going. I was *always* going, Drew."

Drew watched him, his upset obvious as he struggled for words. "So… what?" He stepped closer, close enough for Kieran to see the glistening in the corner of his eyes. "I'm just nothing to you?"

"Christ, Drew, you're the reason, the *only* reason that leaving has become so difficult. Before, it was the easiest choice in the world. Now it hurts like hell."

"So *don't go,* then!"

"It's not enough!" Kieran cried back, not giving a shit that anyone could overhear them if they were to walk by. "If I don't go now I'll never get out of here, I know it!"

"This isn't some hick, dead-end, going nowhere town, Kieran. I don't care what you say; it just isn't as bad as you make it out to be!"

"For *you!*" He yelled back. "I do not *fit*. Okay? I don't fit here!"

"You're making this so much more difficult than it needs to be. When school's done? When you're out of your dad's house and doing your own thing? Your whole world could change, you could *find* where you fit."

"That's what I want to do!"

"But I'm telling you that you can do that here. Kier, you don't have to move so far away…."

"I know I don't have to. I want to."

Drew rolled up his fists and pressed them into his eye sockets as he growled in frustration. He took a deep breath, keeping his eyes closed, and then reached for Kieran, rubbing his arms when he was unable to take hold of his hands. "Okay, okay listen…." He swallowed visibly. "I-I had this idea. What if you stayed in Keys, no—no please hear me out," he said when Kieran tried to pull away with a groan. "What if you went to the community college, like me, and we… we got an apartment together?"

Kieran blinked in shock. "What?" he whispered.

Drew took this as a sign of hope and nodded. "Yeah, yeah, we could live together, go to college together, it'd be great!"

Kieran felt like crying. He hated seeing Drew like this. *Hated* it. "Drew, *don't.*"

"And I swear to you that no one would ever bother you in college. I *swear*, Kieran. I'd never let it happen."

"You can't hold my hand through everything, Drew." He shook his head, biting his lip as he looked away and discreetly wiped at the corner of his eye with the heel of his hand. "You have no business promising me that when you don't know what'll happen. I just…." He swallowed hard, and his voice came out a croak. "I need to get out, Drew, I'm so trapped here."

Drew's brows rose together sadly, and he looked pretty close to defeated. He ran a hand through his hair and then let it fall to his side again. He looked at the ground, then reached for Kieran's hands and held them loosely in his own. "Kieran." He took a few deep breaths, bolstering his courage. "Alright," he said quietly, and when he looked at Kieran his eyes were glassy. "Alright, here's the thing. I love… I love you."

The only sound Kieran made was a quick intake of breath, his eyes widening slightly.

"I love you and I want to be with you for a really long time."

"Drew," he whispered, too shocked to say anything else.

"And the thing is? You're not the only one who's trapped. But the difference is that you have a choice. I *can't* leave. I can't leave my mom all alone. But if I could? I'd follow you wherever you wanted to go. I wouldn't even hesitate."

"You would?"

"Oh yeah." Drew laughed softly, sadly. "But I can't. I can't leave her. The only person here with any power is you, and I'm hoping so much that you choose to stay because honestly? As trapped as I sometimes feel? The only thing that makes it any better is you."

"I-I... if it doesn't work out? If I lose this window?"

"Why do you think this is your only chance to make a change? Your life is just about to *start*."

Kieran groaned and rubbed his hands over his face. He felt like pulling his hair out and screaming. "I don't know."

"Please," Drew whispered, his face filling with heat at the plaintive sound of his own voice. "Please, Kieran," he whispered. "I'd do my best to make you happy, I promise."

"Drew, I... I...." He trailed off with a heavy sigh, oblivious to the tear trailing down his cheek until Drew wiped it away with the pad of his thumb.

"Please let me be enough, Kieran."

"I don't like hearing you talk like that. I don't want you to beg me. You should never beg anyone; you're too good to do that."

"Then tell me you'll stay."

"I... can't. I don't know...."

"Why is it so difficult for you to decide?"

Kieran closed his eyes, forced himself to think and get the words out. "If I stay, it feels like I'm giving in."

"Giving in?" Drew asked, bewildered.

"Like I'm giving up on the possibility of my life ever feeling normal, or just *good*. If I stay, then all the shit I've been through just gets swiped under the rug, dismissed like it never happened. Where, in fact, I want to throw it in my dad's face and make him see what it was like to be me, what it was like to feel unwanted." He let out a deep sigh and shook his head. "Nothing I'm saying is coming out right. I sound childish and pathetic, I know. But sometimes, just the idea of that fresh start awaiting me somewhere else was the only thing that made me feel the slightest bit okay." He looked Drew square in the eyes. "That's what you're asking me to let go of."

Drew swallowed and stepped closer. "Okay, tell me this," he murmured quietly. "Why can't *I* be this fresh start? Why can't I be that for you?"

Kieran looked away sadly, and he took a deep breath. "Because, Drew."

"Because wh—"

"Because people never stay with their first loves."

Drew pulled his head back, and he blinked rapidly, the hurt those words caused him obvious. "So... what, I'm... I'm just your first boyfriend and nothing more? A fucking warm-up for when you get out of here and meet the guy of your dreams?"

Kieran immediately shook his head. "No. No, you're so much more than that, you have no idea."

"I think... I think the problem here is that, well, for me? You make all that shit go away. But... but I don't do that for you, do I?" Drew wet his lower lip and sniffed, looking away for a second to blink hard.

"You *do*. You are that person for me, Drew, I promise."

"Then why—no, *how* can you just leave me behind?" He snapped his fingers. "Just like that?"

"Don't," Kieran ground out. "Do not downplay how fucking difficult this is. I never thought I'd have this. I never thought I'd have to decide—"

"This?"

Kieran gestured between them. "What we have."

Drew pressed his lips together unhappily, nodding. "Right."

"What? What did I say now?"

"Do you actually… I mean, I kind of just assumed… stupid of me, really."

"What?"

Drew stared at him for what seemed a long time. "Do you even love me back?" he asked eventually, his voice quiet.

He could see how much it cost Drew to ask that, and he could see the pride that was sacrificed. He instantly softened. "Yes." He smiled sadly and let out a quiet laugh. "Oh yeah. From the very start I loved you." Heedless of their surroundings, he closed the gap between them, lifting his chin to press a soft kiss to Drew's lips. "Out of all of this, that is the only thing I'm absolutely sure of."

Drew watched him, a certain amount of tension leaving his frame. "So what is it going to take to convince you to stay?"

Kieran let out a deep sigh. "Why are you even doing this? I am so not worth this."

"Yes. You are." Drew sighed, stepped forward, and pressed a kiss to Kieran's forehead before resting his chin there as he pulled him into a gentle hug. "What about if I gave you some time?" he asked quietly with the guise of being calm, but there was still panic, even a hint of desperation laced in his voice.

"What do you mean, *time*?"

Drew shrugged helplessly. "Not long now till graduation. Until then I'll just… I'll leave you alone. To think."

Kieran pulled back and looked at him. "Think?"

"To think about what it is you really want. Without me there to guilt you into anything."

"But-but that means if I go, I won't... we won't... I don't like that."

"Neither do I, and I really do think this is way more complicated than it needs to be, but... if you choose to stay, I want it to be because you've realized it's what you want. Not because your pathetic boyfriend begged you to."

"Don't fucking call yourself that!" he choked out.

"Will you? Will you think about it?" He sighed. "Please?"

Kieran swallowed hard and then nodded. He understood what Drew was trying to do, and he even appreciated it on some level, but he had never felt so at fucking war with himself.

"Okay," Drew whispered. "So, I'll go. You think. If you stay, then come find me after graduation. If you decide to go... just go."

"What, don't even say 'bye?" he asked, his voice hitching.

Drew lifted one shoulder helplessly. "Say good-bye to me now. Hopefully just for now."

Kieran let out a garbled sound close to a sob and ran a hand uselessly through his hair. "Why have I made this so dramatic? It's stupid. *I'm* stupid."

"No," Drew murmured softly. "You're not. You're just uncertain and tired of everything being the same." He kissed the corner of his eye. "You are not stupid."

"I love you," Kieran whispered, mortified that his chin was actually trembling.

Drew didn't answer; instead he pulled Kieran close to press a single hard kiss to his lips, and then to his forehead. "I'm going now," he murmured against Kieran's temple. "Think. Decide. I love you." He turned and headed to his car, then climbed in quickly and pulled away without even glancing back at where Kieran stood shell-shocked.

"I'm so stupid," he said to himself.

THERE were a hundred other things—more productive and important things—he could be doing rather than lying on his bed, wearing a certain someone's Squids jacket and staring up at the ceiling. He could be contacting the American River College to confirm his placement there (if it wasn't already too late to do so——he was afraid to find out). He could be deciding what to pack. He could be trying to at least somewhat smooth things over with his father. But to do any of that would mean to have finally made a choice—to have chosen a future that did not include Drew.

He hadn't spoken to him. At all. Though difficult to begin with, it'd become easier when Drew had more or less disappeared. He didn't know if it was in an attempt to avoid him or if Drew's life had suddenly become busy, but the last few weeks of school had been lonely and not how he'd wanted to spend them. And now he'd screwed up, because tomorrow was the last day of school. Tomorrow he graduated, and it would be the last time he would see Drew, if he decided to leave.

A decent person would have sought Drew out to tell him not to hope and to not worry about going out of his way to avoid him, but he wasn't that guy, he was a coward. And worse yet, he was still as undecided and confused as he'd been the day Drew told him to go away and think about it.

He looked over at where his cap and gown hung against his wardrobe, pressed and ready for the big day. The day after tomorrow was supposed to be the beginning of his new life, the one he'd been imagining for the last few years. He was supposed to feel hopeful.

He sat up, letting out a frustrated groan. He was late for school. He knew he wouldn't be in trouble for it, seeing as for most classes, the teachers were letting them just chillax and take the time to say good-bye. He thought about what and who he would want to say good-bye to. Aside from Drew, there weren't really any other students he wanted to reminisce with or have sign his yearbook, as was traditional in their school. There were no teachers, no classrooms (apart from a particular storage room) that held any relevance to him. He didn't want to see under the bleachers, knowing that to see his and Drew's initials doodled all over would be upsetting. But he liked the idea that they were still there and would probably stay there for many years yet. No, there was only one reason to go to school today, and that was to say good-bye to one person.

Tony. The silent janitor.

He may never have heard Tony say a single word during all their lunchtime meals shared together, but they were friends, and he wanted to say good-bye to his friend.

"TONY?" He poked his head around a stack of chairs and spotted the janitor, in his usual spot, reading a comic and munching on his sandwich.

It was a comforting picture, but this time, it was also bittersweet. "Hey, Tony."

He took his usual spot and catalogued it, as he'd been doing all day. His day hadn't been spent saying good-bye to friends, so much as places. He'd saved away his memory of the last time he'd use his locker or drink from a particular fountain. The last time—hopefully— he'd have to duck down a different hallway to avoid Jefferson. And seeing as graduation was taking place tomorrow during the morning, today would be the very last time he'd have lunch with Tony. He wanted to be cheery and chat like he usually would with Tony, but he didn't have it in him today. He pulled his lunch from his backpack, sitting down.

"So, today's probably the last time you'll have the pleasure of my company. Graduating tomorrow," he announced.

He tore off a corner of his sandwich, nibbling on it but not really tasting it. It was curious how, until now, he hadn't felt at all emotional about leaving this school.

"I figured I'd leave the comics here for you." He shrugged. "Like a leaving present or something."

He was pleased when Tony looked up briefly, away from the *Spider-Man* comic he was reading, and lifted his chin in silent thanks.

"I can't say I'm going to miss this place all that much. I haven't had the best time here, but you probably knew that." He looked at Tony for an answer, and merely continued after receiving none at all.

"It got better for a little while. I actually made a friend or two. I screwed it up, though." He set his barely touched sandwich on its crumpled brown bag, pushing it away. He swallowed hard.

"I was actually intent on getting through high school with no one finding this out but... I don't know, I kind of want to tell you this, just so someone I like knows it about me. So...." He smiled nervously. "So... so I'm gay."

He watched Tony closely for any sort of reaction, but there was no flinch, no looking up from the comic book. He didn't even pause in chewing. It was oddly comforting.

"And I had a boyfriend. *Me*," he laughed. "That's why I disappeared for a little while, but, well, you can probably guess that it didn't work out."

He felt his throat grow thick and quickly blinked against the sudden stinging in his eyes.

"I've fucked up so bad, Tony," he said in a rush. "I've hated school for so long, and home didn't feel much better. So I was all ready and set to take off and move as far away as possible, right? Only now I've hurt the only person who's ever really liked me in this place—who says he *loves* me. So now I have to decide whether to forget college out of state for something that might fizzle out six months down the line, or to let go of the only person who's ever really given a crap about me. And I guess my biggest problem is perspective. I can't see the bigger picture because my head is so full of Drew, but... I mean first loves *never* last, do they?" he asked, not actually expecting an answer.

"And that's not even touching on my dad." He exhaled hard. "All of a sudden he wants to be in my life. He's acting as if his complete and utter lack of interest in me was all in my head this entire time. Now he suddenly wants me to stay, to run his restaurant and be a part of each other's lives, but... but where was he when I needed him, hmm? With his girlfriend, that's where. His girlfriend, who he won't discuss, who he won't introduce to me, and who is more important to him than I am." He took a heaving breath, mortified to realize he was close to tears.

"I've been looking forward to tomorrow for *years*. I hate this school. I hate Keys." He brushed the heel of his palm at the dampness around his right eye. "So why do I feel so fucking sad?"

He looked at Tony, who was actually looking back at him for once. He held his sandwich—a thick, meat-filled sandwich—close to his mouth and was staring at Kieran. Kieran let out a choked sob.

"You always have better food than me!" he cried.

He was startled when Tony's beefy paw settled on his shoulder, and blinked at him in wonder. When Tony spoke, his voice was unexpectedly soft. Deep in timbre, but soft, and almost affectionate.

"You're a nice kid."

Kieran shook his head. "No, I'm really not."

"Yes, you are."

"I don't know what to do."

Tony frowned, glancing away, back at his comic for a few seconds, and then back to Kieran. He looked him right in the eyes. His words seemed deliberate and were spoken slowly. "Grudges are pointless. Talk to your dad." He looked away, his large, boulder-like shoulders falling in a heavy sigh. "People are important, Kieran." And then he was back to eating his sandwich, his eyes fixed once more on *Spider-Man*.

Kieran took a deep breath and let it out slowly. "I guess I'm just not used to having people in my life." He sniffed and fixed his eyes on the edge of the brown paper bag as he fiddled with the corner of it. "I think I'm going to miss you, Tony," he said quietly.

He sensed Tony move and then watched as Tony set the other half of his thick, meaty sandwich in front of Kieran. He let out a quiet, watery laugh.

"Thank you for letting me keep your comics."

"Sure thing."

ORIGINALLY, he hadn't intended to turn up at the restaurant, as his father had requested, for a pre-graduation dinner, but after speaking to Tony, he put his thinking cap on and told himself to grow up. He may not be as close to his dad as he used to be, but they were the only family either of them had, and throwing that away in a tantrum of hurt feelings seemed ridiculous. He was still no closer to knowing what it was he was going to do, but he at least knew he had to include his dad in the decision, instead of merely informing him of his plans.

All his good intentions and open-mindedness were quickly beginning to lose significance however, as he sat in a booth, waiting for his dad to appear from his office. He passed the time by watching the waitresses, wondering which one was his father's girlfriend and unable to picture his dad with any of them. He was hungry as hell, and the restaurant wasn't even that busy—in fact, it was winding down—but he thought he should wait for his dad before he ordered. He watched as one of the waitresses—Sally, if he remembered correctly (it had been a while since he'd seen or spoken to any of the staff)—passed by and did a quick double take. He smiled at her.

"Hi, Sally."

"Kieran!" She came to stand next to him, resting an empty tray against her hip. "Look at you; you must have grown five inches since the last time I saw you!"

He grinned. "Probably, yeah."

"Well, stand up and give me a hug, you!"

He was surprised, but stood and then laughed quietly when he was pulled into a warm hug and had his hair ruffled.

"Look at you, all handsome and grown up. Are you ready for tomorrow?"

He blinked. "Um, tomorrow? You mean graduation?"

"Well, yes, silly. Your dad doesn't talk about anything else these days." She playfully swatted him with a pristine white napkin kept tucked into her belt against her hip.

"He… really?"

She rolled her eyes. "Must be a male thing. I swear, you're all clueless."

"Just him," he joked.

"Do you want something to eat while you're waiting, honey?"

"Um, no. I should probably wait for him."

"I think he's going over the books. He may be a while; does he know you're here?"

He couldn't help but stare at her for a moment as it dawned on him that his dad had most likely *forgotten* they were having dinner. He slid out of the booth. "Actually, I think I'll go find him."

"Okay, well, I have to get back to it." She gestured over to patrons sitting in discussion at the other end of the floor. "It was good to see you, Kier."

"You too, Sally."

He was pissed. Too pissed to remember that just moments ago he felt pleased at the thought of his dad talking about him at work. It had been a while since he'd been up to his dad's office, but when he knocked and then opened the door, it was like going back in time. His dad wasn't there, but the computer screen was lit up. He took a quick glance and saw an open spreadsheet with lists of dates and figures that looked just plain confusing. He threw himself into the chair opposite the desk, and his eye caught on a photo frame. He leaned forward to turn it and then picked it up, handling it with care.

It was a picture of the two of them, taken here at the restaurant. He was sitting on his dad's lap, leaning across the table to blow out the five candles on his birthday cake. His dad looked so happy, smiling down at him like that. It made him wonder just what the hell had gone wrong between them and whether he was a rotten son.

"Kier," his dad said with obvious surprise, a hesitant smile forming. "What are you doing up here? Come to see how this place runs?"

He put the photo frame back where he found it and slouched back in the chair. "No. Where were you?"

His dad sat down behind the desk, still looking pleased and for now ignoring the computer screen. He pointed a thumb over his shoulder. "I was in the bathroom."

Kieran closed his eyes with frustration and let out a small sigh, counting to five in his head. "No, Dad. Where were you? I've been sitting down there waiting for you."

His dad looked confused for nearly two seconds before he sucked in a quick breath and his shoulders slumped, a palm going to his forehead. "Our pre-graduation dinner, dammit!"

Kieran very nearly smiled. He couldn't help it. His dad had always been the kind of father who could make him giggle as a child by pulling faces or doing silly voices for the shadow puppets he made on walls. But Kieran wasn't a child anymore, and he was yet again a second thought.

"I'm so sorry, Kier. I was just checking supplies and going through the numbers and got completely distracted." He looked at his watch. "The kitchen's still open…." He began to rise. "Let's go have our dinner."

"Or we could just talk."

"We can talk over dinner. Come on."

"No."

His dad paused, finally taking note of whatever it was he could see in his son's eyes or hear in his voice. "No?" he repeated.

"Let's talk here."

His dad sat back down in his chair, wet his lip and then nodded. "Let me close all this up." He turned to his computer screen and began clicking and probably saving what he was working on. But Kieran took it as a positive—that he would have his father's full attention for this.

When the screen went dark, they faced each other in the small, quiet office.

"So…," his father began, looking nervous as hell but completely present.

Kieran scratched the side of his neck nervously, feeling that somehow, this would be the conversation that would settle things between them for better or worse. He told himself to be an adult, that he wasn't allowed to storm out like he had every other time, and that what Tony said was true. People were important.

"How'd things get so bad between us, dad?"

"I… they're not *that* bad, surely?" he asked quietly, sadly.

"Considering that you're the only family I have and we say only a few words a day to each other? Yeah, it's bad." He saw his dad's face fall and swallowed hard. He leaned forward in his seat slightly. "I'm not saying that to make you feel bad. I was just… I was lonely, dad. I was having a rough time at school and you kind of made me feel like you didn't want to know me either."

"That is *not* true."

"Then what happened?" He lifted one shoulder, forcing himself to keep his voice even though it so wanted to crack and make him sound as vulnerable as he actually felt.

"Kier," his dad began softly. "You have always been the source of my complete pride and joy, I *promise* you that." He swallowed visibly. "But… you're right. I didn't realize that things had become as… impersonal between us as they had, until we had that talk about college. And we still need to talk about that."

Kieran wet his lips, impatient. "Fine, but we talk about this first."

His dad nodded and said nothing for a few moments, gathering his thoughts. When he spoke, it was with a heavy frown. "Okay. Okay, cards on the table?"

Kieran nodded.

"There are a few things…." He cut Kieran a quick look. "One thing in particular that I've been keeping from you, because I was worried how you might feel about it."

Kieran nodded, encouraging him to get on with it. "The girlfriend."

His dad sighed softly and glanced away, his chin dipping.

Kieran's patience began to waver and he felt that familiar stab of insult. "The girlfriend you don't want to introduce me to."

His father pressed his lips together in a tight line, not looking at him. "I just thought you were getting on with teenage-like things. That you were okay, just distracted by growing up, like every kid should be." He looked at Kieran, looking as remorseful as he'd ever seen him. "I had no idea that I'd left you all alone. I'm so sorry, Kier bear. I feel terrible that you ever felt alone."

Although those were words he'd waited a long time to hear, Kieran couldn't help but notice that he'd dodged his original statement about the girlfriend. "Why won't you talk to me about her?"

His father wouldn't look at him. Instead, he clasped his hands together and leaned forward with his forearms resting across the desk. "It's… Kier, it's not so straightforward."

Kieran slouched back in his chair, looking away, anywhere but at his dad. He felt the familiar dull throb of rejection. "Is she married?"

His dad looked at him in shock, indignation clear in his voice. "Of course not!"

"Then it's me. You're embarrassed by me."

"No! Stop it."

"You know, I can understand other people acting like I've got some sort of disease, but you're my dad, you're *supposed* to like me."

"Of *course* I like you. I love you!"

"That's the shit I got at school, you know. Got called a freak all the time. How do you think it feels to know my own dad thinks the same?" He swallowed hard, forcing himself not to become upset or storm out of there. "*God*, why do you think I want to leave so badly?" He jumped when his father's palm slapped down on the desk.

"That is *not* what I think! I have never thought that about you and it is *not* true. You get that through your head *right* now, you hear me?"

Kieran stood, his chair rolling back behind him. "Then what is it?" He was quickly losing the battle to stay composed. "I get that you're busy with the restaurant. I'd even understand if you weren't around as much because you'd met someone, but why can't you include me in this one part of your life?"

He father pinched the bridge of his nose, his eyes closing. "Kieran, please, it isn't so straightforward."

"Yes, it is!" He glanced at the framed photograph on his father's desk and then back at his dad. "What, do you think I'm going to feel like you're trying to replace my mom? I don't even remember her!"

"That's not...." He sighed and then laid his palm across his forehead. "That's not it."

"Then what is it? Because I'm really at a loss here. I mean, do you think I don't want you to be happy? If you've met someone and you're in love, then that's great, okay? I'm happy for you and I want to be a part of that. But... but it's like you've made yourself a new little family that doesn't include me. And I *know* how childish that sounds, but I really don't give a shit anymore."

Finally getting to the crux of why he felt so unhappy, he took a deep, unsteady breath.

"Why did you have to make it a choice? Why did it have to be her or me when it could have been so much easier as a three? Why was *I* the one that got cut out? Why did you choose her over me?"

His dad rose from his seat, both hands braced on the desk. "I was trying to protect you! I did not choose! There was no *choosing* involved!"

"Then why can't I meet her? Why can't I meet your girlfriend?"

"You want to meet her?"

"Yes!"

"Fine!" his dad yelled, moving from behind the desk. He headed to the door and then paused, pointing back at him. "Sit your ass down in that chair!"

Kieran sat automatically, unaccustomed to his father yelling at him. He sat there for a few moments, catching his breath and feeling shaky. He started when not a minute later he heard voices down the hall. One was his father, dragging someone who was clearly reluctant to be dragged anywhere.

"John, what the hell? My crab cakes will burn!"

Kieran blinked—that wasn't a woman's voice. He stared stupidly when his father reappeared, his hand gripping someone—whom he recognized to be the head chef—by the arm. Silence fell over the room as they stared at one another, Kieran clearly confused, his father fearful, and the chef stunned.

"Kieran," his dad began and gestured to the man with incredibly blue eyes who stood beside him. "This is Steven, my girlfriend."

Kieran stared at them both. "Uh. What?"

The chef—Steven, apparently—stood there looking as dumbfounded as Kieran felt, and weakly waved a hand that still held a greasy spatula. "H-hello, Kieran."

Kieran held up a hand, things slowly slotting into place. "Wait. Wait, are you—are you telling me that he's your… that you're…?"

His dad visibly swallowed and nodded once with determination. "Yes. I'm gay. You have a gay dad. I'm a gay dad," he babbled.

"The amount of times I've pestered you into letting me meet him and *this* is how you introduce us?" Steven then pulled his arm free of his father's grip so he could step forward and offer his free hand to Kieran. "Hi Kieran, I'm Steven. I promise you I'm not usually this greasy and grimy looking, and I am going to kick your dad's butt for introducing me with so little finesse."

Kieran, in a daze, took the hand offered to him and shook it. He looked back at his dad. "You're gay?"

His dad seemed to flinch and then crouched in front of Kieran, his hands resting on Kieran's knees. "Kier, I am the same guy you knew five minutes ago. I am still your dad."

It dawned on him that his father was afraid of his reaction. The idea was so ridiculous, he couldn't even move. "This is why you wouldn't introduce me to your girl—I mean... I guess... boyfriend?"

"It is the *only* reason."

"You're not embarrassed by me?" he asked quietly, feeling an overwhelming relief begin to engulf him. He was distracted by Steven, however, who snorted loudly behind him.

"Oh my God, Kieran, he *adores* you, honestly. All he talks about is the two of you running restaurants together, and about how brave and unique you are, I swear."

"The only reason I've been so closed off and secretive about this is because I didn't know how to bring this to you. I didn't know how you'd feel about it, and I didn't want you to feel embarrassed or even more singled out at school. I am so sorry that you thought it was because I didn't care."

"So... so you're gay. Like... homosexual?"

Steven, who was glancing between father and son and looking worried, took a hesitant step closer and placed a reassuring hand on his father's shoulder. "I know this may be a lot to take in, but ultimately it's irrelevant, isn't it? He's still your dad. Nothing else has changed."

There was something hysterical bubbling up inside of him, and he didn't know if it was laughter or tears. He put his head in his hands and groaned. Things could have been so different if he'd only known. Or if he'd just come out himself. These past few years would have been so much easier to bear, for the both of them.

"Oh my God, Dad...." He shook his head. "Dad, you *idiot*."

His father glanced back at Steven, who shrugged, and then he turned back to Kieran and rubbed his knees. "O-okay, does this... are you mad, or...?"

Kieran snorted, shook his head, and then stood. His dad followed, rising slowly and then blinking in surprise when Kieran was suddenly in his arms, hugging him ridiculously tight.

"Dad, you are such an *idiot*!" he laughed.

His father hugged him back, utterly at a loss. "Uh, so this means you're alright with this? I'm a little confused, Kier."

He let go of his dad, looking up at him anxiously. He shook his head, let out a watery, quiet laugh, and then sniffed. "Dad, do you—do you remember my friend Drew?"

"Drew?" He frowned. "The baseball player? Yes, I think so. Why?"

He bit his lip. "Drew wasn't just... he wasn't...." He heard Steven suck in a quick breath, and looked over at him.

"Oh my goodness," Steven said quietly, his brows disappearing into his hairline and his lips pressing together to smother a smile as he crossed his arms over his chest. He looked at Kieran's father. "You *are* an idiot."

"What?" his dad asked, looking between them, clearly irritated. "What am I missing?"

"Dad, Drew wasn't just my friend; he-he was *my* boyfriend."

His dad pulled back slightly, blinking in shock and looking at his son as if he didn't recognize him. "You're... *you're* gay?"

Kieran snorted, glancing and smiling hesitantly at Steven. "Yeah, have been for a while now."

"But... but how did I *miss* that?"

"Maybe if you hadn't been trying so hard to hide your own gayness, then you might have had a clue," Steven murmured.

"Oh. Oh, I *am* an idiot."

Kieran smiled a little sadly and then sank into his dad's arms again, hugging him tight. "It's okay. And I don't mind if you're gay. It would be kind of hypocritical of me if I did. But the being-an-idiot thing? That *has* to go."

His dad laughed quietly and rested his cheek atop Kieran's head. "What a pair we make, huh?" he murmured.

All three of them glanced to the door when a harried looking waiter appeared.

"Uh, sorry to interrupt, but can we have Steven back, by any chance? Seeing as he cooks all the food...."

Steven gasped. "My crab cakes!"

The waiter shook his head. "In the garbage."

Steven's shoulders slumped and he rolled his eyes heavenward. "I'll be there in a second."

The waiter disappeared and Steven turned back to the pair of them. "Well, I'm going to get back to the kitchen; you two should talk a little more."

"Wait." Kieran pulled out of his dad's arms and stepped toward Steven, offering his hand in a proper handshake this time. "It's really nice to finally meet you, Steven."

Steven took his hand to shake, and smiled smugly over at his father. "I told you he'd like me."

Kieran laughed and let go. They watched Steven disappear with a final supportive grin aimed at his father. Kieran looked at his dad, then let out a loud bark of a laugh. "How dumb is this?"

His dad shook his head. "It's pretty unbelievable. I can't believe I never picked up on you being gay. Aren't parents supposed to innately know these kinds of things?"

Kieran lifted one shoulder, feeling as if the weight of the world had been pulled off of them. "I didn't know *you* were, so...."

His father shook his head and pulled Kieran into his arms once more. "I could have made life so much easier for you if I had just told you from the beginning. I'm sorry, Kier."

Kieran nodded. "It's okay," he said softly. "I feel a lot better now."

"Good. I'm glad."

"I hated being so angry at you."

His dad snorted. "Yeah, me too."

"I wanted to move away as far as possible."

His father pulled back slightly, holding him at an arm's length. "And now?"

Kieran took a moment to find his words. "I... I don't think I ever actually wanted to go. I think I just wanted to leave you, like I thought you'd left me."

His dad closed his eyes against something painful and pulled him close again. "I'm so sorry."

"You said that."

"I'm saying it again. Do you realize we've hugged more in the past ten minutes than we have in the past two years?"

"Maybe it's a gay thing?" he joked.

His dad laughed and ruffled his hair. "How about we close up early tonight? We'll wait for the customers we have to finish up, and then we'll have our pre-graduation dinner as planned."

Kieran nodded and smiled. "That sounds great."

"Because we really do need to chat about college and what it is you want to do in the fall, okay?"

Kieran nodded. "Okay."

"And I *really* want to hear about Drew."

HE WAS confused, anxious, and feeling the very beginnings of desperation. High school was officially done. He'd survived in one piece, and his dad and his dad's boyfriend had been there in the crowd, taking pictures as he received his diploma. He knew what he wanted now; all he needed was to explain it to Drew and to apologize to him for keeping him waiting, but Drew was nowhere in sight.

They graduated in alphabetical order, so Drew should have been the first up on that stage and then him, but they hadn't even called his name. So while his dad stood there with Steven, talking to one of his teachers, he looked around desperately for the one person who could possibly shed a little light on the situation.

He spotted Matt with Travis and who he assumed were his parents, and strode over without a second thought. He didn't even wait politely for a pause in conversation; he merely shook Matt's elbow, a nervous smile playing on his lips.

"Kieran, what are you doing?" Matt pulled his arm away.

"You got a second?" He glanced at Travis and waved.

Matt sighed and turned back to his parents to excuse himself. He looked at Kieran and lifted his chin in the direction of the exit to the assembly hall. "Come on."

They were quiet until they were outside, but as soon as they were alone, Kieran was on him.

"Where is he?"

"I'm fine, thanks," Matt said sarcastically.

"Sorry, sorry. I know you don't... you know, like me anymore, but can you please just tell me where he is?"

Matt sighed. "I've been meaning to apologize for acting like such a dick to you that day, I've just been distracted."

Kieran blinked at him, but though he was pleased to hear the words, an odd sense of dread was settling over him. There was weariness and sadness in Matt's eyes, and Kieran grew suddenly light-headed as something inside of him began to sink all the way down to his toes, cementing him there.

"Why isn't he here?" he whispered.

"Kieran, they're letting him graduate in absentia." He swallowed hard. "He and his mom got a visit from a CACO. Do you know what that is?"

"No." Kieran shook his head.

"It's a Casualty Assistance Contact Officer. His uncle was killed in action, Kieran."

Kieran sucked in a sharp breath through his teeth and he squeezed his eyes shut, covering them with his hands. "Oh fuck. Oh fuck, oh fuck...," he whispered. "Oh God. Drew...."

"He's not doing so well," Matt said, his voice rough. He squeezed Kieran's shoulder.

"Have—" He stopped when his voice cracked, and cleared his throat. "Have you been with him?" *Please say he hasn't been going through this alone.*

"As much as he'll let me. He's been trying to look after his mom, mostly. I was kind of hoping that you'd been... I don't know, looking after him where I couldn't, I guess."

He let out a pained groan. "Fuck, no. No we... after that thing with you at the comic book store? We decided to take a break so I could try to think things through and decide what to do come fall. I never, *never* would have left him alone all this time if I'd known."

"Shit," Matt whispered. "That's my fault."

Kieran was quick to shake his head. "No, Matt, it's not. Honestly. It was a conversation we'd been putting off that you just sort of forced us to have, that's all."

Matt nodded, and neither of them said anything for a few moments.

"Just out of interest," Matt began with a barely disguised hint of accusation in his voice. "What *are* you doing in the fall? Are you taking off?"

"Hell. No."

Matt nodded. "Well, thank fuck for that." He cleared his throat. "Maybe this means we'll get a do-over? You know, considering that you're dating my best friend, and all."

Kieran nodded distractedly. "Yeah, sure." He looked up when he felt Matt squeeze his shoulder again.

"Can you please go take care of our boy? I think he needs you more than he does me right now."

Kieran nodded and was about to leave but paused, and then threw one arm over Matt's shoulder and patted his back in a brief, brotherly hug. "See you around."

"Yeah, see you."

HE'D taken but a moment to explain the situation to his dad, and with one concerned nod, his dad let him take off to look for Drew, postponing the celebratory dinner at the restaurant. The first port of call had been Drew's house. Though he'd never actually been there—knowing it was something that needed to be handled delicately because of Drew's mom—he did know where it was.

He stood so long on the porch after knocking that he'd begun to think no one was home. It was only when he was halfway down the porch steps that he heard the door crack open.

"Who's there?"

He walked back to the door, keeping a short distance, and offered a friendly, if sad, smile. "Hi. Mrs. Anderson?"

"Yes?"

"I'm-I'm looking for Drew. I go to school with him."

"You're a friend of Drew's?"

The door opened a fraction more, and Kieran had to quickly school his expression. Her appearance was honestly that of a woman on the verge of unraveling. Her hair was greasy and uncombed. There wasn't a scrap of makeup on her face, her eyes were bloodshot, and her complexion was gray and worn. Pity flooded him. He knew without a doubt that he was looking at barely concealed devastation and grief.

"Mrs. Anderson? I'd just like to say how very, very sorry I am for your loss. I only just found out about Drew's uncle today, otherwise I would have been here a lot sooner."

Her face disappeared behind the door for a moment, but Kieran could that see her knuckles and fingers, which gripped the open door, were turning white against the wood. He swallowed hard, knowing that Drew not only had to cope with his own grief but also with his mother's, which was so clearly profound and real.

"Thank you," she finally said, her voice raw. "Drew isn't here; would you like me to take a message?"

He could've cried with frustration; all he wanted was to get to Drew as soon as he could. "Um, thank you. If you could let him know that Kieran called by?"

The door opened a fraction, her pale face suddenly visible. "You're Kieran? You're Drew's Kieran?"

He couldn't help but smile at the way she referred to him. "Yes, I'm Drew's Kieran."

A smile, though small and shaky, pulled at her lips. "Oh, oh, hello, Kieran. Drew's told me all about you. Oh!" Her smile quickly fell and was replaced by a look of mortification as her hand flew to her hair, patting it down. "I'm-I'm not usually so unpresentable, I—"

"Mrs. Anderson, please don't worry. I know you've been through something terrible."

"Oh no," she groaned, coming undone right before his eyes. "No, no... I don't want to embarrass him, poor Drew...." She pulled her blouse straight and then went back to her hair, offering Kieran a forced smile that drooped at the edges as her breath hitched with the threat of tears. "As if he doesn't have enough to deal with."

He took a step closer to the door, and when he spoke his voice was as soft as silk. "If it were me in your shoes, Mrs. Anderson, then I would be standing there in nothing but my boxers, sobbing into a Kleenex. You are not an embarrassment to Drew, I promise."

She stopped pawing at her hair, and her expression softened. "He said you were kind."

He smiled gently. "Mrs. Anderson, I want you to know that I'm going to be here for Drew. I'm going to love him and take care of him. And if you ever need anything at all, please, *please* let me know."

She stared at him, and then a small smile that this time seemed genuine changed her face to something very motherly. She was actually quite a beautiful woman, just extremely overwrought. "Drew's devastated, as I'm sure you can imagine. He's trying to take care of me, but he's still just a boy that's lost the uncle that was like a father to him. So if you can offer him any sort of comfort where I can't, then please do."

"I will." He nodded. "Do you know where he is?"

She shook her head. "No, he just said he needed some air. He didn't take the car. And he has his mitt with him."

Kieran sighed in relief. "I know exactly where he is. Thank you, Mrs. Anderson. I hope we talk again soon."

"That would be nice. Take care, Kieran."

It was a wakeup call. He knew Drew didn't see his mother as a burden, but he thought he perhaps understood better now the pressure Drew must feel to take care of her. He thought back to when Drew had asked him to stay because he couldn't leave, and felt his throat grow thick with emotion.

He had a hunch where Drew was. If he had his mitt, Kieran was sure he would be at the park. The park that was one of his favorite places and that reminded him of his uncle. Kieran more or less jogged there, and when he made it over the low fence toward the back end of the park and through the copse of trees, he spotted Drew.

It killed him. He'd never seen anyone look so alone in his goddamn life. Drew sat slouched on a bench, his head down, staring at the mitt he held in his hands. He didn't look up, seeming to not notice Kieran's presence until Kieran was standing right before him. Kieran crouched in front of him, resting his hands on Drew's knees. He wanted to cry for him, he really did.

"Hi," Kieran whispered.

"Hi," Drew said, and then took a deep, shuddering breath just before his face fell and he leaned forward with a pained groan, a sound close to a sob working its way out of his throat.

Kieran moved, kneeling up and pulling Drew into a strong, tight hug, and murmured softly to him. "I know. I'm so sorry, Drew. I'm so, so sorry."

"He's gone."

Kieran only nodded, rubbing his hands in circles on Drew's back. "I know, baby."

"I don't know what to do."

"You don't do anything. You just cry and let the people who love you take care of you, that's it."

"I have to take care of my mom."

"Yes, but you have Matt and you have me to help you."

"You're leaving," Drew choked out.

Kieran swallowed and silently hated himself for not truly realizing just how much Drew had needed him, even before his uncle had passed away. "No. I'm not." He moved to sit beside Drew on the bench, hugging him close when Drew moved without hesitation to lie on his side, his head in Kieran's lap. "I'm not going anywhere," he said thickly, running his fingers through Drew's hair.

Drew shook his head. "You don't want to be here. So you shouldn't be."

"Drew, I couldn't see the forest for the trees, alright? I was so caught up in being the loner that I couldn't even see when I wasn't alone anymore. I'm staying. I'm staying here with you."

Drew gripped the leg he rested his cheek on, squeezing his eyes shut. "I don't want you to feel sorry for me. Don't stay because you feel bad for me, that doesn't help at all."

"I don't pity you, Drew. I love you. I love you and need you, and I'm staying."

Drew shook his head. "I was so sure I wouldn't see you again."

Kieran clenched his jaw. "Drew, sit up for me."

He waited until Drew pushed himself up, and carefully cupped his face, wiped away the dampness, and kissed his stinging cheeks. "I sat down with my dad yesterday and came to the decision to stay. He knows I'm gay, he knows about you, and we came to an agreement as to what I'm going to do this fall. This was all decided *yesterday*." He used the pads of his thumbs to wipe at the dampness under Drew's eyes. "Drew, I found out about your uncle a half an hour ago. I decided to stay *before* I knew about your uncle. Understand me?"

Drew watched him, and then took a deep, heaving breath before throwing his arms around Kieran's shoulders and pulling him into a desperate hug. "Thank you," he whispered shakily. "Thank you."

"I'm only sorry that it took me so long to get my shit together, but I had to work out a few things with my dad." He swallowed hard. "I could have been with you when you needed me if I hadn't been so self-involved and—"

"Shut up." Drew cut him off. "Just… just forget it, yeah?"

He knew he likely wouldn't be able to forget about it, but he nodded anyhow, and smiled sadly when Drew pulled him forward for a soft, tender kiss.

"You're staying?" Drew asked again, and Kieran smiled gently, and nodded.

"Yes. There is a plan."

Drew sniffed. "Tell me about this plan. Tell me something—anything that'll take this feeling away for just a minute."

Kieran slid close and rested his arm on the back of the bench so he could run his fingers through Drew's hair. "Alright, so my dad and I had it out. I called him on everything I've always wanted to, and it yielded some… interesting results."

"Like what?" Drew asked, his eyes closing as he leaned into Kieran's touch.

"Well, he introduced me to his girlfriend."

Drew opened his eyes. "Really? That's great, what's she like?"

"Oh, the usual: blue eyes, short brown hair, about six two, a hundred and eighty pounds, and has a goatee."

Drew stared at him. "What?"

"He doesn't have a girlfriend; he has a boyfriend. His name's Steven. My dad is *totally* gay."

Drew stared at him a moment before snorting and letting out a weak laugh. "That is *too* fucking funny."

"I know, right?" Kieran grinned. "We're ridiculous, both of us."

Drew was chuckling to himself and wiping at his eyes. He calmed down when Kieran reached out to ghost his thumb over the curve of his cheek.

"I missed you so much," he whispered.

Drew held his gaze, and eventually allowed himself a small smile. "Tell me the plan, which apparently includes you having a gay dad."

Kieran grinned. "Okay, so... I'm not going to college come fall. Anywhere. I'm going to take a year off to work at the restaurant with my dad, just waiting on tables and working behind the scenes." He tilted his head and wet his lip. "And to try to catch up on our relationship and just generally become accustomed to what it might be like to run a restaurant." For him, the year coming would mostly be about getting to know his dad again and making up for time lost, but it was impossible to say that now, when Drew would never be able to do the same with his uncle.

Drew's brows rose in surprise. "Seriously?"

Kieran nodded. "He's opening another one and wants me to have the one we have now. Like... legitimately own it."

"That's so cool!" But then he frowned. "But wait, I thought you hated the restaurant."

Kieran had the good grace to blush. "I was being prissy and childish. I don't really know *how* I feel about it."

"Okay, so... what happens after a year and you decide you don't want to run a restaurant?"

"If that's the case, then I'll enroll in college next year. *Local*. I'll still be the owner and so I'll have a hefty income, I'll just hire a manager to run it for me."

A slow smile crept along Drew's lips. "Are you telling me I'm going to have a sugar daddy?"

Kieran snorted. "Please, never call me that again."

"That is kind of amazing, Kieran. Owning a restaurant at eighteen."

Kieran bit his lip. "Yeah, I guess it is." He looked at Drew, sensing that he wanted to ask something but didn't dare. "What is it?"

Drew shook his head. "S'nothing."

"Tell me." He turned Drew's chin toward him and gave him a silly grin. "What do you want? You want the moon? Just say the word and I'll throw a lasso around it and pull it down."

Drew watched him, looking unbearably vulnerable, but eventually cracked a small smile. "Of course you're quoting *It's a Wonderful Life*. That's such a *you* thing to do."

Kieran blinked, a smile splitting across his face. "See, only my freakin' *soul mate* would know I wasn't just being weird there."

"You're not weird," Drew said quietly. "You're perfect."

Kieran couldn't not kiss him then. He kissed his lips, and then pressed soft kisses to his cheeks and eyelids, trying to somehow convey the sum of what it was he felt for him. "What did you want to ask me?"

Drew wet his lip. "Where do I come into this, Kier?"

He frowned. "What do you mean?"

Drew let out a quick breath. "Don't make me ask again."

"Drew, none of this works *without* you."

"So... we're doing this? We're going to be together?"

Kieran smiled softly. "You're going to go study to become a firefighter, and I'm going to work at the restaurant. At the end of the day we'll both be coming home to whatever house or apartment we're renting—which will be as close to your mom as possible." He leaned close for a gentle kiss. "You're going to study, and I'm going to bring home the bacon. Maybe in a few years we'll switch, but either way, yes, we're doing this."

Kieran smiled as Drew surged forward and kissed him hard.

"Thank you. I... I kind of feel like I just might come out of this okay, if I've got you."

"Drew. You have *so* got me." He pulled Drew close, feeling stronger and more at home in his own skin than he ever had before. "You doing okay?" he whispered.

Drew nodded. "I'm doing better now." Drew let out a deep breath, looking around them. "I still love this place."

"I know you love this park."

"No." Drew squeezed Kieran's arm that held him close. "I still love *this* place."

Kieran pressed his cheek against Drew's temple and whispered: "Me too."

EpiLogUE

Five years later…

Kieran leaned against the low, wrought-iron gate outside the restaurant, going through the reminders on his phone.

Dinner with Dad and Steven tomorrow night.

Talk to Drew about a vacation somewhere with mountains.

Pick up dry cleaning for Drew's mom.

"Excuse me, Mr. Appleby? I think we're about done here."

Kieran glanced up, his chest swelling with pride as the men with their ladders moved out of his line of view so he could admire the new sign for his restaurant.

K aNd D's PlACe.

"That's fantastic. Thank you, gentlemen."

"Not a problem. We'll be on our way."

He leaned back against the gate, allowing himself a moment to take in everything he'd achieved over the past few years.

It hadn't been easy and there had been a very real fear of letting his father down and failing. But the restaurant was thriving now with his own unique spin on it. What's more, his father's branch out in Piney Point had adopted his choice of menu and restaurant uniform too. He still got a kick out of seeing his waiters and waitresses in Hawaiian shirts, suspenders, and bowties. It may not be the classic black that most restaurants adhere to, but it lent a more casual, family-friendly atmosphere to the place and played its part in bringing in the customers and tourists looking for somewhere casual to eat. It had taken a lot of hard work and a business degree from the College of Central Florida, but here he was.

Kieran looked down beside him. "What do you think, Tony?" he asked the elderly beagle he and Drew had rescued two years ago. "Do you like the new sign?"

Tony's tail thumped in response and Kieran reached down to scratch behind his ear. "Come on, old man; let's go get you a treat."

Tony carefully got to his feet but then turned to look behind them toward the road, his tail wagging so much that his butt wiggled. Kieran glanced down the road to see four firemen, still in uniform, climbing out of a familiar, second-hand Chevy truck. He grinned, pleased to see one of those handsome firemen in particular.

"Who's that?" he asked Tony. "Is that Daddy?"

He laughed when Drew whistled and Tony took off as quickly as he could on his old, tired legs.

"Hey!" he called out, following Tony, opening his arms for a hug and then laughing when Drew picked him up and squeezed him, kissing his neck before putting him back on his feet.

"Hey, Kier," one of the other firemen greeted him. "If I pick you up and smooch you, can I get some free food?"

Kieran laughed, swatting at the hand that groped his butt. "Behave, you," he murmured smoothly to Drew. He looked back at the three pouting firemen and rolled his eyes. "Go find your usual booth; you know firemen eat for free here."

"Thank you, Mom," one of the other firemen chimed in before pressing a sloppy kiss to Kieran's cheek, making him laugh and push him away.

"Hey!" Drew called after him. "He's taken!"

"Yeah, yeah, Anderson." They waved Drew off and headed on into the restaurant for their free chow.

"Your shift's over?"

"Yep. Just came in for some grub and a quickie in your office, and then I'm off home to catch up on some sleep. I love the sign, by the way."

"Thanks. Me too. Oh! We have dinner tonight with Dad and Steven, remember? So don't sleep in too late."

"Are we staying in or eating at the restaurant?"

"Our place. I want your mom to be there."

For someone who'd been so desperate to leave Keys not so long ago, he was blissfully happy living in the house next door to—for all intents and purposes—his mother-in-law. After Drew's uncle had been KIA, his mother had given Drew, without hesitating, half of the Servicemember's Group Life insurance she'd received. It was flat-out serendipitous that her neighbor, Mr. Gullbeck, the weed-selling weirdo next door, had happened to be moving. And so they bought his house outright, and Drew had been able to stay close by, and Kieran had gained himself a mother—something he'd never had.

"You go on in, get yourself something to eat. I want to take a few pictures of the new sign and text them to dad." He patted Drew on the butt and received a wink in reply. He watched Drew jog up to the entrance, whistling for Tony to follow him, and reflected on just how much he adored his fireman.

Despite his words of reassurance to Drew on graduation day in the park, a part of him had worried about feeling stifled or trapped. But though he had never expected to, he had never felt so at home. He loved his job, he loved his home, and he loved his partner. He smiled to himself, using his phone to take a picture of the restaurant.

Sometimes you do stay with your first love.

L.A. GILBERT currently lives in a small British town where not much of anything ever really occurs. Jumping from job to job, she has no real qualifications in anything and is blithely proud of it. Between spectacularly failing driving test after driving test, she generally spends her free time reading about beautiful gay men, if not attempting to write about them. She is perhaps not the most outgoing of people, but is certainly one of the most cheerful.

Her aspirations are to eventually leave England and see a real, live whale (London's zoo is poorly lacking in that respect) and to perhaps one day hold in her hands a published copy of her own work.

One down.

Find L.A. on Twitter: @L_A_Gilbert

on her blog: http://l-a-gilbert.livejournal.com/profile

on her website: http://lagilbert.WebStarts.com

or e-mail her at L.A.Gilbertmail@gmail.com.

Also from L.A. GILBERT

http://www.dreamspinnerpress.com

Also from L.A. GILBERT

The
Coil

L.A. Gilbert

http://www.dreamspinnerpress.com

Also from L.A. GILBERT

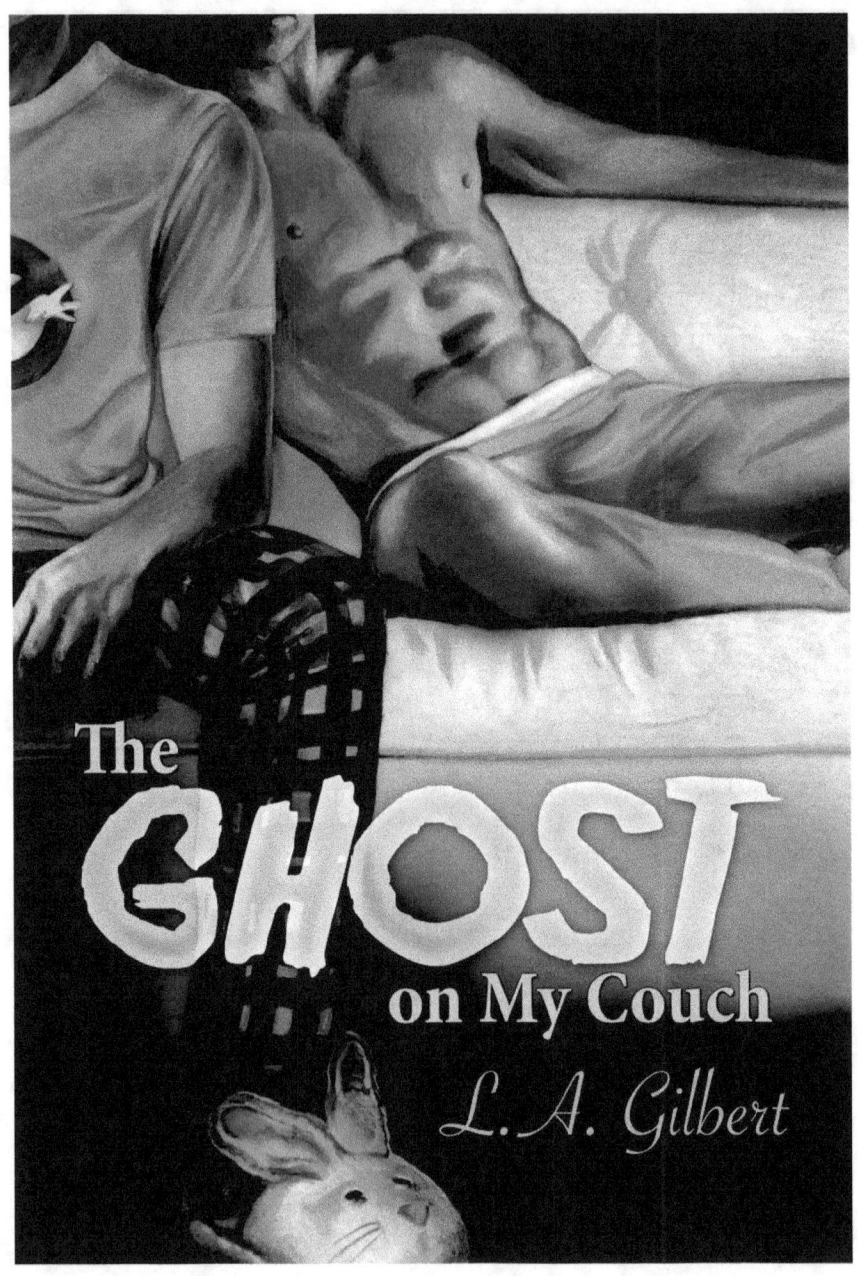

The GHOST on My Couch

L.A. Gilbert

Also from DREAMSPINNER PRESS

http://www.dreamspinnerpress.com